What you promise ...

Joseph McConnell

ProcArch LLC, Ann Arbor

ISBN: 978-0-9886913-8-4

First edition, 2015.

The section headings refer to battles or other events in US wars from the 1840s to the US Civil War. The book's title, on the other hand, is from the Onin-ji, whose unknown 15th or 16th century Japanese author wrote an account of the disastrous Onin war, generally regarded as the beginning of the century-long Sengoku or Warring States period.

"The capital which we believed would flourish for ten thousand years has now become a lair for the wolves."

This book is for Linda, Pat, Charlotte, and the two new Virginians. With any luck, they won't have to choose between their state and their country.

Preface: Major General George Henry Thomas, United States Army

George Thomas (1816-1870) was one of the few Southern regular army officers who remained loyal to the United States during the US Civil War. He is also unusual in that he left us with very little in the way of primary sources. He did not, for example, leave us memoirs or an autobiography, and he died very shortly after the war ended. Everything we know about him suggests a man who valued his given word very highly, even when keeping it meant turning his back on his native state. He was also unusual in his apparent concern for the lives of his troops. Almost alone among generals of that time, he always preferred making clear and complete plans, training and supplying his people properly, and making an attack or a defense that would cripple his enemy without slaughtering his own men.

I try in his sections of this book to write Thomas' autobiography for him, and I do that mainly to contrast him with some of the fictional characters who are also here. If it occurs to you that Thomas might also contrast very strongly with real, current characters in the news, well, draw your own conclusions.

Nat Turner's Rebellion

The beast crouched behind a box. It looked left and then right, its head moving smoothly. Walls cut off the view on both sides, and ahead there was a parked truck. The beast focused on the right rear wheel; something there had just moved! Something was under the truck!

The beast stood up quickly, but it staggered, its hind feet slipping on the ground surface. It flexed its hips, its spine bent like a spring, and it jumped forward. Its chest slammed into the back of the box, and it fell over onto its side.

The action stopped, and a video control bar appeared. "You see that?" Corinne asked.

"Yeah, I saw it."

"You're not getting the traction information right."

"I'm getting it. It's wrong, is all."

"No, it isn't. Rashif's algorithm works the way the spec says. It's giving you what you're supposed to expect. But you're not doing the right thing with it."

"I think the simulation is wrong. It thinks the ground is X-amount slippery but it reports Y."

"No, we reviewed that. You were there."

"Well ... I can look at it again, I guess. But I'm doing it right."

"Not as long as it can't dig its claws in better than that."

"Yeah, yeah."

"Just fix it. We have to demo working hind legs in two weeks."

Corinne walked away. She wore flip-flops in the closed area, and even on carpet they made their usual slapping sound. Engineers dressed as they pleased here. No one who had any concerns about workplace attire was cleared to be in the closed area. She gave one dismissive thought to the conversation she'd just had. She knew she was right, and she'd read the wrong-headed code that was making the cyber wolf stumble. *Arrogant little creep*, she thought.

Ricky closed the simulation and brought up his code for the lower hind legs. With some distaste, he opened an interface specification as well. He didn't particularly like that document's author, and he specifically disliked Corinne, his team lead. *Bitch*, he thought.

Mac MacArthur reacted with some surprise when his phone rang. He got few enough calls at any point in the day, but seven-forty-five in the morning was unusual. He pushed back from the kitchen counter and reached for the phone in its belt clip.

"This is MacArthur." There was a second's pause. He could hear the caller draw in a breath. "Yes, hello," he repeated.

"Mister MacArthur?"

"Yes, it's Mac MacArthur. What can I do for you?"

"This is Mrs. Howard, down the street from you."

"Oh. Okay. Good morning. Are you having trouble or something?" The caller's voice sounded high and weak, and she seemed to be breathing hard.

"Well, your dogs are in my backyard."

Mac closed his eyes tightly and opened them again. It was a habit he had, one he'd picked up in the course of his professional life. It meant he'd been surprised or caught off balance, and it was the outward sign of resetting, mentally.

"Mrs. Howard, my dogs are ..."

"They're out there now, chasing something!"

"Mrs. Howard, my dogs are right here with me." Mac glanced down, unconsciously verifying his defense. Both of his large, intelligent German Shepherds were lying on the floor below his bar stool, ready to defend the household from anything edible he might drop. "They're not outside running around."

"Well ... well ... it's somebody's dogs! Aren't they yours?"

"No. No, seriously, mine are here, inside the house."

"Well, what am I going to doooo?" It was almost a whine. Mrs. Howard sounded as though she was about to break down in tears. "They're out there!"

Oh, Christ! thought Mac. *When did I become the neighborhood dog catcher?* He stood up and tried to see out a window, down the unpaved little street. Another house was in the way, though. "So, what are the dogs doing?"

"Well they came tearing in from the street! I think they were chasing something! And now they're just sitting there, looking at my elm tree!"

"All right, Mrs. Howard," Mac said. "So they probably got away from somebody walking them. Or they got out of somebody's yard. Do you see any people around?"

"No, nobody's here. I think they're after my squirrels!"

"Maybe they are, but squirrels are faster than dogs. They can get away up trees. Now, what you should do is go look out the front of your house, and ..."

"Out the front?"

"That's right. Go look out front and see if there's anybody out there, looking for the dogs. Somebody on foot, maybe, or maybe driving around."

"Out front of my house?"

"On the street, yes. And if there is, wave to them and ask if they're looking for their dogs." A thought occurred to Mac. "Is your husband at home?" Another thought: "Does he see the dogs, too?"

4

"No, he's not here! He went to the store for coffee! Can't you come and get the dogs?"

"No, Mrs. Howard. I can't do that. They'd just get away from an old man like me."

"But you're a policeman! I remember that!"

"Not anymore, no. You remember. My wife told you. I got sick and had to retire. And I didn't have anything to do with catching dogs, even then. You want to call Animal Control."

That was almost a lie, actually. She didn't really want to do that. The city's Animal Control had been downsized and resized and reorganized almost out of existence. The one remaining officer did a nice job of clearing up roadkill when someone reported it, but Mac couldn't remember the last time the dog catcher had actually caught a dog. But if she called the number, maybe Dispatch would have a regular patrol officer who was unoccupied and could drop by. Then his thread of thought was cut off as Mrs. Howard almost screamed in his ear.

"Now there's a man out there!"

Well, now. Maybe, assuming there really *was* someone in her yard, calling 911 wouldn't be a completely bad notion. If there was anybody. If there were any dogs at all. "A man, you said? What's he doing?"

"He's a big fellow. He's got a hat on, and he's trying ... he's trying to catch the dogs! Oh, my Lord!"

"What?!"

"It's David! It's my husband! What on earth is he doing out there!?"

The drama went on for another few minutes. Mr. Howard collared the dogs—there were in fact dogs in the back yard—and called the

5

phone number that was on a metal tag, hanging from one of their collars. A distraught woman four blocks away answered the call and came quickly after her escaped canines. Mac managed to get off the phone long before that, simply by asking Mrs. Howard to let him speak to her husband.

"Yeah, MacArthur," he said, "I'm, um, sorry she called you. She sees you walking your dogs, I guess, and she just links you up with that."

"Oh, don't give it a thought," said Mac. "Sorry I can't come and help, but I think a dog is more likely to catch me than vice versa."

He hung up after a few more polite words. He'd known that Janet Howard was dealing with dementia, but he hadn't realized the progress. *Damn the human body!* he thought.

His dogs gave up on scavenging for dropped toast bits, and they padded silently off to the front room. He followed and found them where they usually would be at this time: sitting quietly at the foot of the long front windows, scanning the street for threats such as terrorists, other dogs, or squirrels. Mac dropped onto a couch. His phone was still in his hand, and he glanced at the time display; it was twenty after eight, and after a few minutes of quiet contemplation, he'd pack himself up, make sure he had a few dollars with him, and take the Shepherds for their morning ride. The Bearclaw Coffee drive-through on the point of land at Washtenaw and Stadium would make him his usual drink and throw in a couple of complimentary biscuits for his entourage. Then they'd go the other way, west on Stadium, and they'd use another drive-up window to collect one of his many prescriptions. He'd just made up his mind it was time to go when ... the phone went off again.

"May I speak to Detective MacArthur?" The caller had just a touch of an African-American accent, and she spoke slowly. She sounded tired, and she seemed to be reading some of what she said.

"Well, I used to be a detective. I'm retired now."

"I see. I'm Deputy Corcoran with the Washtenaw County Sheriff's Department, Mister MacArthur. Do you have a few minutes to talk with me?"

"All right," Mac said. "What are we talking about?"

"Mister MacArthur, I am checking references for individuals who have applied for a deputy position with the Department. One candidate has listed you as a reference. Would you be willing to share some of your views on this person's abilities and qualifications with us, to assist in our hiring decision?"

For virtually all his long career, Mac had been forbidden to do any such thing. Human Resources departments wanted no part of random employees talking about their colleagues. The possibilities for generating legal trouble were just too great. Everyone he knew in any sector—public, private, profit, non-profit—all had the same instructions from above. Refer calls like this to HR.

But now, there wasn't any HR. He was out, retired, on disability, knocked down, to rearrange a line from Jerry Garcia, "like a bowling pin". The only trouble he could cause would be his own problem or, of course, a problem for the candidate if Mac said bad things about them. Still, the habit of caution lingered.

"I'm willing to hear the questions, at least," he said. "Who are you looking into? And what's the job?"

"The applicant who listed you as a reference is Officer Jerilynn Klein. She is applying for a canine deputy position we're seeking to fill."

Jeri Klein. Of course it would be Jeri Klein. An image formed immediately: a tall, fit, black woman, with North African features and a very serious expression. Early thirties, intelligent, and not someone you'd trifle with, at least not more than once. *Oh, yes,* he thought, *I know Jeri. This is going to be ... delicate.*

"All right," he said to the phone. "Go ahead with your questions."

"Thank you, sir. We appreciate your assistance. First of all, can you confirm that you worked with Officer Klein at the Ann Arbor Police Department?"

"Yes, that's right."

"And was your relationship with her as a supervisor, as someone she supervised, or as a co-worker?"

"We worked together on a few specific occasions. I was in Investigation, and she was in Patrol."

"Very well. Can you confirm these statements from her application? She started with the Ann Arbor Police Department in 2010; in January of this year, she went out on medical leave; and she has now returned to duty?"

"Well, I can't say when she joined the Department. She'd been there some time when I met her. The medical leave I was aware of, yes. And I wasn't aware that she'd come back from it ... gone back to work, I mean. But it doesn't surprise me. She was, uh, very dedicated."

"All right, sir. And now I have some questions about Officer Klein's capabilities. In addition to her police training, legal knowledge, and firearms proficiency, she lists several martial arts. Are you aware of those skills?"

"I don't have firsthand knowledge of that, no, but I've heard other people state that she knows at least one Japanese style of unarmed combat." *But what I'll just leave aside is the context in which they talked about it,* Mac thought.

8

"All right. She also states that she's been through the State Police canine training program. Can you confirm that?"

"Yes, the last time I heard from Officer Klein, she told me she'd finished with that."

"All right. I just have one more question for you. If you were in a position to hire or transfer in an applicant for a canine patrol position, would you select Officer Klein?"

Yes, Mac thought, *I would, because I'm the one who suggested she look for a K9 slot. And I suggested it because I thought it would improve her odds.*

That had been part of a conversation during a chance meeting at the University's Cancer Center. He was an old hand there, a frequent flier, their best customer. Jeri was new to the whole cancer experience, just diagnosed. And she was also waiting out an internal investigation, looking into a snowy evening's confrontation in which she'd shot a strung-out addict during an arrest—and then circle-kicked him in the head, too. The investigation had ruled that the shooting was justified; the guy was armed and he'd aimed at another officer. But on another occasion, Mac had seen her knee-drop a mildly retarded boy in the course of his arrest for fleeing a car-hits-pedestrian accident. Something, either crashing his car or that weight on his back, had ruptured the boy's spleen. Another time, Mac had been half a block away when a campus burglar made the mistake of swinging at Jeri; she'd grabbed him and head-butted his nose into a bloody oval all over his face. And finally, although she barely knew MacArthur, she'd told him in that strained, uncomfortable waiting room conversation that she left the army because she couldn't stand all the men.

And I can't say any of that, he thought. *Because I sat there and testified in a lawsuit deposition that I didn't think there anything wrong with the arrest of that poor kid she knee-dropped.*

9

And ... because she asked me for advice and I gave it to her and now I'm stuck with it. When will I learn not to give advice?

He drew a breath. "I haven't done a lot of hiring in my career, but I think Officer Klein might do well in a canine team. I think it might be a very good career step for her." *And that's the absolute truth. She'd go crazy in a desk job, and if she stays where she is, scraping up against belligerent, stupid, fundamentally damaged men on her own, something bad's going to happen. Something worse. But with a good dog there, she'd at least have somebody else to worry about.*

The deputy thanked him for his assistance and signed off. Mac stood up and looked out the windows, seeing a green Michigan-style summer jungle cutting off any detailed view of the street. He glanced at the phone again: ten to nine. He had it halfway back to its holster when the symbol at the top of the screen registered with him. He'd missed a call, and whoever it was left voice mail. "Well, hell!" he said aloud, and the dogs looked at him, heads cocked to one side.

 My name is George Thomas. I hold the rank of Major General in the National Army. I sit down with reluctance to write this document, which some may call a memoir or an autobiography, because although I once said to someone that time and history will do me justice, they have not. Parts of the public, especially in the formerly rebellious states, consider me at best their enemy, at worst a traitor to my home state. Some of the country's new, pushing breed of journalists and unlettered historical writers take a similar tack. And a few at least of my old colleagues, men I served, men who served with me, and some of those I commanded, have made public their opinions regarding my ability and motives during the war of the rebellion.

I am no d'Artagnan, and it is no longer accepted that a man wronged and slandered—I do not think slandered is too strong a word in the case of at least one officer—should challenge another. But just as in years past a peaceful and humane gentleman could be forced by the demands of honor to pick up the sword, no matter how much his faith and education and principles argued against it, so am I driven by respect for my family, my friends, the men with whom I served, and least of all, myself, to take up the only weapon that justice, the law, and a humane civilization allows, that is, the pen. I cannot silence criticism, inaccuracy, and outright falsehood, but I can refute them by a single document that lays out the facts, in one place, with as much clarity and even-handedness as my poor grasp of exposition will allow.

But how hard it is, having determined to write about my life, to begin, and having begun, to find the events and people in my all too human and fallible memory that are important to anyone's understanding of this thing I call myself. However, I have seen other men's personal narratives that commence with early life and childhood experience, and lacking a better plan, I will follow in their path.

I was born in Southampton County, Virginia at the end of July in the year 1816, on land belonging to my father. The farm was near a hamlet called Newsoms with the nearest town of any consequence being Jerusalem. We were well-to-do for the time and place, and even when my father died, the family continued to live well on the land and to work it.

Very early in my memory is a scene and a conversation with an old blacksmith who had been tending to our horses. When he had finished and was leaving, I walked with him part of the way, and he told me that in his view, horses were the most intelligent creatures on earth, second only to men. He said that a horse was large and strong and fast, and if it wanted to, it could rebel, break away from its owner, seize its freedom, and run off to the wild. But instead, the smith went on, horses chose to stay with man and work for us because they were of an inherently noble turn of mind, for an animal, and they recognized us as their superiors in all but strength. There were a few of them, he said, that were disinclined to accept their place in creation, horses that would not work and would defy man and cause damage and injury, but those individuals were kept from doing damage by force, if need be.

As he was speaking, we approached Jack, a tall black man, one of our slaves, who was stripped to the waist, working skillfully to repair a section of fence. He was a man I knew well, and his children were my frequent companions. He was civil, cheerful, and well trusted. I greeted him and he smiled, raised his hand, and greeted me, including a word or two about the heat. I glanced at the smith, and saw that he barely noticed our workman, just exchanged a look and passed by. That was a common thing among the white people of the South, and I thought nothing of it then. Not many years later on, though, I had cause to remember the blacksmith and his thesis on the topic of horses and their place in the world.

There was a slave who lived nearby to us, a man considered by many of his fellows to be at least a thinker if not actually a prophet. He said that he saw visions and heard the voice of God speaking to him. In 1831, the year I had reached fifteen and incidentally two years after my father had died of injuries when a wagon overturned, the family was asleep. There was a sound of hooves and shouting from outside, and we saw that a neighbor, Mister Gurley, had ridden up in great haste. To our shock, we heard from him that the prophet, Nat Turner, was leading a band of revolted slaves in a full insurrection, attacking farms and murdering white people wherever they found them. Mr. Gurley was warning everyone he could reach, advising them to leave everything behind and flee for their lives to the nearest town, Jerusalem. For a few of the adults, memories of Denmark Vesey or George Boxley came to mind, but for most of the people, free or enslaved, a rebellion was terribly unexpected.

My mother and my oldest sister quickly gathered us into a carriage we used, the women mostly, for journeys outside our land. We set our servants to the task of concealing anything that could be used as a weapon, and as dawn broke and we could see some of what we assumed were the insurgents approaching, we set out for the town. I was given the reins and told to drive as fast as I could, but we saw that some of the rebels were mounted and that they were gaining on us. The light still being poor and thus offering us some invisibility, my mother determined to leave the carriage and continue across the country, since by staying on the road, we left ourselves open to being cut off from the town. It was a hard trip on foot, across a marshy area called Mill Swamp, then by the Cypress Bridge road until we judged we were due south of the town. Then we turned north until we struck the river and followed its banks to the Nottaway Road Bridge. It was already guarded by the militia, and they guided us on into the town and to a place where we could rest. In the morning, we learned that our servants had also eluded the rebels and come into town for safety and in search of us. Because the people were so aroused by the revolt of what was, in fact, only a few slaves, our people had to be lodged in the jail to ensure their safety from white mobs.

What people now remember as Nat Turner's Revolt lasted less than a full day, his followers deserting him and eventually fleeing altogether when they met with the militia. Turner himself managed to hide for a month and a half, living in the woods on his owner's farm. He was eventually found by a hunting dog, and the hunter turned him over to the authorities. His trial was brief although carried out in accordance with the law, and he was hanged. In all, from execution and general violence, far more slaves and free blacks died than the fifty or so whites who lost their lives.

Although the event itself is firmly in my mind so many years later, with its hours of fear and our hard march through the countryside, I remember with almost the same clarity its effect on my attitude toward slavery. Leaving aside all emotion, if that is entirely possible for a man of my birth and upbringing, the clear conclusion is that the base cause of the revolt can only have been the institution of slavery. I was not alone in thinking that, by the way, even though I was born in the midst of a society that officially sanctioned servitude. Virginia and in fact other slave-holding states had seen a number of proposals before the law, intended to bring an end to the custom, gradually or abruptly, and I recall that even as a boy I favored the proposals that would result in a gradual fading away of the institution. I reacted strongly against those who were at the extremes of the controversy, either slavery's absolute maintenance or its instant disappearance. To most of the people, civilians and military alike, those I knew and admired right up to the period of the Southern rebellion, it seemed that slavery must pass away, but gradually, throwing the least hardships on anyone, black or white. I

13

realize now, so much later in my life, that my attitudes toward any major question, whether with reference to slavery or not ¹ be expressed in those same terms. I so often find, reviewing m⸝ ⸍rsonal history, that I have preferred a path to achieve the desired en⸝ ⁿd yet cause the least harm to the population affected.

Laura Beth Peakes died at the age of twenty-three, the cause of death being stupidity.

She came from an Alabama family. Her father was an employee of the Pickens County Road Commission, right over on the Mississippi line. He was one of the workers you see standing around a work site, holding a "SLOW" sign and being oblivious to the irony. Her mother worked in retail, specifically as a clerk in one of several stores over in Tuscaloosa County, selling beer, snacks, gasoline, fishing licenses, and beer. Both of Laura's parents had ᵇᵉ described in school as kids who "won't amount to nothi⸝ the two of them lived at least into late middle age, and the fact that they managed to marry, become parents (four times), and usually keep food on the table without public assistance was their refutation of that base canard. But it left little time for more advanced forms of parenting. Life at all was hard enough, let alone the life of the mind. Ideas were worrisome things that other people had.

Their youngest child, Laura Beth, was born during one of the small economic downturns that the Southern rural economy suffers. Mom and Dad had to scrape even harder than usual, and so she got even less tender loving care than her older siblings. Intellectually, she inherited her mother's brains and her father's ambition, social skills, and engineering capabilities. Physically, she got the family's dark brown hair, pale white skin, and a tendency to burn pink in the sun. By the time of her death, she'd had exactly no jobs, no completed educational accomplishments except a misdemeanor arrest for minor in possession, and nothing that would amount to much more life experience than you'd expect in a raccoon of equivalent age. But she'd managed to get married and pregnant (in that order, making her something of an outlier among her peers). Her husband was a man with a career similar to her father's, although he was more advanced in the road construction sector, being allowed to use a shovel. Her son, Richard "Ricky" Peakes, was six months old when Laura Beth decided to flee from a traffic stop. She ran a stop sign out by the Dollar General and became one with the universe or at least that portion of the universe represented by the front end of a truck.

Ricky's father, Duane Peakes, wasn't unkind by nature, but he too had never completed high school, and with a baby on his hands was kept very busy just making a living. Neither father nor son had anything to speak of in the way of a social life until the boy was ambulatory and language-capable. Laura Beth's mother looked after him while Dad worked and, when Ricky had reached four or so, Grandma babysat while Dad took an occasional evening off. This was never anything more than a few beers with his road crew colleagues, over at Jimmy's, in Gordo, and it was almost always a guys' night out, but in the course of one session, he managed to meet a woman, seven years older than he was. She was divorced, and she had a twelve-year-old daughter. The settlement gave her custody of the girl and her ex-husband's very nice pickup truck, plus a reasonable sum of money from the sale of their house. She pointed out to Duane the advantages that a union of households would bring, and without too much more discussion, Duane got to sit down with Ricky and tell him about the new mom and big sister he was going to have.

It would have been better if Dad had remarried earlier on, when Ricky was, say, two. There would have been less adjustment and acceptance for the boy to do. As it was, he hadn't been to school yet, hadn't really met many other children, didn't really understand that having a father but not a mother wasn't the case for everyone. He spent his days with his grandmother, and the nights with Dad were mostly dinner and TV. After the wedding, there was a brief, awkward month in which he and his father and the new person he was supposed to call "Mom" and the new person he was supposed to call "Paula" all lived in the small house where he'd lived all his short life. Then there was a confusing week in which everything that was familiar got packed up in boxes and carried out in batches to the shiny new pickup truck. He got to spend the last couple of nights with Grandma, and then he came "home" to a new, bigger house, one in which he and Paula didn't have to share a room.

During Ricky's first four years, he hadn't had any particular sort of education. Grandma read to him from a few simple, illustrated books, and he watched a large amount of random television. It was a fact of his existence that he wasn't interacting with other children much or adults either. But in some way, he began to absorb language and even rudimentary ethics. There were, the TV told him, bad people, sure enough, but in the end, good people avoided them or even thwarted them. The content—programs or ads — showed him happy folks, wearing bright clothes and doing exciting things. They were in groups, boys and girls together, happy and smiling, sometimes singing and dancing. Every other living member of his family just saw images and heard sounds, and sometimes they felt a vague desire for the things being advertised. But Ricky absorbed more than that. He began to form an idea of what the world was and how it wanted you to be.

What no one remembered about Ricky's family was that back in the early part of the twentieth century, his great-grandfather had not been at all an idiot. He'd actually been a clever man with a reasonable education. He went away to school, studied business and commercial topics, and came home to run the family farm. Unfortunately, he managed to make his mother's housekeeper pregnant. The family and the local minister put him under severe pressure to do the right thing, and so he married her. Ricky's grandfather was born and then the very next year, the stock market crashed. The economy fell apart, a bank called in a loan the young man had taken out, and suddenly the Peakes family were lower middle class. They lost land and other assets, and as the Depression wore on, the family disintegrated. Nothing much remained to be passed down, including even the story. But unpredictably, some of his ancestor's genes did come to Ricky. Ricky was going to be, without anyone's being aware of it, a smart boy.

Now, even at four years old, he was putting printed words together with ideas. He knew what "stop" meant on a road sign. He could read the numbers on the pickup truck's digital speedometer, and he knew when they were larger than the big black letters on the speed limit signs. He knew a few brand names well enough to whine when his parents bought a different kind of snacks than the one he'd seen advertised. Having more people in the house and more people to observe, he began to see how they behaved, how they made rules, and how well they followed them. A year went around, he absorbed new lessons, and in the fall, he found himself in the strange new world of kindergarten.

He already knew that there were things you couldn't do because you were too young or not big enough. He learned that there were other things you shouldn't do because you might get hurt. And he learned that there were many things that you might want to do and other people didn't want you to do, but it was only a problem if they knew you'd done them. He tried out this insight with small crimes around the house, and he discovered that a blunt denial ("Did you eat all the 'tater chips?" "No.") was less effective than having another party to blame. He tried using Paula as a scapegoat, but Paula was older, wiser in the world of childhood crime, and her mother's favorite, anyway. He was schooled early on in forensics when he tried blaming the family's dogs for something, and it was found that the crime would have required an opposable thumb.

17

For these small misdemeanors, Ricky would be scolded or sometimes smacked on the bottom. The consequences were never severe, but he was always left with a feeling of failure. He'd done something he wanted to do, and his measures to avoid being caught at it had failed. In the small world of the home, there wasn't anything he could do that would be especially disastrous. He had no interest in fooling around with the appliances, and Dad was just bright enough to keep his shotgun locked up. But when Ricky entered school, the constraints multiplied. The list of things not to be done got longer, and the percentage of them that were desirable became greater. You weren't supposed to be late, or talk, or whisper, or pass notes in class. You weren't allowed to eat anywhere but the lunchroom, bring toys with you, or go make tunnels in the long grass behind the playground. All of these were things that he wanted to do, and he could see no good reason for not doing them, if he could avoid getting caught at it. The grass tunnels were a great example.

For some reason, the school couldn't be bothered to get the adjoining field mowed periodically. The administration just assumed that naming it "off limits" would be sufficient. The kids, on the other hand, quickly discovered that if your tunnels—just paths made by crawling along and crushing down the three-foot-high grass—didn't start right at the playground edge where they'd be seen, nobody from the official world would interfere. There was a kind of club among a dozen or so of the kids, and you needed to be one of the club to take part in the tunneling and the secret meetings in spaces where the grass was squashed down in a circle. Ricky was one of the inventors of the game and one of the people who got to vote on new members. When a girl named Kelly wanted to join, Ricky voted to let her in. On the second day she'd been in the club, Kelly crawled around a corner in a grass tunnel and put her hand down on a copperhead or a rattlesnake. It bit her on the forearm and escaped through the grass.

The resulting crisis featured a very public blaming of the school for not keeping the kids out of the field. The school, naturally, blamed the families, pointing out the memo to parents they'd sent, telling them to tell their children not to leave the playground. There was an effort to find out who'd started the tunnel game, who was going out there, if somebody was somehow responsible. A few of Ricky's club colleagues talked, but he kept quiet. When the little girl was able to say anything, she named a few names, but by then it had occurred to the adults that the villains they were after were five and six-year-olds, and, as one school board member said privately, "At least nobody molested nobody." The school fenced the playground and hired an additional supervisor. The victim's parents put her in another school when she recovered. Ricky kept his head down and suffered no more than the loss of the tunnel game. He never saw Kelly again, and somehow he came to transfer the blame onto her. If she'd been more careful, it never would have happened.

He began to realize that the things people said weren't always true. His step-sister Paula helped him with that insight, since she was already handy at telling Mom one thing and Dad another. She let Mom think she was doing something academic after school, and she implied to Dad that it was basketball practice. In fact, she was just hanging out with her friends and getting a ride home from someone else's parent. This would have been a simple lie to catch, but neither of the parents really tried. Dad worked, ate, engaged in fairly mundane sex with his new spouse, and slept. Mom frankly didn't give a damn what the girl did. And Ricky wasn't really anywhere in the picture at all. Each parent, if they thought about it, had the idea that a roof overhead, food, clothes, television, and a certain amount of random correction was the essence of child raising. So, when over the years of his childhood the boy did well in school, nobody said much about it. When he fouled up and got caught at it, whatever it might have been, nobody did more than yell at him. Sometimes the scolding included rhetorical questions like "Why are you so damn dumb?" It was unanswerable, of course, and he shrugged it off, usually thinking of the A he'd just received on an arithmetic quiz or the praise the Social Studies teacher gave him. By the time he was twelve, he'd stopped caring what or if his family members thought about him. He had a small number of friends his own age, a group of similar outcasts who had no more interest in sports than he did. They were all boys and, responding to the community and culture they lived in, they all privately thought they should be interested in girls, but ...

That was the problem. Ricky looked around at the girls and women he knew and the ones he saw on television. He contrasted the imagery with the reality and with the myths and dirty jokes he heard from his friends, and he found that it was impossible to connect the ideas with himself. His few clumsy attempts even to talk with girls were painful and embarrassing and unproductive. Although he had unquestionable evidence that people he knew of paired up, went on dates, and "did it", either in the marital bed or in the back seat of a car, the sheer distance in time and effort and courage that separated him from that state of living seemed insurmountable. This was never something he talked about, but he'd try to imagine it, working it through in this mind, going through the motions, and he could never put himself in that picture. It made him uncomfortable and then progressively more angry. He'd look at his female classmates, especially those who seemed to be happy and capable, people whose names he barely knew and who certainly didn't know him, and he'd assign some part of his general pain to them. He was unhappy, and he came to blame women for it.

Mac's voice mail message was from FBI Agent Andrew McReady Patel, a young man he knew and liked, a man who'd shown himself to be a good investigator, and thanks to a stint in the Marines, a more than good shot. Somehow the cases that pulled MacArthur informally back out of retirement seemed to involve Andy, regardless of the Ann Arbor Police Department's policy of rendering unto Caesar any investigation that required Federal attention. The reasons for these entanglements had varied wildly, from drugs to tenuous links to the CIA to the pursuit of rapacious lenders, but in some way or other, Mac and Andy and Ann Arbor always seemed to find their paths intersecting.

Beyond all that, though, their circles were tangent in an even stronger way. One of Mac's close friends was a woman he'd worked with at the Department, a woman who'd initially upset the FBI in her handling of a specific set of affairs. Mac, older and hypothetically wiser, was assigned to help Detective Jennifer Langton with her professional growth, both in investigative technique and in not annoying Federal agencies. Apparently, he'd done well. She'd gone on to become an effective investigator and then a Director of Corporate Security at a STEM company, and she'd done so well at maintaining a good working relationship with the FBI that'd she'd married Agent Patel. Mac and his wife, Coleen, were not parents in the biological sense, and they treated Jenn and Andy as something similar to adult offspring.

Consequently, a voice mail message from Andy could mean any number of things, and as a matter of fact, this one did.

"Hi, Mac. It's Andy. I wonder if we could talk about a couple of things? We've got a kind of ... funny ... case with some Ann Arbor-ness in it. Maybe you'd be able to, oh, I don't know ... talk it over with me? I mean, there's parts we can't talk about. You know how that is. But you might know some people, I guess. And then there's another thing. Oh, and Jenn and I have some great news, too! Anyway, call me back if you can. Thanks. Ah, bye."

Oh, for Christ's sake, Mac thought. *They're pregnant!*

Indian Key

For Ricky Peakes, getting home was a bit of a hike. He procrastinated for a few minutes after checking in his assignment, using a hack to get around the university's browsing restrictions and checking quickly on a few blogs. He was hungry, though, and it was Saturday afternoon. Verbally abusing people was a pleasure, but it was best practiced at night, from a personal machine. In the daylight and especially from a university computer, he felt constrained. The blogger he'd called a "slut" the night before was melting down on-line, but now he just read her complaints with a wry smile and made no response. There were no other items of interest, and he shut things down and left the building.

Tuscaloosa and the University of Alabama campus were, as usual, muggy and hot. He shrugged to adjust his backpack and walked off south on Seventh Street. It was a quarter of a mile down to Capstone and then diagonally across the Diag to University. For another couple of blocks it was still just school buildings and the massive stadium. Finally, shops appeared; it was the point in his walk where he always thought, *Civilization at last*. He passed a chain ice cream store, U of A T-shirt shops, pizza, sandwiches, a bar or two, and far too much faux-historic red brick. At a street named after a football coach, Ricky turned south and ducked into a convenience store. He bought a microwaveable taco and a highly-caffeinated soda. It was another half block to his apartment.

The history of Tuscaloosa is one of recovering from things, war and tornados, mostly. Recovery often becomes a utilitarian process, and Ricky's apartment and the building and the entire neighborhood formed an extreme example. There were students, transient people who came and went and seldom stayed more than three or four years. There was a university, located nearby. There were plots of land that were vacant or could easily be made vacant. Housing the students, for profit, in circumstances they could put up with for a brief period was obviously the utilitarian thing to do. Ricky's building was an example of these circumstances, a single rectangular solid. From the front windows, you saw its parking lot and the side of another apartment structure; from the back windows, you saw the back of a different building. There weren't any side windows. And as you drove or walked in, you saw a blank end wall and a dumpster with trash scattered around outside it. Many people living below the poverty line in northern cities would have rejected the whole area as being too ghetto.

Ricky didn't reject it. All his prior life, he'd lived in single-family homes in a small town. Tuscaloosa was the biggest city he'd ever seen, and apartments were a novelty. And they were so much better, after all, than the dormitory he'd had to occupy in his first year. More expensive, yes, and he had to have some kind of part-time job to cover the rent, but so much better otherwise. No roommate, for example. And a short walk to a café with an Internet connection. In his apartment, Ricky could watch television, but in the year 2000, home broadband wasn't something that automatically came with a cheap apartment. The Internet café was still a concept of its own, not something to be taken for granted. Ricky needed a connection—a $HOME for the $HOMEless, as an earlier era of public connectivity people had called it—as much as he needed money and horrifyingly bad food. Ricky was becoming a *jötnar*: a troll.

Like a junkie or an alcoholic, he hadn't intended to form an addiction. In his last year of high school, someone had shown him a chat room. The users were virtually all boys, and the hypothetical topic was sports in its generic form. Among Alabama high school boys, that meant football, baseball, and basketball. No one he knew used the word "soccer" without snickering, and hunting wasn't "sports", it was "hunting". None of that mattered at all to Ricky; what he saw was the banter and the freedom of speech. He saw that you could win by outsmarting people or shouting them down or insulting them, and that you could do it anonymously, without looking anyone in the face and without getting the ass-kicking you'd receive if you did it in person. For an unathletic, overweight little geek, it was a liberating discovery.

There was no computer in young Ricky's home, but he had friends with AOL accounts and PCs or Apples, things trusting parents had provided on the theory that it would help the children succeed in life. The parents seldom laid a hand on the devices, so the children—Ricky and others—sat around and studied the more obvious kinds of psychological abuse. They picked on people they knew, homing in on self-image or insecurities, and they trolled unknown others, cynically mocking received ideas, enthusiasms, technical inexperience, and any kind of socially progressive opinion. If anyone agreed with them, they'd cheerfully turn on him, claiming he'd fallen for their prank and excoriating him for being naive. Of course, they all acted under user IDs, code names that were designed either to dominate or to suck in the trusting users. It was all juvenile, all as clear as if they'd stood together at a window and shouted, "So what if girls don't like us! We don't like them either! And no, we aren't gay!"

When he graduated from high school (third in the class), a counselor helped him with several applications, and when the boy got an acceptance from Alabama, the man pushed Ricky to take it. There was another counselor, a woman, who wondered if the leap from a small, insular town to big, scary Tuscaloosa might not be hard to make, but the man working with Ricky waved her off, and Ricky followed his inclination and his ego. After all, no one else in the class got into U of A with any kind of scholarship. And so he went off to college.

In his first year, he took the introductory software engineering classes and worked his way through the other requirements. The "humanities" classes were designed to make the point that technology wasn't the only thing people might choose to do, but they failed to make it very well. The message that did come across was negative: this is a class you have to take, and you'd better get a decent grade in it, but nothing you hear about will make you a dime after graduation. That was what Ricky heard, anyway. And by now, he'd begun to understand at least the rock-bottom basics of software as a career. He understood that there was software to be used, games for example, where the effort was in the concept. There was an entire domain of development in which you could hack something together in a few months, using libraries and code generators, as long as you just had a great idea for the content. With a bit of insight from faculty members who'd escaped from industry and gotten teaching jobs, he began to think of applications coding as blue collar.

But there was another kind of career: being the man behind the libraries and the interfaces and the file structures and the operating systems. You could be the one who knew why things worked, not just how. And the faculty deified the serious guys, the guys who could make Linux sing, the guys who hated Windows and wouldn't have a Mac in their homes. Already, even at the end of his freshman year, that became the space Ricky wanted to occupy.

Through his second year, he refined the model. He began to know more about the information industry and about its potential rewards. He came to understand, for example, that decisions you made today could affect your future income, where you got to live, even what you had to wear. And an overheard conversation startled him; it suggested that your basic behavior, now, in your younger life, might keep you out of a whole range of jobs later on. Arrests, for example. Any diagnosis of a mental problem or a record of substance abuse. More than casual contact with foreign nationals. Any of those things might keep you from becoming the sort of strong, self-confident, well-paid engineering god he wanted to be.

The reality was that there weren't many of those gods in the department, although there were junior faculty and graduate students who desperately tried to put on the halo. And there were no acknowledged goddesses at all. Instead, there were a minority of women, some of whom were extremely bright. But bright or not, they lived with a steady, subtle de-emphasis. They got to teach the undergraduate classes, the beginning classes, the "Introduction to" courses. They were the Assistant Chairpersons of faculty committees, not the Chairs. And for Ricky, at least, they were functionally invisible. By the end of the first semester of his third year, he'd had exactly two classes in the department with women instructors, and none of the women students were his friends. What friends he did have were, as in high school, withdrawn and unsocial boys. They were people he'd meet for a beer, perhaps, and a discussion of an assignment, but no one the sight of whom would make him smile. At the end of the day, they were competition.

And so, with a year and a half to go before graduation, Ricky was functionally alone. He studied, he wrote assigned pieces of code, he wrote papers, he took exams. He read little or nothing outside the context of school, and he avoided large scale social events. He wasn't a football fan, and he didn't care for loud music and quantities of alcohol. Being under the influence made him nervous because as he warmed up, he told people things about himself and his background that he regretted later. He wasn't proud of growing up in the boonies or of anything else, really, from the time before he came to college. Even questions about his course work or his plans for later seemed threatening. He was reclusive, ate by himself, watched a certain amount of television, and most of all, he trolled.

🐈

MacArthur set his phone down and made a couple of quick notes. No matter how casual a day he was having, he always had a small paper notebook and a pen; it was another holdover from his detective years. No amount of typing skill nor any imaginable speech recognition algorithm could beat the scribbled, handwritten string of words. All he wanted it to be was a reminder of something, not a treatise and not a tweet, either.

The current page was partly filled with a to-do list from the day before. There were three crossed out entries: "~~Pick up scripts from drugstore.~~" "~~By the Pound: Granola.~~" "~~Dinner.~~" He drew a line under them and wrote the date. Then he added: "Call Andy back" and "Jeri".

He looked at the page, trying to decide which to do first or if calling Jeri Klein was even strictly necessary. He wanted to let her know that she was being taken seriously by the County, but he also thought of her as ... what? Not a villain. Not a loony. But maybe just a bit dangerous, someone whose reaction to anything might not be predictable.

And then, Andy. He had no concern about Andy's reaction to anything. Mac considered him a capable and reliable young Fed and a good friend, besides. But A) he was a Fed, after all, and B) some of that voice mail message had been rather cryptic. And C), Mac had thought—he'd assumed, actually—that Jenn Langton was done with parenthood. She had two daughters from her disastrous first marriage. For most of the time she was working with MacArthur, she'd spoken of them as a pair of burnouts, foolish and borderline-criminal young girls. One of them was showing signs of maturing, now, and he knew that she and Jenn had a substantial *rapprochement* going on. But still, nothing Jenn had ever said to him suggested any nostalgia for child rearing.

But why do I care? he asked himself. *What business is it of mine?* And as easy as it was to ask the questions, so the answers came easily, too. First, it'd mean he'd been wrong about something. He'd have failed to read the signs correctly, and he hated that. Worse, one of them might have imposed on the other partner. It might not be something they both wanted, equally. And weighing up the two personalities, he found that it would probably have been Jenn's idea, not Andy's. That would be contrary to a lot of things he thought he knew about her. *Or hell; maybe they just bought a new car.*

Mac looked at the notebook again, braced it on his left hand and added another item: "Get coffee". He could procrastinate another twenty minutes, go do his drive-through errands, think things over, and make up his mind before he called anyone back.

 My early thoughts about my future and the profession I might seek were somewhat unsettled. I enjoyed making things and repairing things, and although my mother would never have agreed to it, I remember thinking that I was meant for some kind of craft rather than a higher calling. I was very fond of working with my hands, and I remember people expressing surprise at what I could learn to do, just by watching others doing it. I paid attention to the tools and the methods that a saddler used, both the man himself and his apprentices, and after a while, I got some leather and fittings and made myself a saddle. It might not have matched others for its finish, but I rode with it for several years, and it was entirely serviceable.

While my father was still alive, he apparently said to my mother that he wanted me to study law. At least that is the wish that she passed on to me as I approached the age of decision. I made a beginning on it, and I might well have carried on, ending my career as an attorney or perhaps an office holder in the Old Dominion. Things worked themselves out differently, though. Our Congressman in those years was John Young Mason, and as a Congressman he had the right to nominate boys for study in the United States Military Academy. My uncle approached Mister Mason and (as I was later told) sought an appointment for me. While we waited to see what might come of it, I worked as a deputy clerk for a few months. Then I was informed that Congressman Mason had recommended me. I was accepted and, I suppose it is needless to say, I accepted the offered place. I learned later that I was to be something of a make or break candidate as no one from our district had yet succeeded in graduating from the Academy. Our Congressman was very clear with me, when I called on him to thank him, that I had better make it through, or the appointment would be the last favor I could expect.

Thus in the spring of 1836, I entered the Academy. For a first year cadet, I was older than the average, being twenty, but I determined to make little of that fact, since all in my class were considered equally, even though there was a range, in some cases, of as much as four years in age. I remember the time I spent at West Point with the rosy tint of time passed, but I believe we must all have longed to be done with it and embarked on our careers. Some were more forward about their desires and ambitions, but I did what I could to remain serious in expression and speech, seeing quickly that the silly, juvenile, and noisy cadets drew more unwelcome attention to themselves than those who simply buckled down and did the work.

While I was there, I met many young men whose names will be familiar to anyone who reads this, men who served either the United States or the rebellion, men who also served, all on the same side, in the wars that came before, including the fighting in the south and in the west against the natives of our continent and then afterward against Mexico. The list is long, and I will only mention the best known, men such as James Longstreet and William Sherman. There were many others at the Academy who fought together or against each other in the decades following our graduation, and if I tried to name them all, I would fall short somewhere and risk offending those I might neglect.

Of politics during those years, especially the various theories of union and succession, I remember little. It was not a subject that obsessed us, although there were boys on both sides of the question. In those years, it was not one that the nation thought of as passionately as it came to later on. I do recall that one of our texts was an old and not well-reasoned (as I now realize) treatise on constitutional law, called *A View of the Constitution of the United States*. It was a slim volume, written many years before by a man named Rowle or Rawle, and it took the position that remaining within the union or leaving it was up to the citizens. I no longer remember the logic by which its author reached that conclusion, but I remember dismissing it then as ill-considered and

29

old fashioned. Regardless, though, I must remind my readers, my old colleagues and opponents, and even myself that in those years, none of us really thought the dissolution of the Union was likely or even possible. I thought then as I continued to think until the outbreak of the rebellion that slavery would be brought to an end gradually, by processes calculated to bring each freed slave into free society in a way that was in both his interest and those of the country as a whole.

I graduated from the Academy in 1840, thus winning (I suppose, for I never heard from him), the approval of Congressman Mason. Although the army was not a large establishment in that year, it was involved in a long conflict, one that could hardly be called a war, with the native peoples of Florida and other parts of the deep south. I was posted very quickly to the Third Artillery Regiment, and we went soon after that to take part in the last two years of what is now called the Second Seminole War. I will pass over it with little comment, because it was neither a formative experience for me nor a glorious one. Although I was an artillery officer, I spent much of my time in commissary work, organizing the feeding and sheltering of our forces at Fort Lauderdale.

The war was a miserable affair of raids and pursuits, and its objective was nothing less than to force the native population to pack up, leave their lands, and relocate themselves to the Indian Territory in the west. Since they were a people used to living in swamps and forests, they resisted being sent to the prairies, and so a long series of small wars had been going on against them since the year I was born. It would continue with pauses until well into the 1850s.

In the year of my graduation, the war against these several tribes that were collectively called Seminoles was expensive and out of favor with the public, both because of its cost and, to the credit of the country, also because of humanitarian concerns over its injustice to the natives. It sparked up again, though, in one of the larger fights, indeed one of the few large enough to have a name, the battle of Indian Key. On this small island at the very tip of the Florida peninsula, ten Americans out of fifty were killed in a surprise attack by the insurgent population, and even small boats armed with cannon were unable to drive off the Indians. As is usual with this sort of warfare, the attackers faded back into the country while a larger force of troops was sent to find them. A full six months afterwards, some of the Seminoles were surprised in their camp, and their reported leader and a few others were taken, tried, and hanged. This was the sort of dismal, exhausting, expensive fighting that characterized these long and brutally fruitless conflicts.

For my part, I saw no fighting until I had been there almost a year. I was finally allowed to go along on an expedition led by Captain Richard Wade, another of many forays after the illusive Indians. Ours was more successful than most in that we took a prisoner early on who gave us information , and we eventually fell on a camp, killing a few of the opposing force, if it could be called that, taking some prisoners, and capturing a few weapons. Acting on intelligence from our captives, we moved on into the swamps and eventually raided another camp with similar success. We marched back to our base, then, and I was promoted to First Lieutenant. Not long afterward, I left with my Company for refit at New Orleans. A year after that, a treaty was signed, bringing this second in what would become a series of three desultory struggles to an end. That was the story of my first war.

Ricky put his taco in the microwave and his soft drink in the refrigerator. While his dinner processed itself, he flipped through a text book, reviewing the structural differences between C++ and Object Perl. He'd already written assignments in both of those languages, and he was far enough along to appreciate the single-mindedness of one over the organic growth of the other. A final exam that he'd be taking in a few weeks would call for an analytic comparison, something beyond just knowing the different ways of making code connect to a server.

When his food was reasonably warm, he ate it quickly, looking at the book and taking handwritten notes. His laptop was still in the backpack. Without a connection and with no immediately pressing assignment, there was no real use for it. He finished eating, threw the packaging away, and put the pack on again. Swiping his hands around his belt and hips, he confirmed that he had his wallet, his phone, and his keys. It was only just six o'clock, and if he left now, he shouldn't have any problem getting a table at the café. He went out, locking the door as he went, walked out of the parking lot, and turned back north on his street. He was looking where he was going, watching where he put his feet; not everyone here scrupulously picked up after their dogs. He was exhibiting one kind of caution, but neglecting another. Behind him in the lot, a car started, and it drove just to the exit. The people inside watched as he walked down to university University and turned left. Then it moved out and went very slowly after him, being careful not to catch up.

Ricky walked down the south side of the street, and at the end of the first block, he took advantage of a favorable traffic light and crossed. He went west one more block and half way down the next before he stopped at a pink-painted brick building, pushed a door open, and went inside. Outside, the car turned onto the side street and then into the building's rear parking lot. Three women got out of it and walked around to the front, not saying anything. It was still too early for the temperature to have come down much, but they were all wearing long pants or, in one case, long cargo shorts. Two of them were black, with short dark hair, one was white with blonde hair coming just below her ears. They weren't remarkable at all at first glance, although they walked with a sort of rooted assurance. Watching them, you might have thought "runners" or "softball team". They went into the building by the same front door, glanced around, and picked a table. Four tables down, Ricky was setting up his laptop. Otherwise, most of the room was empty. It looked as though it would be a slow night at the LogInn Internet café.

Ricky's game was to jump around among different blogs, assuming different identities and personalities. He kept at least two browser windows open, as well as a small list of his user names. Needless to say, none of them was "Ricky." Instead, the names varied from site to site, depending on what role he was playing. That he kept them in a file on his personal machine didn't worry him.

One of his new targets was a blog intended for gun and hunting enthusiasts. After watching quietly for a few days, noting the themes and opinions and users, he signed in pretending to be a suburban mother, and he began dropping a few gun-control posts into the mix. Every time he said anything about "keeping the children safe" or, even worse, hinted that citizens didn't really need assault rifles to hunt squirrels, he could count on a good crop of outraged replies, second amendment rants, and general threats. Each one was a small victory; every time he conned someone into losing his composure, it was a point for Ricky. The ultimate success would come when, perhaps in a few more nights, he'd say something especially stereotypical and outrageous. That, he hoped, would prompt one of the regulars to suggest that he, Ricky, was a fraud. Then he'd go all tearful in his mom persona and get someone else in the group to attack the first one for attacking Mom. At that point, he'd fade away, he thought. Let them stew. He'd done this to an anti-smoking group, last semester, and his pleasure and amusement were worth the time it took to get them flaming each other.

The NRA boys were only a sideline for Ricky, though. They were almost all men. His real joy came from creating chaos and bad feeling in feminist circles. He'd find a group that consisted mostly of young women, preferably one that focused on discrimination in sports, business, or academia. He'd watch from the shadows until he picked up the terminology and goals. And in particular, he'd note the oppressors, whoever it might be that the members believed were keeping them down, discriminating against women, denying opportunities, pinching or shoulder-patting or making little remarks. When he knew the cast of characters, then he'd join in, sometimes shifting back and forth between male and female user names. He'd stir the pot, sometimes impersonating a victim, sometimes pretending to be one of the accused. Especially in the latter role, he might post contrite apologies; at other times, he'd give out arrogant denials. He could be subtle about it, or he could employ the "You were asking for it!" option. The emotion and fury that these little pranks caused were his equivalent of pornography. He slept best, alone in his cheap apartment, when he could go to bed assured that he'd ruined someone else's night.

It was early enough in the history of the net that a public place could still get away with charging for air time. Ricky's budget was tight enough that he kept himself to a couple of hours a night, and when he'd used up this evening's allocation of funds, he shut down his machine, finished his soda, and got up. The café was doing a better business now, but there were still empty seats. He hadn't seen the three women who came in just after he did, and so the fact that they were gone, their table now occupied by four frat brothers, didn't mean a thing to him. He walked out and back down University Avenue toward home.

When he got there, he unlocked the apartment, dropped his backpack on a chair, and relocked the door. A few nights before, somebody had knocked; Ricky looked out the peep hole and saw a young white guy, holding up a pizza box. Reassured, he'd opened the door and denied having ordered anything. The guy said "Oh. Okay. Damn. Gotta go call, I guess," and went away. It didn't cause any paranoia, but it just reinforced Ricky's general notion that in a big city, you locked the door.

He got as far as turning on the television when there was another unexpected knock. *Damn pizza guys*, he thought. "I didn't order anything!" he yelled. There was a pause, then another knock. "Dammit, all right," he said, and went to the door. The peep hole showed him a young woman, a blonde. She didn't seem to have a pizza with her or anything else. He opened the door.

"Hi," she said. "I'm sorry. My car won't start, and my phone's run down. Can I use your phone?" She had a southern accent, but not Alabama-style. It was softer, and the vowels weren't quite as long as they would have been for a local. She was wearing shorts and a kind of camping shirt, tucked in and with buttoned chest pockets. Oddly, she had a scarf around her neck. "It'll just take a minute."

"Oh ... all right," said Ricky. He didn't really want to do anybody any favors right then, but he was taken by surprise and couldn't think of a way to say no. He stepped back from the door, and then things became very strange. The blonde woman stepped back instead of forward, and two other people came in quickly ahead of her. The first one took Ricky by the shoulders and spun him around. With a practiced movement, she hooked one of his feet with one of hers, swept it out from under him, and suddenly he was on the floor. The third woman dropped down beside him and helped keep him from moving.

The blonde whipped the scarf off, knelt quickly on Ricky's back with one knee, and grabbed him by the hair. She pulled his head back, yanked his jaw down, and put the scarf in his mouth. In another second, it was tightened and tied behind his head. She got up, and the other two women got his hands behind his back. He felt something bite into his wrists. He heard the door close.

There was a pause. The blonde and one of the two others stayed behind him, out of his sight. One of the others, tall, black, looking like an athlete, squatted down in front of him.

"Now you listen to me, little boy," she said. "I'm only goin' to say this once, and you better believe every word you hear. We are very, very serious." Ricky had been cycling through idea after idea, starting with "prank", going through "robbery", and ending up nowhere. He had no explanations, no plans, no concept of what the hell was happening to him. He felt his feet being pulled together and then constricted. There was a zipping sound.

The woman in front of him stood up, looked around, and then picked up his backpack. She was out of his sight for a moment, and when she crouched down again, she was holding his laptop. She opened it and set it on the carpet directly in front of his face.

"Now you watch." She put one hand on the keyboard and one on the screen, and then she leaned forward so all the weight of her upper body came down on the device. With a plastic crunch, it literally broke in two. It dawned on Ricky that she was wearing surgical gloves.

"You are done," she said. "You are finished with the net. You ever log back on to anything, and we will come find you. It won't just be your piece of shit laptop we break." One of the women behind him was stretching his right index finger back up, away from the hand. "You won't ever type your shit again." The finger was painful. Then it was released.

"Just so you believe me, sonny, listen to this. RogerU. BigBoy. Ophukov." With horror, Ricky realized she was reciting his user account names. "We got you cast in concrete. And here's some other people who might want to know about you. Doctor Cargill. Debbie Corcoran. Doctor Branch. You get what I'm saying?" The names were those of faculty members Ricky had trolled. "Now you lie still right there." She stood up again, paused for a second, and then walked away.

Ricky's fat-and-sugar lifestyle hadn't had time to catch up to him. He was still a reasonably healthy young man, overweight and out of shape but too young for any of the consequences to have shown up. He'd never been really ill. Now, though, he felt paralyzed. It wasn't just the cable ties around his wrists and ankles or the scarf jamming his tongue against the roof of his mouth. He really felt as though he was immobile. He could move his eyes but beyond that, he was frozen in place.

The woman came back, coming from the direction of the kitchen. To his horror, Ricky saw that she had the only sharp knife he owned. She went to the small table by the couch and picked up the landline telephone. The knife wasn't all that sharp, but it cut the phone cord without too much trouble. She walked back to the middle of the room, bent down, and laid the knife on the floor. It was eight feet, more or less, from Ricky's nose. "Give me his cell phone," the woman said. One of the other two patted his hip pockets, then reached under him and pulled it loose from the clip on his belt. It was a flip phone, hinged in the middle like the laptop. The first woman knelt back down, showed it to Ricky, and then broke it in two, just as she'd done with the computer.

"Now, boy, you are really off the grid. We're goin' to loosen your feet, and then we go out the door. You get yourself over to that knife and get loose the rest of the way, as best you can." She bent closer and looked hard into Ricky's eyes. "And after that ... well, you just remember. Just remember it all."

MacArthur got home and let the dogs out into the back yard. Usually the sound of the door wall opening was enough to send smaller creatures of the wild running up a tree or down a hole. This time a squirrel was brazen enough to sit up and stare. That lasted less than a second as a pair of enthusiastic, motivated apex predators came charging out like Scarlett's Heavy Brigade at Balaclava (the brigade that actually did something useful, not the idiot-led Light Brigade). The squirrel, playing the role of the Russian cavalry, withdrew in disorder, first to the rear and then up a tree. The dogs established a perimeter and began trying to stare him down.

Mac turned around and went back in. He'd made up his mind that just sending Jeri Klein an email message would be sufficient. And he had at least an outline of how he'd respond to Andy's "great news." First, he'd have to be absolutely nonjudgmental, congratulatory, prepared to say nice things. He would ask no questions about the lack of room in their small house, Jenn Langton's old bachelor quarters on the city's west side. He wouldn't ask which one of them would take time off for child care, whose career would go on hold, what Jenn's daughters (at least the one with whom she was on speaking terms) thought about it. No, he'd just be the positive, rational, happy-for-them old friend, the one they'd show the baby to but never, never ask to babysit. He ran over those ideas one more time, and then he tapped "return call" on Andy's voice mail message.

"Hi, Mac. Thanks for calling back."

"Not at all, not at all. I was actually talking to someone else when you called."

"No problem. So ... things going all right with you folks?"

"Yeah, in general. Dogs are out repressing the rodents, Colleen's off at work, obviously. How about, ah, how about you two?"

"Oh, we're great! Jenn's doing really good stuff for Holcombe, kicking ass and taking names, really getting their ... their systems squared away."

Holcombe was Jenn's employer. She was their Director of Security, something they needed rather badly, since they were a technology company, doing contract work for both the Navy and another agency she wasn't allowed to name. Mac could make a guess or two about who it was, but he had a newly-learned aversion to investigating things he wasn't being paid to investigate. Andy's reluctance to say that what Jenn was squaring away was their security compliance procedures wasn't just a matter of being coy. There was a general understanding that people talked to their spouses, but that the spouses didn't let it go any farther.

"Good. Good. I said they were getting a bargain when they got her," Mac said. *That didn't sound very new-parent-like*, he thought.

"So, I wanted to talk about a couple of things," Andy said. "One is I've got a case that, well, it touches on Ann Arbor. I just wanted to see if we could have coffee somewhere, maybe see if you, oh, I don't know, knew some names."

"Sure. I know a lot of names. You want to make a time and talk about it in person?"

"Yeah, that would be good. Might be best to talk in person."

"Okay, good. Sweetwaters, downtown? You want to do it today?"

"Sure, if you can make it." Andy knew, of course, that Mac could make it. The only scheduled things he was likely to have on his calendar would be healthcare events.

"Say four-thirty? Catch you on your way home?" Mac knew that Andy's job took him all over the Detroit metro area. "What was the other thing?"

"Four-thirty is fine. That'll be great. Um, the other thing. Well, I wanted to see if you had any ideas about, you know, other kinds of places, I mean other kinds of jobs, I guess. For me, I mean."

Ah, ha, thought Mac. *He's the one who's going stay home with the kid.* "Other kinds of jobs? In, say, law enforcement, still?"

"Well, I suppose. I mean, I don't really know. I can't really take a huge pay cut, really."

No, I bet you can't. Pieces were falling into place. "Look, do you want to talk about this over coffee, too? Might give me some time to think of things."

"Oh, sure. Sure. I didn't expect any kind of instant, um, solution. Yeah, we can talk about it this afternoon."

"Okay, good. But what's the big news you said you had?" MacArthur wasn't going to let him off the hook that easily. And if Mac had until the afternoon to think it over, he might have an even more subtle, nuanced facade to put up.

"Oh, yeah. Well, we finally got a confirmed bid on my condo. So we're going to start looking for a bigger house up there, up in Ann Arbor. And when we find something with a yard, we're gonna get a dog!"

Mac blinked hard. *I am an idiot,* he thought. "That's ... great. Really good. Glad to hear it." He was astonished at just how glad he was, in fact, to hear it. "Well, uh, see you at Sweetwaters, then. Four-thirty."

"Right, four-thirty. See you then." They hung up. *Funny,* Andy thought, Mac sounded a little bit ... scattered. Hope he's all right.

Monterrey and Buena Vista

Dr. Karolyn Holcombe was not, in person, what you'd expect from seeing only her name in print. The Anglo-Saxon idea you might get from her business card or from reading her name on her company's website was not at all the reality. Her mother was from Mexico, the daughter of an academic family, and her father was an expatriate Venezuelan oil executive. They came to Southern California, bringing assets and jobs with them, and Karolyn was born there. Her last name now was by marriage, acquired from a young man who was born in Connecticut, educated in Boston, and employed at Michigan State University. That she could have kept her maiden name, Rojas, just didn't occur to her.

From there, with a new doctorate in computer science, she walked a dusty and potholed road to Ann Arbor, to the University of

Michigan, and eventually to tenure. Late in that game, she had a set of ideas about how to deliver a package of program management and system design to customers who might have grand technical dreams but who lacked the ability to fulfill them. After the fourth grant application to study it was turned down, she said to her husband, "The hell with this! I'm going to just *do* it!"

Five years after that, Holcombe was what it was, with its own building, a hundred and fifty-eight employees, and a confidential balance sheet; the Holcombes were the sole owners. Technically, it was Holcombe, Inc., but the name on the building was just "Holcombe".

This particular morning, she was sitting down with the people she considered the inner team. They all walked in at about the same moment: Dr. Holcombe herself, Vivienne Keyes, Israel McLeroy, and Jenn Langton. They were in a larger space than four people needed, but it was the only actual conference room in the closed area. That none of them was carrying any of the usual executive technology—no phones, no laptops, no pagers—could be explained with the phrase "closed area". This was the part of the building with a pair of locked doors, both activated by different badges. In the space between, there were shelves to drop off anything that could store or transmit information, and there were several pieces of signage using large capital letters to remind you that your outside gear wasn't welcome inside.

McLeroy was the last one in, and he shut the door behind him. He dropped into the chair beside Jenn. Dr. Holcombe, sitting on the other side of the table, held up a piece of paper. It was very plain, just a few numbered lines with the heading "Canis Lupus Cyber Introduction Agenda".

"I just got this," she said. "I'm not crazy about the first two items." She slid it to McLeroy; he looked at it and passed it to Jenn.

"I, uh, don't see the issue," he said.

Jenn scanned it and gave it a shove to Viv Keyes. The first two points seemed like standard first-meeting stuff: "Introductions and Welcome: LifeRigor" and "Summary of the Subcontract: Holcombe".

"It's our meeting," Jenn said. "We're the Contract Lead. Sounds like they think it's their meeting."

"That's my point," said Dr. H. "I'm going to send it back with that all changed around. We're only going over there to make sure their closed space is up to specs, anyway. Otherwise, we'd have them over here." She looked around at the team, making "Right?" eye contact. McLeroy was the Vice President of Engineering, very good at technology, very good at staffing and getting results, politically clueless. Viv Keyes didn't have a Director title, but she might as well have. She ran the company's PMO, its Program Management Office; she reported directly to Dr. H. and got paid as much as any of the top people. Her job was to take bright ideas, wild pipe dreams, "You know, this guy in the Air Force thinks he wants ..." situations, and make them into programs you could pitch, concrete offerings that might actually get funded. And then when something did get funded, she directed the planning and team building that would make the something really happen.

And then there was Jenn Langton. Jenn was the newest one, recruited away from a position as a lowly detective with the Ann Arbor Police and dropped into a Director of Security job. Besides the security things most companies had—guards, malware defenses, firearms policies—she was also responsible for the much bigger realm of information security: what can't be exposed to the outside world, and how can we be sure it won't be? The closed area and its upcoming expansion were hers. The secure network and its few and tightly closed connections with the outside world were hers. Looking very closely at subcontractors such as LifeRigor,

Inc. and evaluating the quality of *their* security establishments: those were hers. And of course, when something went wrong, cleaning up afterward—"conducting an investigation and remediation" to speak formally—was hers.

"All right," said Dr. Holcombe, "We're going over to see them, and we'll sit in their chairs, but we're paying for the chairs, and we make that pretty obvious. Jenn gets a tour, peeks under the desks ... peek under the chairs, if you want to. Izzy, you talk about how we're going to move things back and forth. Documents, code, people if we have to. You need Jenn for that, too."

"Right, okay. Yeah, we need to get them connected with our guys," McLeroy said, nodding at Jenn. "You want to get Peter hooked up with them right away, or ..."

"Done," said Jenn. "He got their secure network information early, under non-disclosure. He can flip the switch any time."

"Oh. Great. Fast service."

"I think you'll find that Jenn's group is working about a month or so out from signing, these days," said Keyes. "We put that into our subcontractor evaluation process, what, last quarter?"

"Right," said Jenn.

"Ah. Super. Great," said McLeroy. Holcombe smiled. Izzy wasn't any kind of conscious sexist; he wouldn't have survived in her company if he was. He was just drifty.

"Viv," she said. "Your agenda ... the usual?"

"Yes, plus. I want to make sure they know the difference between being a sub and being a partner. That if we want partners, we sign partnerships. And I want a handshake on that from their Program Manager."

"Did you drop the pups bomb on them?"

"No, they're not read into that. It's far enough down the road that we can look at some other subs, or do it ourselves."

Jenn looked at Karolyn, then at Izzy. "Pups? What ...?"

"Oh. Oh, I'm sorry, Jenn. Did I not send you that addition?" he said, looking embarrassed.

"Not that I saw."

"It's, uh, another little brainstorm from the customer. As a phase two sort of thing. They don't have any kind of requirements yet, just some concepts."

"Okay."

"They think it would be nice if the cyber wolf could carry a couple of mini-wolves. Deploy and recover them. Communicate with them, you know, autonomously. Pups, they're calling it. The concept." Izzy looked more uncomfortable. For Jenn and Viv, it was scope-creep. For him and his people, it was a whole new universe.

Karolyn Holcombe stepped in. "We can go over that—we'll be ramping up another whole program—and I don't want to get into that yet. But, Izzy, make sure all of us are on the list for new and brilliant ideas from our beloved customers, okay?"

"Right, yes. Sorry. I thought you were on my list for that, ah, sort of thing, Jenn. I'll fix that."

"Please. And so we're not talking to LifeRigor about it yet, if ever?"

"Nope, not yet," said Karolyn. "But back to this briefing, Viv, are you happy with their committed staffing? They gave you names, right?"

"Yes. I have a print copy." She passed over a document with a classification cover sheet. Dr. H. flipped a page or two and found the list of people LifeRigor was promising to assign. She had a habit with documents like this, especially when two Ann Arbor companies were doing something together: she scanned for names she knew. On this list, except for the execs she'd met during negotiations, there weren't any familiar techs or team leads. She skimmed down a list of developers: Byron Kelly, Janet Kromer, Rasif Arundel, Corinne Dupuis-Baker, Richard Peakes.

The rebellion of the Southern States has so occupied the attention of everyone, including the public, the Army and Navy, and our historians that the earlier war of 1846 and 1847 has almost fallen out of our national memory. It was not a war with clear causes, although we thought at the time that it was, and the governments on both sides, ours and that of Mexico, were at odds with themselves. In Mexico, a revolution had just occurred, overthrowing Antonio López de Santa Anna, their President. In Washington our President, James Polk, was faced with resistance to his intended annexation of Texas and distracted by a crisis with Great Britain over the northwestern boundary, the demarcation dividing territory claimed both by ourselves and by Canada. England was not in a position, economically, to fight a war with us, but her Minister in Washington refused to be guided by his government, and the two countries rattled sabers at each other. Mexico was ill-equipped in any way to fight a war with anyone, but she conspired with Great Britain to continue Texas as a sovereign state, an act which contributed to our determination to confront her. The war, when it took place, was universally a disaster for Mexico, and it had the unforeseen cause of establishing the United States as master of the entire North American continent, south of the Canadian border.

Further, its effects were not limited to the expansion of the Union nor the ruin of Mexico. It led to the absurd adventure of France, as it used unpaid debt as an excuse to take over unhappy Mexico for a short time. Even more critically, the fighting we did from Palo Alto to the Mexican capital gave our Army and its young leaders a sharp seasoning in war.

Many of the commanders in our later national conflict served with Generals Scott and Taylor, and I count myself among that number, for I went into the Mexican war as a First Lieutenant of Artillery and come out as a Brevet Major. Ulysses Grant and Robert Lee were there, as were James Longstreet, William Sherman, William Rosecrans, and even Jefferson Davis. The man I would oppose in our war during the fight at Stones River, during the advance on Chattanooga, in the bloody mess at Chickamauga, and finally at Missionary Ridge, namely Braxton Bragg, was my commanding officer in Mexico.

This war was fought with the ideas and methods and even the weapons of Napoleon, transplanted into a dry, thinly populated, and often unwelcoming climate. It was fought with much smaller armies and much less effective supply arrangements, and on our part, it was fought with a blend of national and state volunteer units. Unfortunately for their cause, the Mexicans again and again sent large, poorly-led conscript forces against our smaller, better-trained regiments and divisions, and over and over our opponents were driven from the field. In only a few more years these same armies of theirs, led by honest and well-intentioned leaders, soundly defeated other foreign invaders, but by trusting their forces to amateurs and politicians, men of great ambition and little experience, they doomed themselves.

I will not dwell on my part in the strategy, since it was never under my control. I went where I was ordered to and fired on the targets that presented themselves. It is enough to say that I commanded guns defensively at what is now called Fort Brown, and at the taking of Monterrey and at the bloody fight at Buena Vista. I saw men die, both beside me and in front of me. I gave orders that sent men to their deaths, whether they were my troops or the enemy's. I will just state in the simplest terms what we did, the men around me and myself.

In the battle for Monterrey, I went with Bragg to the support of General Garland's force on the left. Since the Tannery had already fallen to us, we carried on into the town and found ourselves in a different kind of struggle. Working six-pounder field pieces on a field is one thing, taking them down narrow streets flanked by fire from housetops and windows is a very different one. We lost men and horses, and much of the time we were manhandling the guns back and forth. We were called back, eventually, and we removed everything we could preserve, guns, harness, and all.

That was the first day, and we spent the next day in our camp, refitting and replacing our horses and men. We remained on the left, and except for the troops left to garrison the Tannery, most of us saw little fighting there. On the right, General Worth's force had steadily advanced, taking the ridges and forts that covered the city and the Mexican lines of supply. On the third day, we went back into the town again, fighting our way through the streets in the same manner as before. Our Texan volunteers were used to this sort of fighting, and we advanced with them, learning to run the gun out of one street into another, fire it off, and use the recoil and our gunners' muscles to pull it back into cover. Eventually, there was a ceasefire, General Worth's men having broken into the city and begun to flank the forces who were opposed to us.

The Mexican commander, Ampudia, bluffed our General Taylor with tales of an armistice between the two countries, and under the terms of surrender that was eventually signed, he got off more lightly than some at home thought he should have. Monterrey was a clear victory for the United States, but it gave the administration an opportunity to dilute General Taylor's authority and presence. General Winfield Scott was sent out to take over the war in total, and he promptly withdrew a large part of our force for another campaign in the south.

At this great distance in time and with the events so clouded by our later great conflict, I will not try to explain the maneuvering between what were now our two armies, those of Generals Scott and Taylor, nor will say I anything about General Santa Anna's actions in our front. He was then back at the head of the country and its army, since it appeared to the men of politics in the Mexican capital that he was the least of many evils. As was so often the case in that poor country in that time, they had cause to regret their decision not long afterward.

Although I had by then been given a Brevet promotion to Captain, my position was no higher than it had been, that is, a mere Lieutenant of

Artillery, commanding a single gun. Neither our strategy nor our tactics were in my hands, and I will limit myself to the very lowest level of description, that is to say what I saw take place. The reason that there was a fight at all was that General Taylor had moved further west after we took Monterrey, and when our light cavalry and our gathering of information from local people and prisoners told us that Santa Anna was coming to us with a large force, we withdrew from an open, unconstricted position and into the strong narrow places south of a rancho called Buena Vista. There, under the immediate command of General Wool, we placed our infantry and our guns, and we waited for Santa Anna to advance against us.

Of the fight itself, I remember only the part of it that took place directly ahead of my gun. We were placed on the right of the Second Illinois, and Lieutenant French with his gun was on their left. The Mexicans had masses of infantry, trained in the European style, but their leadership was not of the quality that could inspire them to sweep us off our hill. They came on obliquely at first, more in my opinion because of the terrain than in any intentional way, and our force where their blow fell gave way. The enemy, however, having broken our line at one point failed to turn in and strike at us, and the Illinois troops and French's gun dealt them a flanking fire that stopped their advance. Soon, the Mississippi Rifle Regiment and more of our guns came up and together the attackers were, in almost the literal sense of the word, blown back off the hill tops.

At this point, Santa Anna could still have finished us. He had troops not yet exposed to fire, and he sent them, under an officer named Lombardini, in force up and out of a ravine. They came on with the bayonet and crumpled up the infantry we had to oppose them, but our guns, both Washington's and Bragg's, many standing alone without other troops nearby, opened a fire on the attackers that eventually broke their will.

I remember that period only as a haze of firing with our six-pounder, a blur of sponging the barrel, ramming down the canister round, men running back for the next shot. At one point, my gunner and my number three man were wounded, and as there was almost no aiming or traversing to do, I put number four in the gunner's position and had him thumbing the vent as well. I took over the lanyard and the primers and gave the orders to fire. Each discharge rolled the gun back several feet, but as long as the muzzle was pointed at the nearest Mexican troops, we left it alone and kept up our fire. My only concerns, I seem to recall, were just the lapse of time between my orders to fire and whether I yet had the men to work the gun. After the fight, I gathered from several sources an estimate of the length of the engagement, and by comparing it with the number of rounds expended, found that we had been firing at a rate of twice a minute or perhaps a bit more.

The enemy had with this attack twice inserted a force, unsupported by other simultaneous attacks, into the heart of our position, defeating the units directly opposed but being themselves overwhelmed by the fire of our artillery into their front and flanks. They fell away, and the fighting ended for the day. Overnight, we were reinforced by troops that General Taylor had kept behind us, in Saltillo, and we all prepared for a renewed attack in the morning. As we arose, though, and as we sent out scouts, we found that Santa Anna had slipped away and left the field to us. We heard after the fact that he felt his supplies on hand, there at the Narrows, were insufficient for another battle, and he withdrew under that pretext.

Some who have written about the battle consider it a draw, and for a while, the Mexican government called it a victory, but no one who was there could see it in those terms. Fewer than five thousand of our troops stood in the path of a force that was, at a minimum, fourteen thousand, and after a day of sending his army into the face of our positions, Santa Anna withdrew. Our losses were severe, and some of our horse and foot were displaced, but in the end, we remained in possession of the field and our losses had been made up by a timely reinforcement. If I had to name the lesson of that sad day, I would say that the fight was won by men who could load and fire and make use of defensive ground, and it was lost by men whose leaders were at odds with each other, driven by political necessity, and careless of their soldier's lives. Virtually every man who fought at Buena Vista, American or Mexican, conscripts, national troops, or volunteers, had taken an oath in some form. Their oaths brought them there, and those that kept them and lived could say afterward that they either won the battle or stood until they were called off. Those who ran, on either side, may have saved their lives, but they lost the knowledge of having kept their promises. Remembering it all at some later date, I recall thinking: "Even if his officer is a fool, the soldier who runs is still a soldier who ran."

Although Mac was a devoted patron of his neighborhood coffee drive-through, it wasn't an ideal place to sit and have a conversation. For meeting someone, Sweetwaters—the old original location downtown—was preferred. Its afternoon trade leaned toward realtors and grad students, all of whom were absorbed in their own affairs. If you chose your table wisely, your talk could be reasonably confidential.

Andy was already there, in line at the counter when Mac came in. They got their drinks and went into the back room.

"So," he said. "Long day?"

"I did a lot of driving around," said Andy. "To no real purpose, I guess. Sometimes it's just hard to find people."

"Specific people, I assume? Not just any old people?"

"A few specific ones, anyway."

"You guys are looking for a new house, I think you said?" Mac was in the habit of referring to couples as "you guys", regardless of the assortment of genders that might be involved. "Guys," in fact, could mean any group of beings, human, animal, or a mixture. When he walked in the door at home, he usually said "Hi, guys" to his dogs.

"Yeah, we are. It's kind of scary, what things cost, but we need another room or two. Like, home offices for each of us. Maybe a ranch, or one of those old west side two-stories."

Mac smiled internally. The Old West Side, decidedly spelled with initial capitals, was usually the first neighborhood name people learned when they came to Ann Arbor. It was a good place but not the only one. When Andy started throwing around "Packard Hills" or "Broadway" or "Water Hill", he'd have a bit more street cred. Mac himself wasn't much of a home shopper, and he enjoyed not having to know about markets and prices. But he did know, just because people were always saying it, that an inside deal was the best way to buy an existing house in Ann Arbor. "I'll keep my eyes open," he said. "Any particular neighborhoods?"

"No, not really. I mean, we'd rather be close in, but the prices ..."

"Yup," said Mac, and he took a sip of coffee. He put it back down and switched to his changing-the-subject tone of voice. "So, what's this about jobs?"

Andy was in his late thirties, and his moderately dark skin and jet black hair were genetic gifts from his Gujarati mother. He went clean-shaven, something that took daily attention thanks to his father's Irish-Austrian genotype; Andy's beard was fast-growing and persistent. He'd been born in Massachusetts and went to school there. He'd been a Marine, and then he'd joined the FBI. His accent was as neutral as possible for an East Coast man, and unless you were listening for it, you'd never catch the dropped R. He liked a variety of food, certain wine grapes, Celtic folk music, and Jenn Langton. And for a while, he'd liked being a Fed.

"Well," he started. This wasn't a conversation he'd practiced. In fact, he hadn't talked about it with anyone, including his wife. That he was bringing it up first with MacArthur seemed both odd and right. Mac was a kind of universal solvent: not a family member, not a colleague, just an old guy with a relaxed way of talking and no interest in the outcome. That Mac *was* highly interested in the outcome never occurred to him. "I'm not, you know, in a panic. I mean, I haven't really gone through it with myself."

"Yeah," Mac said, giving the word no emphasis or flavor at all.

"I mean ... I'm not sure I make any kind of difference. I *do* lots of things. I ask questions, I find people, I talk to lawyers."

"But ... " said Mac.

"But what good is it?"

"I suppose you get to stop somebody from doing something awful, once in a while."

"Yeah, once or twice. And usually we go get 'em *after* they did it. But ... well, didn't you ever think 'Drop in the bucket'? Or 'One down, infinite more to go?'"

"Sure. All the time. Like pulling up garlic mustard. And I used to think I'd be happier getting people to do things instead of stopping them."

"Like teaching?"

"Oh, I never got to specifics," Mac said. "By the time I started to add up the alternatives, something would come up."

"Like what?"

"Dog would need a walk. Domestic violence complaint. Tomatoes would be at peak; time to make sauce for the winter. Requalify with the sidearm. Couple of friends get married. Life. And you know what?"

"What?"

"You keep that up, year after year, and suddenly you're done. Knocked on your ass."

Andy started to say something, changed his mind, and took a sip of his coffee. "I'm sorry, Mac, I didn't mean ..."

"Of course not. But the point is, first think about what might be better, then make the changes. Don't do it the other way around."

"Right, right. You're right. I'm jumping the gun."

"And make sure you talk to Jenn about it. She might actually have an idea or two."

They both used the coffee as a distraction. Andy felt an unexpected relief. He'd been given permission to be dissatisfied, a sort of path to start down, and a reason to soldier on while he thought it all out. And all that in just a few sentences. Mac was also relieved; he might have done some good, after all, and if you had to give advice, it was a pleasure to give it to a person who actually seemed to be listening. He set his cup down first.

"I wanted to ask you about all this ... secrecy, I guess."

"Oh, yeah," said Andy. "The, uh, case I was mentioning."

"The case you didn't mention, you mean."

"Right, yeah, I didn't mention it."

"Does this stuff really do any good?" Mac asked. "I've never had to deal with it, except on the low end. Gag orders, not naming the victim until the relatives are notified, like that."

"Well, it's the Federal Government, so it's complicated. But yeah, I see value in it, some of the time."

"Like what?"

"Well, how about an analogy?" Andy said.

"Sure."

"So, you're out on the street and a guy asks you for directions to the bus station. Do you tell him?"

"Um, sure. I do."

"But you've never seen him before, and he has a backpack. What if he's a terrorist and wants to blow up the station?

"Why would he do that? I mean, why would I suspect he'd do that?"

"You wouldn't. That's natural. The chance that he's some kind of anti-bus lunatic is tiny. And it's not your job to defend the bus station, anyway. I mean, if he had the bomb right out in the open, or if he had a "Busses must die!" T-shirt or something, maybe you'd call somebody. But beyond that, it's not really your job to decide if he should know or not."

"I hear a 'but' coming, though," said Mac.

"Yeah, there is. *But* suppose it *is* your job. Suppose you're getting paid to keep the bus station safe. In fact, you're required to. Your charter, under the law, says that. And any incident—anything bad at all—that happens is your concern. You're, I don't know, The Bus Security Agency or something."

"Okay. So then I *don't* tell him how to get there?"

"Not right away, you don't. You take into account that some people, maybe most people, have a need to know where the bus station is. A legitimate need. Their taxes paid for it. It's their bus station. So all you can do is try to reduce the chance of a bus hater getting that critical information."

Mac took a pull on his coffee. "So it's a game of keeping the odds in your favor?"

"Well, to keep the analogy going, here's what you have to do. This is what's being done now, anyway. You get the guy's name, and you peek in his backpack. You check his background and his friends and his family and what websites he looks at. You see if he owes a lot of money to somebody. And then you sit down with him and go over all that. Maybe you even do a polygraph."

"A what?" asked Mac.

"A lie detector test. So-called."

"Ah."

"And if all that tends to show that he's not a bad guy, you make him sign an agreement and swear an oath and promise that he won't tell anybody else where the station is. At least anybody who hasn't been through all this checking, too. And then you look around and over your shoulder and you maybe wait for traffic noise to pick up, and then you whisper the directions to the bus station."

"And after all that, you're still not sure he isn't a terrorist."

"No, you're not. All you've done is raise the odds against it. And what's worse, you can't possibly afford to repeat that stuff very often, so you don't know if he might *become* a terrorist while he's walking over to the station. But there's an even bigger problem."

"Which is ...?"

"He doesn't have to blow anything up himself. He doesn't even have to want to blow things up. All that has to happen is for him accidentally or maybe even deliberately to pass the directions along to someone else. Someone else who really is a bad guy. And who might be willing to pay for it."

"None of that's very confidence-inspiring."

"Right. Because if there's some information that you really want to keep, oh, 'not generally known', I guess is the way to put it, the rock bottom truth is: you're relying on people keeping their promises. You can threaten consequences, but that's just after the fact. If the bad guys find out where the bus station is, punishing the guy who talked is almost pointless."

"Well, it might keep him from talking anymore. Or discourage other folks from running their mouths."

"But the damage is still done. The thing you were trying to prevent happened."

"You know," said MacArthur, "you're not the only person I know who thinks about this sort of thing."

"Right. Jenn. She's up to her ears in exactly this stuff."

"So what are we really talking about?" Mac paused. "Tell me you're not investigating your own wife."

"No. Actually, that's one of the promises *I* had to make—not to work on cases involving my family. This one's close, but technically there's a loophole."

"A loophole?"

"Well, that's, um, one of those *serious* aspects of it. I think I mentioned that?"

"You can't tell me?"

"There are some things I can't, yeah. I'm sorry, Mac. I don't think you'd blow up any bus stations, but ..."

"You never know. But the amount of help I might be is going to be proportional to the amount of facts I have."

"I know. I'm sorry, again. I wouldn't even bring it up, but, you know, they kind of think of me as the Ann Arbor guy. Between you and Jenn, they think I can find out things that somebody else couldn't."

"All right. So what kind of intel are you trying to get?"

"Well, there's a company up here. And we think some ... actually one ... of their people might be doing some, uh, bus station directions things. Or thinking about it, anyway."

"Okay."

"And I wondered if you could just sort of ... think about who you might know working there. You know, just 'He worked there, and then he moved to this other place'. Or 'he used to be married to this other person, but they split up'. Just that kind of Ann Arbor gossip, really."

"That isn't something you guys can look into?"

"We could, but again, nobody down there really has a lot of Ann Arbor, um, exposure."

No, I imagine not, Mac thought. *Not with Doug Markowitz retired.* Agent Markowitz had been the Detroit FBI office Ann Arbor guy for years. Mac had worked with him—so had Jenn Langton, for that matter—and he'd been Andy's mentor, of a kind. But the sort of gossipy intelligence Andy was asking for now wouldn't have been anything even Doug would know.

57

"All right," he said. "Do you need it now, this minute? Or can I think about it?"

"There's some time," Andy said. "Anything you might come up with will help. Say, a week? And, uh, if you could be kind of discreet about it, sort of not really saying why or who or ..."

"Understood. But I have to ask: is there a reason you can't ask your wife about this?"

Andy looked MacArthur straight in the eyes. "Yes," he said.

"Okay. I see. Got it. What's the company?"

"It's called LifeRigor."

🐎

Gray wolf female P51 stretched out on the grass. She yawned, curling her tongue and showing a set of highly capable teeth. There was just this small slope of open ground running down to the lake, and it was a favorite place to lie in the sun. Both her yearling pups were down at the water's edge, wrestling in the sand. The air had been still when they came out of the den, but now a breeze was beginning to ruffle leaves in the taller trees. Pine needles were starting to make their flat hissing as the air moved past them.

A treetop moved slightly, deflecting a puff of wind down and across P51.The air moved down the bank toward the pups, carrying a range of interesting smells. First one, then the other of the juveniles came to attention. *Deer blood!* P51 had licked her muzzle clean after last night's meal, but the mesh strap of her tracking collar was still stained red.

The yearlings came charging up from the lake and tumbled over her, growling and snapping. One of them, the male, managed to get his lower jaw under the strap, and he bit down on it enthusiastically. His bite went cleanly through it, and the whole

58

tracker came away in his mouth. P51 shoved him away with her paw, and both the pups went tearing off to the water again, the male shaking the tracker wildly. His sister shoulder-checked him, and he went under. He sprang out again, sending water in all directions, and jumped on her head, ducking her. The tracker sank to the bottom. P51 and her family went off the grid.

Ricky Peakes spent a month recovering from his experience with the women. That he hadn't suffered any physical injury was irrelevant. In fact, it was just an example of how efficiently the attack had been planned. If he'd had bruises, broken bones, cuts and scrapes, there might have been some chance that he'd work up the courage to report it. But the idea of walking into a police station and saying, "Some girls knocked me down and broke my laptop" was out of the question for him. The first thing the cops would ask would have been, "Are you hurt?", and that was intolerable. He'd been made an object of contempt, and he could never admit that to anyone, let alone an officer. For a long time, shame far outweighed anger, and having to acknowledge being made helpless was just nothing he could allow inside the walls of his denial. If Freud himself had written out a prescription, the furies couldn't have administered a stronger dose.

Of course, it fell short of being a cure. It didn't occur to him that the women he'd mocked and slandered on-line might have felt what he was feeling. His education was interrupted for a term while he gathered up his poise and just enough self-confidence to finish up and graduate. He didn't consider that he might well have driven someone else away completely. A graduate assistant he'd Internet-publically called a "closeted lesbo" dropped out of the doctoral program rather than face questioning looks from the faculty. Ricky didn't see the parallel. Instead, he drew into himself, stayed religiously away from social media, and finished his undergraduate work.

He went back to Pickens County for the summer, and he spent his time applying to graduate schools, most of them far away from Alabama. Flight from danger or even just an awkward situation was in his nature. Technical difficulty was another matter; when he was up against a software challenge, he became another sort of person, keeping at the conflict until he'd bent it to his will. But that used up all his self-esteem. It was hard answering the life goals essay questions on the applications.

Fortunately for him, his academic performance was quite good, and somehow he'd learned to write clearly. He had a few rhetorical and persuasive tools already, and a couple of Internet sources helped him gain more. He'd returned to a sort of consumer on-line presence, searching and reading only and never supplying any comment. By the end of July, he'd knocked out several grad school applications, all of them focused on masters' programs in computer science.

To his surprise, he started getting acceptances. The worldwide panic over the so-called Year 2000 Bug was subsiding, and CS applications were down. Ricky had good undergraduate results and the low-income status to qualify for financial aid; he wrote coherently on the applications; and he had a couple of polite and moderately enthusiastic letters from his UA professors. By August, he had three schools to choose from, all of them with winter term, not fall term, starting dates. One was from the University of Tennessee at Knoxville. Another came from the College of Engineering at Texas Tech. And the third was from the University of Michigan.

As we've noted before, Ricky wasn't all that cosmopolitan. He'd never been to Texas, and he'd never heard of Lubbock. But somehow, the place sounded wrong to him. A school in a town called Lubbock seemed as though it wouldn't be much of a career launch pad. He set aside the Texas Tech letter.

Knoxville was more familiar. The requirements and the apparent quality of the faculty seemed all right. The brochures and newcomers' guides showed nice pictures of the campus and the town. But the offer letter was signed by the Dean of Admissions, and she was a woman. The letter had a picture of her, dressed severely; her smile was tight and, to his eye, a bit satirical. He held the Tennessee material in one hand and the paperwork from the University of Michigan in the other as if he was weighing them with a balance scale. Ann Arbor seemed a long way away, but he set aside the UT documents and looked over the general U of M materials again. Most of the illustrations were carefully selected to show the campus and the town in the summer, and those that did show winter featured winter sports, giving the impression that you went away some distance to experience snow. He picked up the Engineering school brochure. He'd gone through the data long before, adding up the numbers and assessing the value of each program. Now he just looked at the pictures. There were two or three shots of happy students, smiling and doing things on computers. In each one, the women were seated and the men were standing, looking down. He lingered over one in which a man, older, obviously a faculty member, was leaning with one hand on the back of a woman's chair, pointing something out with his other hand. Ricky drew a long breath, something like a sigh, and made his decision.

California, Texas, and the Comanche

Oleksiy Shulyayev looked somewhat wistfully across the Detroit River. He wasn't longing to be on the other side; what he could see of Detroit wasn't calling to him. Given many factors, his home here in Canada was preferable. Nor was he homesick for Kyiv; things in the Ukraine weren't welcoming anymore. Where he wished he could be was back in his home, back in Yalta, back on the southeast shore of the Crimea, back where modest little crimes, the kind that victimized no one but Russian tourists, were a recognized trade. *At least,* he thought, *the connectivity here is better.*

He was sitting in one of Windsor's many riverside parks, typically small green spaces between a street and the river bank. From his bench, he had a view directly across to the United States, with the Joe Louis Arena on the right; an equal distance to the left was the Ambassador Bridge. While he waited for his phone to establish a connection, the irony of it all came to him again. *I make my living from America. I could take my car and drive over the bridge, less than a kilometer. And I will never do that.*

Ricky's father drove him into Tuscaloosa with a couple of big duffle bags and a backpack. The luggage was stuffed with nearly everything Ricky owned: clothes, books, and so on. He had a hundred and forty dollars in cash, a credit card with a low limit, and a bank account where his financial aid money lived. Other than that, he had what he was wearing, a new cheap cell phone, and an interstate bus ticket to Ann Arbor. It was December, 2002.

For a Pickens County boy with no more sense of the world than he had, it might have been exciting, leaving home, setting foot on the great highway of life, et cetera, et cetera. In fact, Ricky got a left side seat by a window, opened a text book, and tried to read his way through the trip. Once in a while, he'd look out the window, but there was a great deal of the same thing outside. For mile after mile, the freeways followed low paths between mowed banks, and the line of sight stopped just beyond, usually ending in a stand of trees. Going through Birmingham was just a blur of endless residential streets, dead-ended against the highway. Then they went north on I-65, and all that meant was that the sun came in from a different angle. Even crossing the Tennessee River at

Decatur was anticlimactic; it was just a flat, four-lane bridge, east of the town.

Nashville was briefly interesting just because it wasn't more countryside. There was a distant view of downtown from the Cumberland Bridge, but then 65 went northeast again on its long slant up to Kentucky and Louisville and the Ohio River. By then, Ricky had managed to fall asleep, and he slept through Indianapolis and a sidestep eastward. The lights outside woke him when they skirted west of Fort Wayne, and then he nodded off again. The highway took him, unaware, between a pair of battle-named towns, Sedan and Waterloo, and then due north across the Michigan line. He woke up again when the bus slowed, angled off to the right, and merged onto I-94. The sky in the east was just beginning to lighten up, and he looked out the window, rubbed his eyes, and looked again. There was snow on the ground.

The bus came off the highway and immediately dove under Jackson Road. Then it headed east for the heart of downtown. Ricky was wide awake now. He'd been in a kind of suspended state for the better part of twelve hours. Nothing slipping by outside had suggested any aspect of his life, present or future, but now this place certainly did. He'd be here, somewhere in this new town, for two years, maybe more. Suddenly, he had to sit up and pay attention.

Except for the evergreens, all the leaves were off the trees, and the semi-tropical lushness that the town showed in the summer wasn't apparent. But there were a lot of trees, anyway, leaves or not. The bus went through an intersection that seemed at least a little like Tuscaloosa—there were shopping centers on three of the four corners—but then it was residential again, houses close to the street, sidewalks shoveled or not, apparently at random. The road went on east, flanked by nothing but houses and snow, straight into the rising sun. Finally, something that looked like a downtown rose up ahead. Ricky blinked, trying to get a view. The bus stopped for a red light; on green, it made a lurching turn left, then immediately a right into what seemed to be an alley, and then it pulled up.

"This's Ann Arbor," said the driver. "If you goin' on to Dee-troit, stay on the bus."

Another morning. MacArthur came stumping up the garage stairs and put his key in the door knob. The dogs crowded him from each side as he got the door open, and then they pushed past to get at their individual water bowls. The coffee shop's complimentary biscuits were delightful—they were food, after all—but a bit dry. Mac followed them in, shut the door behind him, and headed for the couch. His notebook was handy, left there on purpose since sitting in the sun with coffee was the necessary prelude to thinking things through. A loud sound of lapping came from the kitchen.

I know how to do this sort of thing, generically, he thought as he settled in. He took a sip of the coffee. *But I'm not sure I know how to investigate things I can't talk about.* He opened the notebook, found the first blank page, and took a pen out of his pocket. He looked at the page for a second, then wrote the date at the top, followed by "Andy". He took another pull on his thermal mug, and then drew an oval, right in the center of the sheet. He labeled it "LifeRigor."

He looked at his work briefly, then drew a second bubble and called it "Execs". He connected it to the first one with a line. He kept going, giving the diagram "Pres.", "Engineering", and "Oth. Mgmt". Then he went back to the first node and gave it another child, "Security". He connected that one to "In charge?"

In twenty minutes, he had a diagram that would have confused anyone except its author. It covered the page with labeled bubbles and a network of connecting lines. There were things scratched out, and the lines weren't neatly arranged; some of them had little bridge-like bumps where they crossed others. It was messy and it seemed incoherent, but it was a record of the thoughts-leading-to-thoughts mental process that he'd just gone through. He closed the notebook and stretched. He heaved himself up off the couch, cursing quietly at his joint pain, stepped over a dog, and headed for the bathroom. Step one was finished; on to step two.

When he came back, he found his page again. He started to work through the diagram, turning it into a list of things to be learned. There were plenty of obvious questions, and he took it for granted that Andy could get answers for them himself. But Mac would need them, too, if he was going to find any of the more obscure bits of dirt. For example, the organizational info would be easy to get off the net, but if he wanted to ask somebody, "So, what's up with this company Mr. X started?" he'd have to know who X was. He stopped writing when his list covered the sort of things a job applicant might look up: who owned the company, who ran it, what it did all day, who did it think its customers were, and had it been in the news? He levered himself up again, stepped over another dog, and went up the stairs to his office and his desktop. The phone was handy on the couch, but for anything that took accurate typing, he preferred the big screen.

He budgeted three-quarters of an hour for this initial snooping, and it didn't take much more than that. When he was done, he knew who owned LifeRigor, that the position of Engineering Vice President was "open", and that the company's mission was "To apply the discipline of automated bio-reverse-engineering to real-life design and implementation challenges". He knew that the President was a man named Witthaya Metharom, a man who held PhDs from both the University of Michigan and from a university in Thailand. And he knew, to the extent that he could understand the description, that bio-reverse-engineering was a technique that claimed to record motor nerve impulses and convert them directly into robotic control software. According to the website, Dr.

Metharom had successfully captured data from a moving flatworm, and then he'd used it to control movement in a worm-robot without writing any code. Mac noted his first reaction, typically cynical: *"They steal intellectual property from worms."*

 In August of 1847, the Third Artillery was ordered back to the United States. The war with Mexico was finished, at least in the sense that my part in it was finished, although it took until May of the next year for a treaty to be signed. In that time General Scott was relieved, General Santa Anna was relieved, and a new Mexican government came into power. General Taylor went home to great honor and was being put forward for the Presidency. I, however, remained for a while, performing my old duties in supply. I finally got to return to my home in Virginia in February of 1849.

My old battery commander, Braxton Bragg, tried at this time to secure an appointment for me as an instructor at West Point but another candidate, an officer with more seniority, received the position. In August I rejoined the Third at its post in Rhode Island, and not long after that, I went again to Florida where the Indian Chief, Billy Bowlegs, was causing concern. This was not yet the Third Seminole War, but nevertheless we spent time in the South again, trying to keep the peace. During that period, we were under the command of General David Twiggs, a man whose displeasure I had earned in Mexico. He gave improper orders for the transfer of some government property, and I refused him some mules he wanted to use for personal purposes. He seems to have resented it. I had no conflict with him during our time in Florida, but he will appear later on in a similar role and then, at the outset of the rebellion and as an elderly man, he will be seen behaving very poorly indeed. All that, however, is for a later page.

In the next year, I left Florida for New Orleans once again, following the same route as I had after my first Indian war, the difference being that this time I left in command of two companies of the Third Artillery Battalion. Shortly afterward, we all took ship for Boston, and we had a close call on the way, thanks to weather and a ship's captain who chose the wrong time to make himself intoxicated. I had to intervene in favor of the First Officer who then managed to bring us safely into port. We took up our place at Fort Independence, and settled into the peacetime routine of regular troops. However, less than a year later, the officer who had been assigned to West Point instead of myself became ill and most unfortunately died. Another acquaintance of mine, then-Captain William Rosecrans, recommended me for the vacant post, and I was ordered to the Academy as Instructor of Artillery.

I was very pleased to be back at the school. I thought I would be able to give the benefit of my experiences in the late war to our officers in the making, I welcomed the chance to expand my own knowledge, and of course, it was fascinating and gratifying to return as an instructor to the place where I had been a student. What is more, during that time I had splendid colleagues on the staff, including John Reynolds, fated to die at Gettysburg, and from 1852, our Superintendent was Robert E. Lee, the man who would not fall but rather fail in that same fight. Many of the cadets were also notable men, including Phillip Sheridan, J.E.B. Stuart, and a man whose name I would come to know well, and he mine, John Bell Hood.

All in all, I felt myself very lucky, but how lucky I was to be, I had no idea, for it was there that I became acquainted with the Kellogg family, one of whom, Frances, was to become my dear friend and my beloved wife. Our vows included the usual pledge to love, honor, and obey, and although in my mind obedience is something one requires from a soldier, not a spouse, still we have both lived by those oaths throughout the remainder of our lives. The nature of my profession and the accidents of history meant that we would spend many years apart, but a homecoming has always been a matter for rejoicing, and today, as I write this inadequate script, Mrs. Thomas is with me, here in California. She professes as she always has done to be happy and satisfied with the life we have led, and I will rely on her to read and correct this simple account, once I have it in a form I would dare show anyone.

The good fortune, at least as far as my service is considered, lasted only a short time. I was required to leave the Academy just before examinations, and I was placed in command of a quite undesirable post, located in the newly-won California territories. The place was called Yuma, and there is little to be said about it, except that I took two companies of the Third Battalion there, as ordered. It was a blazingly hot and distant post, with little to do, militarily or otherwise. I got the men there, overland, in some shape, mostly by leaving a cache of supplies and using the wagons to convey the troops. They would not have survived the last marches if they had been required actually to march. We sweltered there while elsewhere in the world a war among the great European powers began. The British, the French, Savoy, and the Ottoman Empire struggled, in the far reaches of Eastern Europe and Asia, to prevent the Russians from exerting influence along their border with Turkey and, most importantly to the allied powers, to prevent the Czar from having access to the Mediterranean. I remember writing to William Sherman that I believed Russia would be quickly defeated, and I also remember the extent to which that prediction was incorrect. No one in that brutal and poorly-managed war distinguished himself except for the individual soldier. The leadership on all sides was foolish to the point of mental deficiency. On the prompting of Mrs. Thomas, I mention that one person at least, a British woman named Nightingale, managed to take charge by force of personality of the pitifully inefficient medical service and make it into something that a wounded soldier might actually hope to survive. Beyond that, it seems to me that there were few positive lessons to be learnt.

My time in Yuma was not all that long, although I remember that it seemed long enough. I have already said that my assessment of the war in the Crimea was decidedly inaccurate, and it is likely that I may miss the mark again here. I have never heard anything but supposition and conjecture about his motives, but the facts are plain enough. Jefferson Davis was certainly aware of the rising tide of antagonism regarding slavery and the potential fate of that institution. Davis was, in the year 1855, the United States Secretary of War, and he pushed through the authorization of several new cavalry regiments, one of which was staffed with officers of Southern origin. Whether this action was in some form a preparation for conflict or just a natural preference for men of his own background is not likely to be settled. However it came about, the Second Cavalry Regiment of the United States Army was made from the first into an elite unit, officered by men who were, at the very least, above the normal quality. The first commander was Joseph Johnston and the second, Robert Lee. John Hood was a junior officer, and even if I must blush to say it, I was accepted into it with the rank of Major. My appointment was in 1855, and we built it into exactly what it was intended to be, that is a crack unit of horse.

By the next year, I was sent back to New York to recruit, and with Mrs. Thomas cheerfully accompanying me, we returned from there to Texas and to the task of creating posts, encouraging the Indians to accept their reservations, and preventing settlers from taking revenge on the natives for any crime, no matter who committed it. For myself and also for Colonel Lee there was an almost unending round of court martial duty. Mrs. Lee was there as well, and when we could, we shared accommodations and larders. For a period of time, Lee was absent, and most unfortunately General Twiggs was in charge of the Department of Texas. In that role, he interfered in my exercise of command repeatedly. I will say in fairness to the man that during that time, his actions seemed to be simple dislike of me and dislike of having his incorrect decisions overturned by higher authority. I do not believe that there was anything more in it during those years. Upon Lee's return to command, the situation resolved itself, and I thought little more of Twiggs.

As to fighting, there was nothing that could be called a war, but there was constant cavalry work, pursuing one or another kind of livestock thief or tracking down the occasional murderer. I have no numeric records to consult, but I would guess that the cavalry and the Comanche alone traded shots on thirty or forty occasions, and the number of fights between settlers and Indians are innumerable, in the literal sense of that term. Some of the events we passed through during those months I look back on now with a form of amazement.

I have been a soldier since I was twenty years of age, and I have fought in two great wars and many small ones. I have been on battlefields along with tens of thousands of men, men armed with rifles, pistols, cannon, howitzers, and mortars. Many of those weapons were aimed at me or at least in my direction. I have seen cities assaulted and taken, mountains overrun, forts destroyed. Death and injury were all around me. Yet the only wound I ever got in warfare I received in a fight between a handful of my troopers and one lone Comanche warrior. We were chasing a band of his people who were making off with some stolen horses. He stopped, dismounted, and waited for us in order to let his companions escape, and he faced us on foot with just a bow and a lance. He refused to surrender, and of course he eventually died, having been shot twenty times or more, but he wounded several of my men, and he hit me with one of his arrows.

That was the only time, no matter what the carnage around me might have been, that I was ever hurt at the hands of an enemy, and there is an even greater irony, one that puts my arrow wound in the shadow. The cut in my chest healed quickly, and it left only a small scar. My second injury, sustained shortly afterward, nearly ended my career, and its effects are still with me even as I write this. That injury was inflicted by my own hand or rather by my own foot, as I stepped wrong in the dark and fell down a railroad embankment in Virginia. No man who ever aimed a weapon at me has done as much damage or caused as much pain and inconvenience as that sharp tumble did. I spent many months of the year 1860 resting, being nursed by Mrs. Thomas, and trying to think whether my injured back would let me ever again serve as a cavalryman.

A young man without any serious attachment to beer, sports, or dating and with an extremely cautious attitude toward social media can get a lot done. Ricky went through his coursework and his projects with a detached efficiency, and although it was still an issue, he dealt with his misogyny by avoidance. Whenever he could, he stepped aside from women. He discovered that the less he knew about a person, the less he disliked her. Simply seeing a female colleague was no longer distressing. If he crossed paths with someone on the Diag, he could at least nod and then look down. He avoided classes taught by women, and he did his best to stay out of project teams that weren't all male.

In his last year in school, he served once as a teaching assistant for an undergraduate network class, but he did such a half-hearted job of assisting that the department found other things for him to do. It had been a stressful experience, trying to avoid or blow off questions from the female students and, in order not to be obvious about it, giving the boys the same short shrift. He got out of it in the end by being very good and productive with technical assignments. He was credited as a contributor on two different papers, just in his last year.

He managed to finish up in the advertised twenty-four months. One of his few friends convinced him to go to the graduation ceremonies—he wouldn't have gone otherwise -- and he heard *the* Bill Joy of Sun Microsystems say encouraging things about accomplishment. Ricky wasn't especially impressed. He thought of Sun, when he thought of it at all, as old news. His concerns were centered more around personal income and career growth. He'd already found a job, locally, through a friend of that one same friend, and he dug into it.

His actual employer was a supplier of bodies, an organization that hired promising, young, and not too expensive software engineers. They hired Ricky for a specific contract, building drivers to sit between Linux and Windows on one hand and a medical device on the other. He did a good job, and after two years the client wanted to bring him on as an employee. The job shop refused to let him go, and so Ricky resigned. Within a few weeks, he had leads elsewhere; one of them led him into defense work, and that led him to his first security clearance. He was still there, doing work he couldn't discuss outside the building, when he happened to see a position listing. It was from a small, newly formed company (it said), that needed software architects (it called them) with exposure to device control systems and experience in a secure environment.

He thought about it. It had a scent of university spinoff, and it was local. The work he was doing now wasn't moving at much of a pace, and there were rumors that the client might lose funding. And of course, he had that clearance.

He interviewed with the new company's president and the office manager. It was going to be a startup in the classic sense; there were only five employees on board so far. The office space was still being cleaned up after the previous tenant, and the three of them talked in the founder's living room. The slot for an Engineering Vice President was still open, but they were actively recruiting, they said. Until they filled the position, development staff would report right to the founder. To demonstrate the business concept, they showed Ricky a video of a small robotic tube following generic instructions to crawl around, rather than executing specific code. *Wasn't there something like this ... SmallTalk or something ... already?* he thought, but he kept his mouth shut. In fact, there was some similarity between the new company's core idea and that forty-year-old teaching language from Xerox PARC, but the details went beyond. In fact, as the President, Dr. Witthaya Metharom, explained, it was a huge leap in the dark, a venture with substantial risk and enormous potential. If Ricky was interested and would sign a non-disclosure, they would show him what they had in mind.

Half an hour later, Ricky walked back out to his car. He had an offer letter for a Senior Engineer position, with an attractive salary and a small, symbolic stake in the new company. Everything about it appealed to him. The financial picture was fine, better than he'd ever had. The title was bigger than he'd expected to get for another five years. He was comfortable with the security aspects of it. And there was the environment; he'd have an actual office with an actual door he could close, and until they hired an Engineering exec, he'd be almost completely on his own. True, it was a startup, and there was only funding for two years, so far. But he judged the resume material alone to be worth the risk. He wanted a day or two to think, but essentially his mind was made up. He looked at the letter again; the name on the stationery was "LifeRigor, Inc.".

South of Bear Lake, well off in the woods, there's another body of water. One human family has a cabin out at the end of a peninsula, but otherwise the shores are empty, and the woods come right down to the water. That summer, a traditional wolf pack—a mated pair and four surviving offspring, plus a two-year-old female wanderer who had joined up—were living around the lake, taking young deer and anything else the woods had to offer. They were just outside the bounds of P51's territory. She knew about them and they knew about her, but since both of the packs were adequately supplied with food, they respected each other's turf.

Unfortunately, the one human pack in the area chose that year to bring its own pup, a fifteen-year-old male, up to camp, and he brought his birthday present with him. It was a bright green jet ski, and it was incredibly loud. After a week of nervous moments, the southern pack began to shift north, away from the not-quite-naked ape, and as they moved, their evening howls began to be more nervous-making for P51. They were the only pack she could hear, and her hearing told her precisely where they were. Finally, it was too much. Early one evening, after they settled down at the northern edge of her core territory, the howling made its point unmistakable. They stayed put for six or seven more hours, but well before dawn, they moved.

They trotted east through woods, dodging across small open areas and looking for cover. Their course followed a stream for a while, then crossed it and swung north. They kept on until they came to another watercourse, treed along each side and providing a wolf highway. There was a human highway off to the east, but P51 herself, if not her yearlings, had heard vehicles before. This was a small highway, and it wasn't well travelled. So they kept on, ignoring it and staying out of sight. They kept on until their path got too close to one small farm; it blocked them from going farther north, so they rested for a few minutes, until there was no sound of machines or movement, and they then dashed east across the highway and back into shelter. They kept on, then, invisible to anyone on the ground. They crossed one small dirt road, then another, picking places where the trees came close on each side. By evening, they'd come to a peninsula of woods, sticking out into some cleared land, and there they bedded down. P51 howled tentatively as the darkness settled in, and the only response was some barking. They were closer to a farm than she'd have liked to be, but the woods behind them left an escape route.

In an isolated house, a male human rolled over in bed. "You hear that?" he asked his mate.

"What?" she said. "Hear what?"

"Damn dog's barkin' at something. Wonder if we got coyotes, again."

"I don't hear nothin'. Go back to sleep."

Secession

Oleksiy Shulyayev lived on a very quiet residential street. His house was narrow, single-storied, and gray. It had a paved alley behind it, giving him access to a parking space in his back yard. On the other side of the alley, there was a run-down urban park; it was nothing more than a mowed open space with two softball diamonds and an equipment shed. Going east, the alley ran by some kind of hockey rink, not a sport Oleksiy understood at all. The alley ended on a larger street with a convenience store. Going the other way, it ran into another street and the blank wall of a commercial bakery. The neighborhood might have been a post-war block in any older American city, except that it seemed not quite so decayed. From his front door to the Canadian side of the Detroit River was just over half a mile.

Today, though, he walked out his back door, past his car, and out into the park. It was deserted and open, with only a few adolescent maple trees along the alley. He got out his phone and dialed an international number as he walked. A woman with an Asian accent answered, speaking Hungarian. Oleksiy strolled across the grassy parkland, carrying on the kind of conversation he was used to. Both parties were using a foreign language, and neither party believed more than half of what the other one was saying. Neither one trusted the other at all. One was in a park in Windsor, in Canada; the other was in an apartment in Ma Tin Tsuen Village, in Hong Kong's New Territories.

Oleksiy opened with a rather pointed query about funds that were supposed to have been paid to him. The woman said reassuring things until he was tired of hearing them. He moved on to a discussion of potential new offerings, the expansion of an existing product line. The person on the other end of the call had no reason to believe that any such goods existed, but if they *did* exist, she would be interested in them, and she said things that would, if you listened carefully, give you that impression. In fact, the terms of her agreements with other people demanded that she be interested. Her job was to be interested in things of this general kind. There was a short, preliminary discussion of pricing, and a renewed series of questions and non-answers about payments due. Finally, the call ended, with each party satisfied that some minor progress had been made. Oleksiy considered that he'd done what he could to extract at least some of his money. The woman in Hong Kong sent an obscurely worded text message to one of her associates, hinting at a future offering.

Oleksiy walked slowly back toward his house, making another call, a short one, to a man who appeared in his contact list as "Ricardo". Ricardo was actually a waiter and a very, very low-profile data thief in Ann Arbor. His real name was irrelevant to their relationship. Oleksiy needed to know how things were coming with a little personal finance research on the executives and managers at LifeRigor, Inc.

While the young man's mother was carrying him, she'd been convinced that she was going to have a girl. When the nurse presented her with her newborn son, she was extremely surprised. And when she was asked for a name, she was caught flat-footed. She had half a dozen girl's names in mind, but she'd done no work on naming a boy at all. Her eye fell on a book she'd been reading, something about passion and flaming love in New Orleans. Her favorite scene so far was a seduction taking place in a café, with the handsome rogue sipping something called "chicory". The nurse cleared her throat and held out a pen. The new mother panicked and wrote "Zachary".

Zach had turned out pretty well, kept himself out of trouble, and generally behaved. Now though, on this sunny Friday evening, he was playing with dynamite and he knew it. The woman sitting in the passenger's seat of his car was freaking out, demonstrating distinctly irrational behavior, and acting exactly as a meth head does. This was not good, not at all, since they were stuck in one of the horrific M-23 and M-14 traffic jams; if anything happened, if a cop even took a quick look in the window, it would be a very bad thing.

The woman, someone he'd met just a day ago, called herself Laguna or something that sounded like that. She was in fact a methamphetamine addict, an occasional prostitute, and when necessary, a smash and grab thief. When they met at a party, she'd been nicely high, and Zach took her for just a wacky white girl. When she knocked on his door at four-thirty the next day, already shaky and sweating, and asked for a ride to a place in Ypsilanti Township, he'd been fool enough to agree. The deal was, he'd take her to the general neighborhood she wanted, but not to any specific house. He'd drop her off, and after that, she'd be on her own. This sounded fine to Laguna, since she'd expected to have to pay for the ride in some way or other. That she'd score and then be functionally homeless was not especially important. But now the good deal had gone sour in the sense that they were still stuck on some damn highway. Her desire for drugs was getting worse with every passing quarter-mile. She read every sign obsessively, over and over, hoping for one to say "Ypsilanti". Infuriatingly, the one that was slowly coming up kept stubbornly saying "Plymouth Road".

A little less than a half-mile away, Ricky Peakes badged himself out of the LifeRigor building. He was tired and hungry, having skipped lunch to make sure a key piece of code was working. It still wasn't, but he'd learned to recognize when he was done for the day. Nothing else he could do without some food and sleep would make things any better. He'd been a software engineer long enough to understand how his own work processes functioned, and the signs now were clear. Get the hell out and go home.

There were only a couple of cars in the lot. His Hyundai was parked straight in, and he stretched his neck muscles back and forth, thinking about code. The lot wasn't all that big, and there was a car right behind him; it took a bit of backing and filling to get out. When he got pointed in the right direction, he ran his side window down for some breeze and turned out of the lot, going right. Left would have worked, too, here on this quarter-circle street, but there was a car coming. A right turn was a freebie, though, and he went briefly east. Where the street met Green Road, he slowed, took one quick look off to the left, saw only a car a full block away, and turned out into the right lane. His attention was still deeply involved with a piece of malignant C++, and he neither signaled nor carried out even an approximation of a stop.

The car that Ricky ignored was an Ann Arbor Police patrol vehicle. Most of the time, it would have had one officer, but this evening, Jerilynn Klein was in the passenger's seat, carrying out one of her last assignments at the AAPD. She was observing the performance of a new officer, a man named Phil, taking notes for what would be his six months' evaluation. That made her nominally in charge. She had her head down, looking at what she'd been writing, when he said, "You see that?"

"What?" Her head came up fast.

"That Hyundai blew off the stop sign. No signal, either."

"Let's go talk to him," said Jeri, putting the clipboard on the floor.

They kept their speed, since they could see Ricky's brake lights come on, slowing for the Plymouth Road traffic light. As they rolled up behind him, Jeri said, "Let's let him go right, if he wants to. See if he signals this time."

"Right," said the new guy.

Just five minutes before, Laguna had slipped her last grip on patience. Zach's car had been creeping along with traffic, well under twenty-five miles an hour. Now something up ahead of them caused a rolling chain of brake lights, and their car came to a dead stop. Laguna broke.

"God DAMN it all!" she yelled, and she yanked off her seat belt. "I'm gonna walk to god damn Ypsi!" She opened the car door.

"Now hold on!" Zach screamed at her, but he was drowned out by her own incoherent shouting. Her purse was still in the car, her shoes were on the floor mat, and she was running away, looking up and to the right, trying to see a way to get off the freeway.

"I can walk faster than that, dammit to hell!" she said, now talking to herself. At one moment, she had nothing in her hands, and then suddenly she had the steak knife that she usually carried, stuffed recklessly in her waist band. Waving it around, she kept running south, away from Zach and then up the exit ramp. It was also packed with cars waiting for the light at the top, and people were staring at her. Some of them had the presence of mind to try calling 911, but a real accident had just happened, at the next exit down, and the general dispatch center was getting a boat load of calls about that. A crazy lady with a knife wasn't the same thing as a personal injury collision, at least not right at that moment. So Laguna wasn't interfered with as she stumbled her way up the ramp, up to and through a parking lot and straight west, with no plan whatsoever, toward the intersection of Plymouth and Green. Back in the car, Zach shoved Laguna's possessions under the passenger's seat. Short of abandoning his car and running away himself, there was nothing else he could do.

Up on the surface streets, the traffic light that Ricky was waiting for was a long one. He was paying only moderate attention to it, and suddenly he had a thought about his software problem. He leaned over to his right, fumbling to get his pack open, grab something to write on, and take a note. Back in the patrol car, Jeri said, "He's reaching around. Looks like he's going for something."

"I see it," said Phil.

"Light him up." The flashers went on, and he gave Ricky a couple of short blasts on the siren. Ricky's head snapped up.

At that point, Laguna came running across Green Road from the far side. She'd made it through a long set of parking lots, jogging and stumbling and waving her steak knife around. She came out onto the street and focused on Ricky. He was alone, he had a car. His window was down. He might be useful. Every lane was at a stop, waiting on the light or for a chance to turn left. Nobody was moving. She ran up to his side door.

"What the hell?" said Phil.

"Let's go," said Jeri. Laguna was now leaning with one hand on the side of Ricky's car, screaming at him about needing a ride. Her other hand was making swooping movements with the knife. Ricky was frozen with utter terror. *A crazy woman with a steak knife!*

"Stop! Drop that knife!" Jeri was out and around the right side of the patrol car. Her hand was on her sidearm, but she still had it holstered.

"Drop it!" Phil shouted, and Jeri glanced at him, seeing that he'd drawn his pistol.

"Arrrgh! Yarrrah! Gotta geta Ypsi!" said Laguna, very loudly. Ricky flinched away to the right, screwing up his face in fear. He lost control of his bladder.

Jeri was thinking at lightning speed. She had three unknown quantities to deal with. The crazy woman, her rookie, and the guy in the car. The tone of Phil's voice sounded wrong. He was excited, he was probably afraid, and he had his gun out. She flicked her eyes once at the car and realized that Ricky was out of sight. He'd lunged over on his side, trying to get into the passenger seat. Jeri didn't know that. All she knew was that one subject was no longer visible. And Laguna was suddenly moving in Jeri's direction. What little grasp on reality the woman had was gone, and she was acting with her last small amount of animal cognition. Although she had no awareness of the knife at all, it was still in her hand and it was highly visible.

Suddenly, Jeri knew what was going to happen. Phil was going to shoot the crazy lady. It was as clear as if it had already happened, and she had maybe a second to prevent it. Her world slowed down.

"DON'T SHOOT!" she shouted at Phil, putting every decibel of command voice she had into it. It was an army skill and a useful one. Phil looked over at her, even more startled than he'd been, and Jeri took the opportunity to step into his line of fire. She had time to consider that he might go on and shoot *her* in the back, measured the risk as small, and decided to accept it. Laguna made a bestial sound—"YARR-AR-AR-AHHH!"—and took two more steps. Jeri let her come on. With the third step, she moved in and sideways, quicker than a meth-ravaged nervous system could see, let alone counter. She put one hand high and one low on the knife arm, shifted weight quickly to one and then the other, and put a foot behind Laguna's calf. It twisted her around and moved her diagonally away, even farther out of Phil's line of fire. The moderate pain in her arm and loss of balance made Laguna drop the knife. Jeri had just time to see that a straight line from her own body through the crazy person's would end against Ricky's car trunk. She sent her weight down that line, and Laguna found herself face down against the Hyundai.

"CHECK THE DRIVER!" Jeri yelled at Phil. Phil, who didn't have Jeri's experience or her military background, still knew a command when he heard one. In two running steps, he was at the driver's door and shouting his own commands at Ricky. Jeri got Laguna's hands behind her back. The woman was easy enough to cuff. Without a weapon, she was harmless, weak and confused, shaking with fear and need. Except that she might infect you with something, she was no longer an object of concern. Jeri held her against the trunk of the car with one hand, using the other to trigger her shoulder radio.

"I need another unit and an ambulance out at Plymouth and Green. And a supervisor. We had to go hands-on with an armed subject. Weapons drawn."

The grotesque traffic and the working accident slowed things down. By the time a sergeant showed up, Laguna was babbling and twitching, restrained in the back of an ambulance. He glanced at her, made an experienced diagnosis, and walked over to Jeri.

"So," he started, "What ...?" He knew that she knew what he'd need to know.

Ricky was sitting on the curb with his head in his hands. "Phil and I saw the driver," Jeri said, pointing at Ricky with her nose, as a dog would, "blow a stop sign and fail to signal his turn. We both stopped at the light, here, and we were just going to light him up, when the female," again she nose-pointed at the ambulance, "ran out into traffic from over there." One more gesture toward the east side of the road.

"Just ran up? And then what?"

"She went up to his left side window, started yelling at him, waving a little knife around." The knife blade was about three and a half inches long, and Jeri's description of it as "little" was intentional.

"Okay. And ...?"

"We both exited number twenty-one over there." This time she actually pointed with one hand, indicating their patrol unit. "We ordered the subject to drop the weapon, and she refused."

"So who drew a side arm?"

"You understand that I'm evaluating Phil?" she asked. "So I was nominally in command ... I mean, in charge?"

"Oh. Okay."

"He drew his weapon. I made the decision that the subject could be subdued without lethal force, and I applied a hands-on technique. She dropped the knife, and I was able to cuff her."

"Yeah. So what about the driver?"

"He's clean as far as the incident goes. Says he's never seen her before. Nothing in the car. No priors. Works right over there. I gave him a warning on the traffic offenses."

"But she ran up to his window? She wasn't trying to buy something?"

"His car was clean, and so was he. Oh, and he holds a security clearance. Says he's going to have to report the incident to some agency or other. He's some kind of engineer at a company over there."

"All right. So he's wrong-place-wrong-time, as far as you're concerned?"

"That's my take, yes, sir."

"There you go again. I told you not to 'sir' me, Jeri. Especially now you're leaving us."

"Force of habit, si ... Sergeant."

The sergeant walked over to Phil, looking for his side of the story. Jeri went over to Ricky. He seemed to have calmed down a bit. At least he wasn't shaking anymore. She told him he could go, repeated the warning about stops and signals, and reminded him that he might have to testify if anything ended up going to trial. He was able, by now, to control his voice enough to thank her, and he drove slowly and very legally away. He got back to his condo, flopped on the coach for five minutes, and then booted up his home workstation. He started a browser and did a search on the string "Michigan concealed carry permit".

I come now to the time in my life that saw the greatest amount of uncertainty, for me without question, and I believe for the country as well. Although there are many now still living who went through it, that will not always be the case. For those reading this who were not alive or who were still in their youth during those years, let me offer this analogy. Suppose that you are a citizen of a country and an officer in its army. Your country is at peace, but there is a dispute with another country, and there are parties in each place that argue for an entire spectrum of possible measures: peace, war, compromise, negotiation, and many shades of each. Regardless of the decision, it will inevitably affect you and your family. Consider what your feelings must be and how troubling the uncertainty would be to you. I suggest that you would find it hard to concentrate on other topics in the midst of the swirling rumor and report.

Now imagine that the dispute is not between two countries, but between two parts of your own homeland. If you can form this image in your mind, you will have some sense of how our country was and of how everyone was caught up in the question of slavery.

After my injury, I spent a great part of the fall and winter recovering or attempting to, both in New York with Mrs. Thomas and for a short time in Virginia with my family. Through those months, I of course gave thought to the national question, but I can say with my hand on my heart, I did not believe that the extreme ideas on either side would be put into play. I did not think it possible that the radicals would prevail and send the country into a maelstrom of war and destruction.

More of my efforts, though, some of them conducted from my bedside and some if not all with the assistance of my dear wife, were to determine what sort of career would be open to me, injured as I was. I believed that I could no longer do the entire range of activities that were required of a field cavalry officer, and that if nothing else offered, I would have to find employment of another kind. It was these efforts and the correspondence involved in them that has caused doubt to be cast on my intentions, and I will try as clearly as I can to counter those ideas.

First, I will say that I had always thought of Virginia as my home. I felt then a sense of allegiance to the state and to its people and to its land. I thought of myself as a Virginian, and that feeling continued up to the point that it became something exclusive of my other allegiances, those to the United States and to the United States Army. That was not a thing that I had anticipated happening, since it had always, until that fatal spring, been possible to be an officer and an American and a Virginian. When that was no longer possible and when the men of extremes on either side of the great question had forced my hand and that of every other serving officer, I then had no choice.

When I entered West Point all those years prior, I took an oath. When I made it clear that I was determined to remain a soldier of the United States, I considered it wise that I take substantially that same oath again, and so I did, in front of a magistrate. Then, after the rebellion opened actual hostilities by firing on Fort Sumter, and after I succeeded in command of the Second Cavalry, I took my oath a second time as all newly appointed officers had to do. Ten days after that, when I was appointed a full colonel, I took it a third time. One of my captains expressed surprise that I was being called upon so often to repeat my words, but I told him then what I would still say, that the condition of things being what they were, I would take the oath before each meal if the Army wished it. That is the sense of what I said to him, anyway. Others have quoted it often enough.

I mention above that I was appointed to command my old regiment, the Second Cavalry. That came about because of the actions of two men. One of them, Robert Lee, resigned his commission and allied himself with the Southern Cause. He was a man who had been my commander and my friend, and to this day, I cannot simply dismiss him. He made a choice that I could not make, but at least he did it in a manner consistent with his conscience. The other man, however, I can only look on with contempt and with the point of view of having been betrayed. David Twiggs, a man I had served with and under, justified my low opinion of him by conspiring with the rebellion and surrendering his command in Texas. That command included most of the Second Cavalry, and only the men and their personal equipment were allowed to be evacuated by sea. Twiggs died of disease in the next year and that spared him the consequences of his unfaithfulness, but nevertheless it left me with an ill-equipped and angry regiment to reform and place in the field. That we managed to report ourselves for duty as quickly as we did owes more to the men than to any efforts of myself and my officers. I did not know it at the time, but that would become a trademark of the war as it was fought over much of its duration. The individual soldiers, both the regulars and the volunteers, would win the battles.

There was a gentleman in Ann Arbor who was, in a modern sense, the keeper of tribal lore. Leo had grown up with the technical revolution, and he could be said to know everyone. With the coming of the Internet, "everyone" became a much larger set, and by now, no one could really claim universal acquaintance, but still Leo's tribe was vast and widespread. Tribe it was, too, in a strict sense, although there wasn't a recognized leader. It wasn't a *karass* as Vonnegut imagined it, since many of the members knew they were members, a point that MacArthur had made to Leo on at least one occasion. Inevitably, the two of them knew each other, both having been steeped in the town's history and characters for thirty years or more. Now, Mac arranged his Saturday trip to the farmer's market so that he'd run into Leo.

After greetings and asking-after-spouses, Mac brought up LifeRigor. "Kind of a nifty idea, it seems like. UM prof. Says he can record nerve signals and turn 'em into code."

"Yeah, yeah," said Leo. "That's Doctor Metharom."

"You know him?"

"Not myself. But Marian K. was with him for a while. Marian Kasimir."

"Where was she before?" asked Mac, pretending he knew the woman.

"She was at the U. I think she's back there, actually."

"Back?"

"Yeah, she was head of engineering for the LifeRigor thing for a while. But her daughter knows Maggie from school, and she told Maggie her mom wasn't there anymore."

Mac untangled those references, remembering that Leo's daughter, Maggie, went to Community High, right across the street from the market. "Really? Did she say why?"

"Not really. Maggie said she quit."

"Huh. Startups." said Mac, dismissively. "So ... asparagus?"

"Asparagus!" Leo held up a bunch of bright green spears, bound with a blue rubber band. Behind him there was a double-booth of the iconic spring vegetables, manned by "Doug", so called because his potatoes, when they were ready, were always accompanied by little signs saying "Dug Yesterday". What the man's real name was, Mac never knew, but his tall Amish hat, beard, broad smile, and ironic T-shirt slogans were a brand in themselves.

"But you know," Leo went on, "somebody else mentioned Doctor Metharom. I'm not remembering who, but somebody said he might not be the most enlightened guy, gender-wise."

"Ah," said Mac. "So maybe not a great place to be a woman exec?"

"I'm not sure. I mean, I wouldn't take that too seriously. I can't even remember where I heard it." Leo was infallibly polite, and it occurred to him that he didn't know why Mac was interested in LifeRigor.

"No fear. Just curious. Colleen heard about the place from somebody at her shop. It was a new one on me." Mac was a good liar; he didn't do it often and he always mixed it with truth. "Gotta go get the traditional Saturday chicken, though. Best to Meg and Maggie and ..." he tried to recall the dog's name. "... and the dog."

So, Mac thought as he walked away. *Two academics. One of them bails out. Give that to Andy. And Leo didn't contradict my notion of the recording-animals idea.* He glanced to the right as he passed one of the large organic produce vendors. A head of red hair, attached to a woman standing with her back to him and looking at mushrooms, struck him as familiar. Then she turned, apparently rejecting the fungi, and he recognized her. Velvet Underground came to mind: *Pale Blue Eyes.* "Hello, Alice."

"Oh, Mr. MacArthur," the woman said. She had, as Mac's unconscious had pointed out already, pale blue eyes set in a Celtic face. Her hair, he guessed, was never under a great deal of control, and this morning's moderate breeze had unleashed it. She was Alice Graves, partner of Jenn Langton's daughter and a post-doctoral archaeologist at the great educational empire up the street. "How are you?"

"As well as can be expected," said Mac, using one of his standard answers to that question. People who knew him and asked after his condition were, he assumed, just looking for a binary "nothing new" or "something new and awful" response. No news was good news, after all, when you were talking to someone with Mac's health record. The trouble was, though, he didn't know what to ask *her.* A cousin of hers had gone missing, back in the dark winter, and Mac hadn't been any help at all, really, in locating him. Hers wasn't a face on which grief would sit well, and he looked closely at her to see if it had left any visible traces. "How are you? And Jackie?" was the most neutral thing he could think of to say.

"Jackie's doing well. She's really digging into the International Business program. She might try to transfer here in the fall. And I'm ... as *you* said, as well as can be expected."

"I'm sorry, you know. About being useless. Can I assume you talked to Andy Patel about your cousin?"

"Well, yes. Twice, actually. Once in his FBI role, and then again, when we were all being, oh, I guess 'new family'. He was able to be a little less formal, then."

"Andy's a really smart guy. And he's very straightforward. Did he tell you why I just dropped off the planet on that ... problem?" Mac didn't want to say "case" or "investigation". His part in looking for Alice's cousin had been completely ad hoc, with no formal status at all.

"He told me that his, um, employer didn't want anyone else looking into it."

"Right. And they told me the same thing, rather emphatically." Mac had gone on one expedition into the Detroit suburbs, poking around, trying to find out why Alice's cousin had vanished. Then, he'd gotten a call from the FBI, asking him to back away and stay away. Not long after that, the firm that the cousin had worked for showed up in the news, with two of its executives exchanging pistol shots at a highway rest stop.

"Well," she said, sounding rather lame, "I'm grateful for what you did, anyway. And give my best to Mrs. MacArthur. I need to ..."

"So do I," said Mac. He was about to make the chicken excuse again, but he thought better of it. For no reason at all, he'd labeled Alice as a likely vegetarian. So he just finished with, "Good to see you."

"You, too," and Alice turned one way. Mac turned the other and stopped short. Another step and he'd have run into Jeri Klein, head on.

"Hello, Detective," she said, stepping back.

"Klein! I didn't see you. I'm ah, glad to hear you got the Deputy position."

Jeri was dressed for the market, wearing jeans and a tan sportsman's shirt with a pair of chest pockets. From behind Mac, somebody barked once, deeply. "Cara! Be quiet" Jeri said. Mac turned and saw a yearling German Shepherd, tethered to a fire hydrant outside the market's no-dogs zone. He turned back to Jeri.

"That isn't your duty dog, is it?"

"No, that's *my* little girl," she answered. "She's learning to sit and be patient, but she's not quite there yet. My patrol canine is Marty."

"Well. This is ... " He turned the other way to do an introduction, but Alice was gone. "Hmm," he said. "I was just talking to somebody, but she's on her way." Jeri had a canvas shopping bag on her arm, the badge of the serious market patron. "Finding anything good?"

"Yes." She didn't elaborate. "Detective, I'd like to thank you for your help with the County. I think this is going to be a better assignment for me."

"I was happy to help."

"Can I ask you ..." she paused. There was almost no expression on her face, and her voice was neutral. Mac just canted his head, like a dog listening to a human.

"Do you think the department ... I mean, the Ann Arbor department ... has a discipline problem?"

Because she was right there in front of him, looking at him closely, Mac didn't do his tight-closed-eyes face. Instead, he drew in a breath and let it out again. "What kind of discipline?"

"Two evenings ago, an officer put me in a very bad position. He drew his sidearm in response to a subject who was out of control, yes, but in no sense a threat."

Mac looked around. "Do you want to walk over there and introduce me to your dog? There aren't quite so many people over there."

"If you want, yes." They walked the ten feet out from under the market roof. Mac knelt, not without his usual twinges in the knees, and greeted Cara, looking down and not straight into her eyes. She neither backed away nor bared her teeth, and when he held out a hand with the fingers curled down, she sniffed it politely. He stood back up and took a step away. Cara relaxed and stuck out her tongue. Jeri stroked the dog's back, and told her she was a good girl.

"That's a nice Shepherd," Mac said. "There's some brains in there." He paused one breath's worth, then said "What ended up happening?"

"I put myself in his line of fire. And then I disarmed the suspect and took her into custody."

"Her?"

"Yes. She was intoxicated. She may have been having a psychotic break."

"You disarmed her? What did she have?"

"A useless little knife. A steak knife."

"Okay. What's the question, though?"

"I believe that if I hadn't been there, he'd have shot her. If I hadn't ordered him not to fire, he would have."

"Klein," Mac said, "We don't know each other all that well, but I don't think of you as ... as somebody who'd reason from one incident to a broad conclusion. Am I right about that?"

"What do you mean?" She kept her tone level and neutral, making the question sound literal, not like the beginning of denial or disagreement.

"I mean, do you have a larger reason for thinking of a ... systemic problem?"

"I shot a suspect. You remember that, I'm sure. I fired because a subject was about to kill another officer. And that officer wasn't taking any steps to save his own life."

"I remember."

"I took the responsibility, because that other officer wasn't taking it. And I took the responsibility this time, because another officer was about to overreact."

"Okay. I see. I think I see."

"So now I'm going to the County. What if it's the same thing there?"

"You know, I don't think I can even guess at an answer. But ... how well do you know Jenn Langton?"

The Holcombe building was a simple structure. From outside, it was another single-story technology space, right at the back of a tech park. The street that led to it ended in a circular turn-around, and Holcombe and its nearest neighbor had driveways leading out of the circle. Trees marked the end of the property, and even though a five-minute walk through them would bring you into a subdivision, the effect was still one of being out in the countryside.

For Doctor Witthaya Metharom, it had a worrisome aspect. It was the headquarters of his company's only real customer. His theoretical work had some small grants, and he'd managed to round up a certain amount of capital, mostly from people and funds that were willing to place little bets on wild notions. But the subcontract he had with Holcombe was the bread and butter of his company. That was troubling for several reasons.

The structural problem was that he was committed to delivering working, deployable software to drive the mobility of a robotic quadruped, essentially a combat-ready android wolf. The actual hardware would be years down the road, and it was someone else's job. But LifeRigor had to get a demonstratable simulation package in place in less than a year. And to make that happen, he'd had to bring in people to write code from scratch, since code that could be captured and converted from crawling flatworms wasn't even close to usable in this application. And quite frankly, he had no good idea how capturing algorithms from anything like a mammal would work. He thought he knew what would have to be done with it, once you had it, but the mechanics of getting a large predator or even a domestic canid to cooperate with the recording technique were not at all clear to him.

Even worse, as long as he had to keep people at work on a normal software project, he couldn't put them to work on his own ideas. He hadn't clearly understood that, but the bidding process made it very clear. His company's hourly rates had to stay as they were bid, and he had to pay the coders what he'd offered them or they'd leave. He'd tried to get around that, tried to cut his costs by using offshore development for the contract, but ... well, that blew up on him. His development chief, that impossible woman, Kasimir, had reacted very badly to that. The people he wanted to talk to in India had no clearances, of course, and she'd driven that point home very forcefully. The contract, the contract ... she was always waving the contract at him.

"What is the difference?" he'd asked her. "If we deliver good code and save money, what does it matter?" But she wouldn't agree. She kept saying it was illegal. Saying that the contractors would have to know things about the project that were classified. When she got to the point of hinting that companies "like that" couldn't be trusted, well, he'd had enough of it. The separation papers left it deliberately unclear if she'd been fired or had resigned. Unimportant. She was gone, and he was having to deal with all this by himself. Oddly, he found that easier.

Now, though ... now he was having to take up the same things with the source of his contract, essentially his customer, this Holcombe company. And except for their engineering chief, they were all women, too. Difficult women. He parked his car in the visitor spaces, and he and his passenger got out. The man was a senior developer and a newly-named team lead. *Best to get this over with,* Metharom thought, *this 'Design Review' that Holcombe wants. That they say the government wants.* Walking a step or two behind, Ricky Peakes carried a secure laptop.

Inside, they were met by Vivienne Keyes and Jenn Langton. Jenn had a couple of red visitor badges for them. Viv did the greeting.

"This is our team leader for the ambulatory ..." Doctor Metharom began, nodding in Ricky's direction, but Vivienne cut him off.

"Let's keep any technical discussion for the closed area," she said. He glanced around. The lobby was entirely empty except for a young man in a black uniform shirt, sitting at the reception desk. *Foolish, foolish,* the doctor thought, but he just nodded.

"This is Mister Peakes," was all he said, doing a reasonably good job of seeming unperturbed.

"Let's go back to the area," said Jenn. "Doctor Holcombe will catch up with us there."

"It's always a pleasure to see her. As you say, let's go back."

There was a brief delay while Jenn's staff got the presentation files off Ricky's laptop and onto the secure network. While that was going on, Jenn signed them all into the closed area. They arranged themselves in the conference room, and Viv handed out a printed agenda. Jenn picked up a copy and looked at Ricky.

"Mr. Peakes, is it? Are you presenting instead of Ms. Dupuis-Baker? Or will she be joining us?"

Ricky had been rehearsing his PowerPoint deck, mentally, and missed part of the question. "Um, I'm sorry, Mrs. Langton? Will what?"

Doctor Metharom stepped in. "Corinne will not be attending. Mr. Peakes is now leading the software team."

"She's left the program? Has she been de-briefed?"

"I beg your pardon?"

"If she's no longer working on the subcontract—not charging time to it—she needs to be taken off the list of cleared personnel. Formally. We need to tell the customer."

"Oh, she's still working on it. She hasn't left the program."

"No," said Ricky. "She's just, um, doing regular work. On it. Not being the team lead."

"All right," said Jenn. "But, Viv, we still need to update the list of personnel, right?"

"Yes. We need to give the sponsor that change. Your security guy, Mister ... Todas? I think?"

"Todarcz," Jenn said. "I'll send him a note. He needs to tell me and I'll tell Captain Gordon."

"My, oh my," said Metharom. "All this paperwork." At that point, Doctor Holcombe arrived.

"Hello, all," she said. "Sorry to be late. Hello Doctor Metharom." She looked at Peakes. "And I don't think I've met you."

Ricky opened his mouth, but Metharom again preempted him. "This is Richard Peakes," he said again. "He is now leading the software team. We have been talking about the formalities of making that change, ah, formally."

"Oh. All right. Viv, are you okay with that?"

"Mr. Peakes was on the original proposal, just not in the lead role. I don't have any particular issue with a change, I suppose. It's LifeRigor's decision. We just have to update a document or two."

"All right. Now, before we kick off, there's one thing I have to make very clear." She was looking Doctor Metharom straight in the eye. "We all know that this is a catch-up review. It should have been done, what, Viv? A month ago?"

"Yes."

"And we have to do it. The minutes, the assessment, the materials we review—those are all deliverables. The contract requires it. And LifeRigor signed off on that contract. It's your responsibility to make this kind of thing happen. You need to have the reviews and reports on your project calendar, you need to be scheduling them with us, not the other way around. You've got money for it in the bid, you get to charge for it, you get paid. So make sure Mr. Peakes or Mr. Dormanski or whoever is running the show over there knows what's in the agreement and makes it happen."

It had been a long time since anyone had spoken to Doctor Metharom in a tone like that. No; he corrected himself. Marian Kasimir had been just as rude, just as out of line. The difference was that he couldn't fire this Holcombe woman or her arrogant people. The best he could do was to nod in a way that he hoped would convey agreement and strong disapproval at the same time.

Ricky Peakes, for his part, was rigid in his chair. He saw Karolyn Holcombe speaking, but his mind was hearing the young women in his old Tuscaloosa apartment, that lunatic hag at his car window, and that rigid, strong, capable, black policewoman talking to him as he sat on a curb, out in public, with his pants wet.

The wolves slept poorly, curled up together in an unfamiliar place. At the first light in the east, they moved off, dodging from one woodlot to another. There were traces of deer and smaller game everywhere, but P51 was intent on making progress, getting out of this patchy territory and into real forest again. Motor noises of any kind were a signal to seek cover; she had no real understanding of land vehicles versus aircraft, but they all made a convenient set of warning noises, and she had memories of avoiding them, whenever they came close. She'd done a trek like this before, when she was a pup herself, and she was beginning to remember things about it and the associated lessons.

By mid-day, the open spaces were outnumbering the woods, and a line began to show up on the horizon, whenever you could see ahead more than a few hundred yards. The group stopped for a rest in a last grove of pines in the center of an open field. Ahead of them, trees stretched in a line, north to south, literally unbroken.

From beyond the line, there were motor and rushing noises, not constantly, but in small windows of sound that moved one way or another. P51 knew that it meant a road and humans, but it was still a woods, and in a natural and almost unconscious way she was confident of her ability to hide. After a few minutes, they bolted in line ahead formation across the open field and into the trees.

The strip of woods was less than a quarter mile wide, and when she peered carefully out from behind a last tree, her ears and nose had already told her what was there. Down a shallow bank straight ahead was a wide road, and as she watched, a car and then a very large truck sped by, heading southwest. But looking the other way, northeast, over her left shoulder, was the bank of a river. And the road, plus another one running alongside it, crossed the river on a pair of bridges. The riverbank below those bridges was open for just a few yards, and then the trees closed in. One at a time, moving quickly from tree to bush, slinking carefully across the open, P51 and her pups slipped under Interstate 35. Instead of dashing away, they turned south and found, in less than twenty feet, what an unmistakable scent had promised them: the road-killed carcass of an adult deer.

Mill Springs

Yet another coffee with Andy Patel. *People will think I'm having an affair with him, next,* Mac thought. It was late in the afternoon, and he'd switched to *caffè latte* from his usual black. The milk was easier on his stomach, now that he was on his third cup of the day. They were in a window seat this time, the last available table, and their view was of the Ashley and Washington intersection.

"So," Mac started, "you said a 'guy' at LifeRigor might be suspicious?"

"Um, I might have said that, yes," said Andy.

98

"Well, I turned up a couple of bits of dirt, but one of the cast isn't a 'guy'. She's the ex-Chief of Engineering."

"Oh. No, I probably meant 'guy' generically. What's up with her?"

"It turns out that the President—the one with the big ideas—has a sort of reputation as a sexist."

"Okay," said Andy, taking notes.

"And what I got from a couple of people is that there may have been a problem along those lines. Either with him or with the administration-and-money guy. Somebody named Dormanski. Roger Dormanski. Nobody I'd ever heard of."

"I was aware that the CTO, Marilyn ... no, *Marian* Kasimir, quit."

"She did. And one of the people I talked to hinted something about a lawsuit in the works."

"That we, ah, didn't know." Another note.

"There's another thing."

"Another thing?" said Andy. So far, Mac had given him exactly one new piece of intelligence, interesting, maybe, but not really germane to his case.

"Yeah. And it might slop over into the ... the family side of things. For you. So I'm just going to start talking and you tell me when to stop."

"Okay. I'd be less than candid, I guess, if I pretended not to understand that."

"Right. So just hold up a hand or shoot me or something if I run off the rails." Mac had been in awkward conversations like this before, but always with lawyers who were good at shutting off the faucet. He wasn't sure what Andy knew or wanted to know.

"I talked to an old bar pal of mine—ours, actually, Coleen knew him from high school. Faculty member, now. He knows Doctor Metharom. And he explained something to me about IR and D. You familiar with that?"

"Well, R and D is Research and Development, usually. IR and D, no."

"The I is 'Internal'. Internal Research and Development. And according to my friend, the company has a problem with it." Andy was scribbling.

"I didn't know any of this, myself. According to him, there's this complicated process you go through if you want to be a government contractor. It's about documenting your billing rates, and not low-balling your quotes just to get the award, things like that."

"Yeah," said Andy. "We get into that, sometimes, when somebody's really off the path with it. You know, low-ball the quote, start the work, then stick up the DoD or whoever for more money if they want the job done. And the customer goes along because they'll look bad if it goes public."

"Yup, that was how he described it. So everybody's really interested in your rates being real, the money you quote on your proposal being real. I mean, *really* based on your costs. And that means, you have to keep your overhead down, or your rates go up and you get out-bid by somebody else."

"Right."

"And that means, I guess, that you can't do a lot of R and D on your own, stuff nobody's paying you for. Or else it drives your rates up. And he told me that LifeRigor has a problem that way."

100

"Okay." Andy was running out of one-word ways to say, "Yes, I understand. Keep going." He had a feeling he was repeating himself.

"The deal is, he tells me, that Doctor Metharom's worm-recording idea isn't even close to ready for anything more than tormenting worms. So the company's a way of getting revenue to pay for R and D. But it needs so much R and D, that he can't keep the rates down. So maybe the rate bids aren't exactly, completely, utterly kosher." Mac looked closely at Andy. The Fed was writing quickly, and seen upside down from Mac's point of view, it was illegible. Whether it was some kind of code or just bad penmanship, Mac couldn't tell.

"And here's the part that you might not want to hear. Formally, anyway. LifeRigor isn't contracted directly to the gummint, right now." He paused. Andy just looked at him.

"They're a subcontractor. To another company in Ann Arbor." Nothing from Andy.

"And your wife works there." Andy nodded his head.

 Many wild ideas swept across the United States, north and south, during the first year of the war. There were so many mistaken notions and erroneous principles alive in the minds of men that listing them all here would be a tedious job and even more so, tedious reading. A few examples will be enough.

First, the public on both sides believed that the other side must obviously fail, and that their own forces would march gaily to victory in the first battles. The fight at Manassas or First Bull Run as it is sometimes called showed the error in that idea. Neither side demonstrated any grasp of coordination or grand tactics, and the rebellion blundered into victory as our National forces blundered into defeat.

Next, there was the perception that the war would be short. Many of the state volunteers, at least in the north, were men recruited for three months' service. In sober fact, it would take longer than that simply to gather, equip, and train them. Many battalions on both sides went into battle with obsolete muskets or none at all, and by the time we had the volunteers equipped, when they knew which end of a rifle to point at the enemy, and when they and their officers were ready to think about marching to war, their terms of enlistment were almost up.

Also, it appeared that in the west, neither the Confederacy nor the Union had an accurate appreciation of the civilian point of view. In Kentucky and in East Tennessee, both parties counted on their adherents to carry the day, politically and militarily. The rebellion in particular overestimated its popularity with the people, and although the Governor of Kentucky played a treacherous game himself, the citizenry were mostly for the Union or at least for neutrality. Across the Cumberland River, in the eastern part of Tennessee, a large part of the population also wanted to remain within the Union. Both of these unlucky states were directly on the dividing line between north and south, at least west of the mountains, and both sides took a political determination to make them part of their faction. To keep Kentucky loyal and to help the Tennesseans expel the rebels, the President turned to General Robert Anderson, the defender of Fort Sumter, and named him Commander of the Department of the Cumberland. I and William Sherman were sent to help him build an army.

For the first time in my experience and certainly not the last, I served under a rapidly changing series of commanders. General Anderson was succeeded quickly by General Sherman and he, suffering in health, was then relieved by General Don Carlos Buell. Each of those gentlemen was subjected to pressure from the national government, from local politicians, and from East Tennessee volunteers. All of those factions wanted immediate action, whereas doing anything immediately was difficult, impractical, unsupported, and dangerous. We were all fortunate, all the soldiers of every rank within the Department of the Cumberland, in that the rebellion in our part of the world was not well served, and we were spared several chances to fail, simply because their local command, Generals Zollicoffer and Crittenden, were as uncertain as we were and because they received as bad information and as scant supplies as did we.

The composition of our war, then, was one of threatening or being threatened over a period of time, not one of pitched fights. To the west of us, Ulysses Grant and General Halleck were preparing to begin their assault on Forts Henry and Donelson, and in our department, General Buell was planning an assault on Nashville. Meanwhile, partly to thwart us and partly to accommodate his enthusiastic troops, Felix Zollicoffer moved across the Cumberland and threatened to cut off one of my advanced positions. General Buell ordered me to push Zollicoffer back across the river, keeping him from threatening any move on Nashville. This led to the battle of Mill Springs. For many men on both sides, this would be their first serious fight or as the saying came to be, their first sight of the elephant.

At this point, General Buell's force was called The Army of the Ohio, and I was in command of its First Division, including the First, Second, Third, and Twelfth brigades, plus artillery and cavalry. I was getting sound information from my scouts and from my advanced positions regarding the rebel movements, and so I concentrated as much of the Division as was with me and ordered more of it to join as soon as possible. I was anxious to engage the enemy quickly because of the dangerous position in which he had placed himself.

To understand our fight, imagine a flour sack. The sides of the sack were defined by a northward bend of the Cumberland River and a stream called Fishing Creek. Zollicoffer chose to bring part of his force across the Cumberland and into the bottom of the sack since it offered him a crossing place where he could not be easily flanked. Unfortunately for him, it also kept him from making flanking movements himself. His superior, General Crittenden, joined him and apparently was unhappy with the position, since the whole force that was north of the river would have to withdraw straight back across it if they were forced to retreat. Zollicoffer, I am told, argued for an advance and an attack on my forces without regard for any withdrawal, since he did have a local superiority in troops and, I again assume, because he was filled with the notion that southern soldiers were inherently better

103

fighters than ours. This idea was at that time widespread, north and south, because of the defeat at Bull Run and other things.

In consequence, the rebel force on our side of the river moved north at night, up the throat of the sack and toward our position. I had concentrated three regiments of infantry, one of Kentucky horsemen, and some of our guns at a place called Logan's Crossroads. This was a force only about half the size of the enemy's, but I was confident that if I could keep the men in hand and in confident spirits, we would be a match for the rebels, partly because I knew that we were better trained and better positioned, and partly, I confess, because I was aware of the other side's serious deficit in equipment.

I settled the command down for the night, stressing the need to keep close watch and pushing out guards and scouts. In the early hours of the morning, our camp was roused by the lookouts, and the two forward battalions went into defensive positions across a road that ran south, toward the bottom of the sack to the river and to a place beyond called Mill Springs. Shortly, the vanguard of Zollicoffer's force attacked us vigorously out of some woods.

My leading battalions, the 10th New York and the 4th Kentucky, slowed the attack and then fell backward in good order. The confederates tried repeated charges with their infantry, delivered well, but they were handicapped by the poor quality of their muskets, their seven mile march in bitterly cold and wet conditions, and by their artillery never managing to get into action. As the head on fight continued, I brought up our artillery and positioned them on our left, situated to take in flank any attack that might be made across a hayfield that was there or, for that matter, anywhere along the front of the battle. The fire from our guns broke up numerous attempts by their infantry, keeping them from getting to bayonet distance. As my other two regiments arrived from camp, I fed them into the line, allowing them to relieve the original two, now running low on ammunition.

At an early point in the fight, General Zollicoffer became confused by the mist and smoke, and he assumed that some of his men were firing on another one of their regiments. This was not the case, since they were actually firing at our dismounted Kentucky horse, but he rode out into the middle ground of the battle and got within shouting distance of Colonel Speed Fry, in command of the Kentuckians. Zollicoffer shouted at him to cease fire, still thinking he was one of his own officers, and Fry, less deceived, shot him. The wound was fatal, and some writers have cited the lack of leadership as a cause in the Confederate failure. Of that, I have no opinion. I do not know if General Zollicoffer was well-loved by his men or if his death disheartened them or if they were let down by a night-long march in bitter weather, an attack against a prepared enemy, or the antiquated flintlock muskets that many of them carried. Personally, I consider all of it to have been equally discouraging, and I honor them for making as good a fight as they did.

All I can say with certainty is that shortly afterward, our Colonel McCook arrived on the field with his 9th Ohio regiment, and I ordered him to throw them in on our right flank, wheeling in and taking the enemy infantry on its left. At that, the rebel force crumbled and fled. In short order, their whole army was in uncontrolled flight back down the Mill Creek road, seeking the shelter of defensive works they had made on the north bank of the river. We pressed them closely, but declined to storm their trenches that night, preferring to wait for the morning when we would have more of our guns up and ready to support an assault. Unfortunately, with the help of a river steamboat they had on hand, General Crittenden was able to get them away in the darkness, leaving his wounded, a great deal of supplies, and a number of guns and flags. When we advanced, there was no resistance, and the victory was thus mostly complete. Although we did not take his position by storm and smash his army with force, those that escaped accomplished that for themselves by dispersing to their homes or anywhere else they pleased.

Mill Springs, as it came to be called, was a small battle by the standards of those that were to come. There were fewer than twenty thousand men on the field, all told, and including the pursuit it lasted a single day. Nevertheless, it was the first engagement worthy of the name that could be called a Union victory, and both the administration and the press were enthusiastic. Because of events to the west of us, notably

General Grant's seizure of the rebel-held Forts Henry and Donelson and the subsequent near-run-thing at Shiloh, neither my Division nor any other was allowed to advance into Eastern Tennessee, and the chance to pacify at least that part of the state, if not all of it, was lost. For me, it was a fight of great instruction, the first one of any size in which I had held independent command. I will try to list the most important of the lessons it brought me. They were all things that my later experience would prove to be correct.

First, I was confirmed in my belief, one that I had held through most of my prior career, that nothing but hard, thorough, unrelenting preparation can even make success likely, let alone assured. Going into any fight, even against savages, without a well-armed, well-fed, and well-trained force courts disaster. I have always tried to follow this principle, even if it has cost me the favor of commanders and politicians who, perhaps for good reasons of their own, are anxious for quick adventures and easy solutions.

Next, the whole campaign prior to the actual battle confirmed for me the need for clear and reliable intelligence, good scouting, and judicious placement of outposts. At most times, we were informed of Zollicoffer's movements. I was prepared to counter them, and if he had not been so rash as to attack us, we were at that moment preparing to attack him. Although I was confident of defeating him wherever we met, his advance up the sack towards an alerted force bought him a defeat that cost us less than it would have if we had attacked him in his entrenchments.

Finally, it accustomed me to patiently obeying orders that were often given without reference to facts. The campaign leading up to Mill Springs was a chaotic exercise of commands and counter-commands, with both Washington and the Governor-in-exile of loyal Tennessee demanding haste. Whichever General officer was commanding the Department of the Ohio at the time felt compelled to resist or even countermand some of these orders, based on their perception of local realities. I obeyed the legitimate orders I received, including one that required a brief and unnecessary withdrawal. That bitter retreat could have cost us many of our Kentucky and Tennessee loyalists, but I and my brigade commanders did as we were told while trying to reassure the state unionists, and in the event our local troops fought well and skillfully when they were finally allowed to do so.

On the other hand, General Zollicoffer was given or assumed too much independence at first, and by the time General Crittenden arrived, their force for the invasion of Kentucky had already been moved forward recklessly. They were, they appear to have felt, compelled to push ahead and engage us in what was a position of no great advantage to either side, but one that favored us slightly by making it difficult for them to bring their larger force against us all at once. The defeat that occurred would not have happened, at least not in the way it did, if Zollicoffer had not been allowed to operate quite so independently.

The conclusion I draw from these circumstances is very simple. An order is an order, and your only recourse is to protest it with logic and factual analysis to the extreme point, that is to the point where you are convinced that the higher authorities will not be moved. At that point, having expressed your views, you must obey. You must assault the ridge, charge for the guns, or swim the river, doing your best to achieve the desired outcome. Afterwards, if you live, you must neither gloat at having been right (when the effort fails) nor apologize for having been wrong (if it succeeds).

MacArthur's phone told him that he had a call from Jenn Langton. Having pointed Jeri Klein at her for advice and counsel, Mac wasn't surprised that she'd be calling.

"Mrs. Patel," he said. "How are you and all the little Patels?"

"Mr. MacArthur. There's only one little Patel, and he's off in the suburbs, somewhere, serving his country. How are you?"

"No worse than can be expected, thanks. What can I do for you on this ..." he glanced out the window "... somewhat gray and muggy day?"

"Why does Jeri Klein think that you think that I have advice to give her?"

"Because I once made the same mistake I always make and gave her some advice. Now she wants more, and I'm trying to phase out of the advice business. So I outsourced it to you."

"I really don't know her very well."

"No, nor I. But she's moving to the Sheriff's Department, and she seems to be concerned that there'll be professionality and gender-bias issues out there. Frankly, you're the only woman I know who's worked that shop." *And*, he added privately, *What the hell do I know about gender bias? Or the Sheriff's Department?*

"Oh. Well, ... I guess I could talk to her about it. But you know what I think?"

"No."

"I think I'll get Alice to join in. She's a woman in academia, and from what I hear, that can be pretty grim, in the bias category. "

"Not a bad idea. Funny, though. I almost had the chance to introduce them. Ran into Alice at the Market, then I turned around, and there was Jeri. She's got a nice dog, too. Jeri, that is."

"Really? Andy said he told you about us getting a doggie? After we get a real house?"

"He did. I mentioned it to Snacker and Goose, and they were enthusiastic." The Shepherds, who usually stayed close to Mac when he was in the house, heard their names and looked up, smiling. "They're confirming that."

"All right. Well, got to go to another meeting. That's my major responsibility here. But I'll see if I can set up a lunch or something with Jeri. Take care of yourself, and say 'Hi' to Colleen."

"Likewise. Give my best to Mr. Langton."

Jenn hung up. *Mr. Langton,* she thought. There had been a Mr. Langton, a Deputy Langton, in fact. She'd been young enough and dumb enough to marry him, and one of the few positive aspects of that was that she'd been spared whatever advances other men out there might otherwise have made. But that hadn't been sufficient, not by any measure, and she'd divorced him, left the Sheriff's shop, and come to the AAPD. If there were any wounds from his crude behavior and constant infidelity, they'd healed by now, especially in the light of Andy. Also: one of her two daughters was becoming a charming young person, blooming in a relationship with Alice Graves, and the other one was having the basic courtesy to stay out of touch. *No,* she thought, *Unless you count being conned into marrying that first schmuck, I haven't seen a whole lot of harassment. I really think I'll get Alice to join in on this little chat.*

Jenn admitted, privately, to a bit of relief. At work, getting a meeting set up was as simple as asking an Admin, a very bright young man, to do it for her. Getting a time and a place together for herself and three other women, all of them with unrelated and demanding jobs, had been difficult. The time and date had been tough enough, and selecting a place where they could actually hear each other ... *well, that was damn near impossible,* she thought. Colleen MacArthur had solved that, finally, by offering her living room. Now they were around a book-laden coffee table, strewn with a range of volumes reflecting the MacArthur clan's bookshelf shortfall. Mac and the Shepherds were off on a dog park mission, and the four women sat in a lopsided rectangle: Jenn, Colleen, Alice Graves, and Jeri Klein.

Jeri was talking, making a kind of half-meant apology for taking up their time. She'd been slightly flattered when Jenn was setting up a chat for her with "some friends who might have suggestions". Now, talking to these other women, she began to appreciate the range of people in the room. Jenn she knew from the Ann Arbor department, a smart detective and now a Director of something. She'd met Colleen MacArthur once before, and knew she was an executive in some sort of technology. And she'd just met Alice Graves, a woman with academic credentials. They were the kind of people she used to meet when she was still at home. Recently, not so much.

There were the inevitable afternoon drinks: tea, coffee, "just water, please". Jenn, being somewhat at home in the MacArthur household, helped with cups and glasses and put out a plate of biscuits. Colleen made a comment about how the goodies would have go up on a higher table when the dogs came back. The four of them sat down and, a little stiffly at first, they cooperated in getting the conversation moved off into the topic of gender in the workplace. Everyone had a story or two, all ending, more or less, with no real theory or general plan of action.

"I think," Alice said, "there's an analogy here. Can I set it up, just as briefly as I can?"

"Sure," Jeri said. She shifted focus onto Alice.

"Forget about gender for a minute. Let's just think about people. Imagine that you're part of a large group, living in a society where things are run by another group. You can live, eat, have a family or not, but you haven't got any power. You can't vote, you can't run for office. If you just sit still and do your work, you'll get by. But you haven't got any ability to ... step up."

"Like a slave society?"

"It doesn't even have to be that bad. Think of places today where there are two or more ethnic groups, or a couple of different religions. And one group holds all the cards."

"I can think of places like that," Jeri said. "Some countries in Africa, for example."

"Right," Jenn put in. "Or the Middle East."

"Or," said Alice, "North America. After the French were ousted, after Britain won those fights and ended up taking over. There were Native Americans. And white colonists. And Africans, slaves and free. And only Britain had any power, technically."

"Okay," said Colleen. "So, haves and have-nots."

"Well, *power* haves and have-nots. Some people were enslaved, some were being thrown off their lands, but not everybody. The white colonists had property, ways of making a living, a certain amount of freedom. But they had no power, at least in theory. Britain had the whole political deck of cards." She stopped for a sip of coffee. "That's nice, Mrs. MacArthur. We have terrible coffee at the Department."

"'Colleen,' please. Everybody, first names."

"Thank you. Anyway, one thing you can decide, when you're in that powerless situation, is whether you *want* power, in the first place. Do you care? You can go on as things are, taking your paycheck, paying your taxes, saluting ..." she nodded at Jeri "... the commanding officer."

"You mean, just accept the situation?" Jenn said. "Just let it go?"

"You could decide that, yes. Millions of people are doing exactly that, right now. All over the world. But it's only one of the ways to react. You could try to run away, for example."

"Refugees. Or people who change careers."

"Right, Colleen. Exactly what I mean. But what's another option?"

"You can try to change things." Jeri's voice was flat, expressionless.

"Yes, you can revolt. Thousands of people are doing that, too. Mostly against violently repressive states, but sometimes for other reasons."

"But ... I'm sorry, but we're still just talking about an imaginary situation?" Jenn asked.

"*I see*, I think," said Jeri. "Are you going to talk about different levels of, I guess I'd say, 'action', next?"

"That's right. Because if you, being powerless, revolt against power, you'll lose."

Colleen chuckled. "Have you heard Mac on that subject?"

"I think *I* have," said Jenn. He quotes, ah, Rudyard Kipling, I think."

"*An order is an order until you are strong enough to disobey*," said Colleen.

"When I was thinking about leaving the Army," Jeri said, still in her flat, precise way, "I did some reading. And I found some things that made ... a little bit of sense, I guess."

"What were you reading?" Jenn asked.

"Things in political philosophy. I liked this: *the power to think and the desire to rebel.*"

112

What? thought Colleen. "That's Bakunin, right? *God and the State*?"

"Yes. I didn't agree with everything he had to say, but ..." she paused. "Is that what you're talking about, Alice?"

"Well ... I haven't, um, actually read ... he was an anarchist, wasn't he?"

"One kind, yes. He was born in the upper classes, and ... a lot of the other people who were talking about revolution then didn't trust him."

"Well, anyway ... " Alice was caught a bit off balance. "Where I was going was just to say that if you ... if someone revolts, it needs to be in proportion to the, to the power you have. Or the power you can gather together. Or you lose."

"And so you take it easy, to start?" said Jenn. The room hadn't relaxed, particularly.

"The trouble with that," said Jeri, "is knowing when to turn up the volume. If you hang back too long, you can get comfortable. And you can lose something ... credibility. And you gain things along the way, things that make it hard ... that are hard to give up."

"Yes," said Alice. "That was where I was heading. You got there before me."

"Do you know anything about the Community Colleges around here?"

"Oh, well, no. Not all that much. Jenn, Colleen?"

Colleen cleared her throat. "Well, I know a few people at Washtenaw. But, were you thinking of taking classes, or ..."

"I was thinking of trying to teach," said Jeri.

"Teach?" Jenn asked, realizing she'd sounded more surprised that was entirely polite.

"I got an undergraduate degree before I went into the Army. And half a master's. I dropped out, sort of. But it wouldn't take a lot of time to finish up."

"I didn't know that," said Alice. "What was your field?"

"Political Science."

"Oh, that's … great. Where were you … where were you studying?"

"The University of Virginia. My father was in the State Department."

Norman Todarcz—"Norm" to everybody—was the sole manager at LifeRigor who wasn't an academic. He had an undergraduate degree in electrical engineering and a lot of experience in buying and lashing together computing equipment. He'd had a stint in a manufacturing plant, doing installation and maintenance, and for a short time, just before the job at LifeRigor, some consulting IT at the university. If a thing transmitted, emitted, rotated, or reciprocated, he could bend it to his will, and that was exactly the job he hired into. He was the facilities guy.

But then the Engineering VP left, and the Operations Manager put him in charge of security, too.

"You can handle it, Norm. It's just a bunch of forms and badges. I gotta do the Engineering job, now for a while. So I gotta hand off something, and this is really up your street. Good experience, too. Keep the lid on it for, say, six months. And then if we don't get a new EVP in here, we'll bump you up and get you some more money. Maybe some help, too. It'll be fine. You'll do great."

Norm had heard this kind of pitch before. It was couched in enthusiastic, congratulatory terms. Higher level managers used it to send part one of a message: *we need you to take on more work while we fix a problem*. If you argued, you got more of the same happy, back-slapping camaraderie, covering the second part: *suck it up and do the extra job*. And so he said okay.

He went off and took a week's briefing from a consultant. He got his head around the basics, and he brought back a box of white three-inch binders. He called a list of vendors—the badge people, the badge reader people, the secure net people, the phone people—and told them to call him now, not Marian Kasimir. Shortly after that, the company signed its subcontract with Holcombe, and he got to meet Jenn Langton. He didn't sleep very well the next few nights.

Now, on a day when two important things were broken and the software team lead was bugging him and that creep Dormanski the Ops Manager was excited about some meeting with a customer, his phone kept ringing. He had to answer because it might be a vendor calling back with a solution to something. But this time, it was somebody he didn't know, calling from an organization he hadn't heard of. And they were asking for Ms. Kasimir.

"Ah, sorry. She's not here anymore."

"What? She is not?"

"No, sorry. What do you need? I mean, what're you calling about?"

"I am from DSCC. I need to speak with your software program security officer."

"You said DS ... what?"

"Defense Systems Compliance and Control. Who is in charge of your software compliance program?"

"Ah, that would be ... " Ricky Peakes had just been in Norm's office, acting like a big shot. "That would be Mister Peakes. He's in charge of software. You want to talk to him?"

"Yes, certainly. Tell me again his name?" Norm spelled it.

"All right, 'Peakes'. Yes. Go ahead and transfer me."

"Sure. Hang on." Norm sent the call out into the local net. It would ring into the open phone on Peakes' desk. He knew just enough not to send it to the closed area system. Ricky answered, and Norm handed off the call. He gave it one more passing thought before diving into the day's ordinary chaos. *Government jerks. Wonder what kind of accent that was, the guy had?*

Back in the closed area, Ricky heard the call connect. "This is Peakes," he said.

"Yes, Mr. Peakes. Thank you for taking my call to you. My name is Clarke," said Oleksiy Shulyayev.

Odocoileus virginianus is to *Canis lupus* as *ragù* is to the people of Bologna. A gray wolf in North America looks at a white-tailed deer and thinks "lunch". But, fortunately for both parties, it's not as simple as see deer, eat deer. Adult whitetails are fast, and if pressed, they can use their hooves as striking weapons. A doe who sees her fawns threatened will defend them, and any deer will run, fast and far. A pack can take turns chasing and harassing and running in for quick, damaging bites, but an individual wolf or a small group will invest more energy in a long chase than they'd like to.

116

These constraints are good for both species. Healthy, mid-life, breeding deer stay alive and keep the population going. If they were all easy pickings, wolves would have a great time for three or four generations, and then, having over-bred and depleted their food supply, their population would crash, too.

No, the ideal opportunity for a wolf, at least in return on investment, is a deer in poor health, an unguarded fawn, a deer slowed down by deep snow, or a dead deer that can be stolen from another predator. Best of all, even if it carries some secondary risks, is a deer killed by some natural force and then thrown aside and left for you. Roadkill falls into that last category. P51 had never seen a car hit a deer, but she'd eaten many deer who died that way. She'd learned that roads were scary things, but that they frequently carried a reward for a wolf who was cautious and sneaky.

Once, on a rainy autumn afternoon, she'd seen her own mother lie behind a downed tree, watching a group of humans wandering around where a car had hit a young male deer. He'd fallen on the road, out in the open, and she wasn't prepared to just run out into plain sight. So she waited. Two of the humans finally approached the deer, grabbed it with their strange front paws, and pulled it off to the side of the road. They turned back and continued doing whatever it is humans do. Not long after that, a State Trooper walked back to where he'd left the deer and was amazed to find it gone, vanished into the dark, wet woods, leaving nothing but a drag mark on the gravel shoulder and a streak of blood. P51, then a six-months pup, remembered it all clearly, along with the meal that followed.

Now she and her own pups were well fed and ready to move again. One deer by a road didn't make this a good place, a place where there'd be plenty to eat and little competition. It was too close to humans, human noises, human smells. And in fact, as they padded down a slope toward a stream, another drawback presented itself.

Twenty yards upstream, an adult black bear stood up and looked hard in their direction. Neither party made a sound, but his stare carried a generic message: "Mine!"

P51 and her pack kept moving. They had only a near-in, tactical sense of their course, but they'd chosen a reasonable path. Ahead lay four massive national forests, the Chequamegon, the Nicolet, the Ottawa, and the Hiawatha. Even allowing for small patches of human population, the pack was heading into three and a third million acres of wooded wilderness.

Shiloh

"Ooooh, Lord," Andy said, stretching his arms above his head. "I hate Wayne County."

"Any *new* reason for that?" Jenn asked. She hooked two fingers under the far end of a corkscrew arm and pulled straight up in line with the long axis of the bottle, letting leverage ease the cork out. Her husband could control an assault rifle in fully automatic, but he was useless at opening a bottle of wine.

"They've got patches of road scattered around among the potholes. Makes for tricky driving."

"So, nothing new, then."

"No, not really. And Washtenaw's not much better. Behind you." He swung around with the pasta pot in hand, headed for the sink. Jenn turned off the heat under a pan of red sauce. "To paraphrase something you said once about a bigger bed, we're going to need a bigger kitchen. One of us is going to get parboiled."

They ate, sitting across from each other at a table that was sized for one and a half diners, not two and a large bowl of penne, bread, a bottle of lower-end Montepulciano, and a dish of olive oil. It was cramped. Their conversation was mostly news of the day, personal and public. There'd been a couple of highly satisfying Supreme Court rulings; one of them could, at least in the legal sense, mean another marriage in the family. Jenn summarized the Jeri Klein round table, cast a few aspersions on brilliant engineers who couldn't remember to leave their cell phones out of the closed area, and showed Andy a notice for a singer coming to the Ark, Ann Arbor's iconic old folk club. Andy ate his pasta, talked briefly about an especially stupid and optimistic piece of civic corruption in the suburbs, and begged off watching the city council meeting. "I'll get the highlights on Twitter, anyway."

"But I meant to ask," he said, in his changing-the-subject voice, "How wide is your big bag? The one you carry?"

"How wide is it?" she asked. "Oh, a foot, thirteen inches, more or less. Why?"

"Have you ever seen these?" Andy passed his phone across the table. "It's not a great web site, not on the phone."

Jenn saw a truncated display: "ShieldU Ballistic Pan...". The two images that were visible seemed to be featureless black rectangles. "What, ..." she started, then scrolled sideways. "Oh. I see. No, I haven't really looked at them."

"We were talking about it yesterday at work. I don't carry anything that big around, but ..."

"Yeah, but I do." She scrolled down. "This would fit. How heavy ..." More scrolling. "Ah. A pound and a half. Man, I don't know. That's a ton of extra weight."

"True. But, that's the ... what? The level two? The one that stops a .357? You could go down one level and assume it would act together with your laptop. That might save a little weight."

"I suppose. But ... you know, dear, it's not exactly a jungle in there. It's been a week or so since there was any random violence in the office. Random, anyway."

"Really? That long? I thought the tech world was bloodier than that."

"Cheery and violent," she quoted. "But, I'll think about it. There's always parking structures, after all. And road rage."

"Right." Andy was not, of course, just bringing this up as a passing topic. He didn't recommend things often, especially in the professional arena. Jenn was a cop, after all, an ex-cop but a cop. He knew what she knew, at least in terms of defense and being prepared. Unfortunately, he also knew a few specific things she didn't know. He'd be happier, himself, if she had a Kevlar panel in her work bag. But he couldn't say why. All he could do was start a drip, begin leaving hints and planting ideas. With any luck, she'd pick up a general thread. He took the leftover dish of *rotini* back to the counter.

Jenn handed him a plastic freezer box, began sorting the dishes out, and thought over the issue of personal armor. She could see a hint from her beloved a mile away, but the question remained unanswered: *why does he think I need it?*

In keeping with evening rituals, Andy turned on their receiver and speakers. They had a range of favorite music on one of their personal machines, and he skipped over the folk directories. Both of them had a secondary enthusiasm for the eighties, and he picked a playlist designed for evenings. It was heavy on Eurythmics. Annie Lennox began the set: "*Jennifer, with your orange hair. Jennifer, with your green eyes. Jennifer, with your dress of deepest purple. Where are you tonight? Where are you tonight?*"

"Right here," said Jenn, putting her arms around him from behind.

Mac and the dogs came in the garage door, or to be more precise, the dogs came in wagging and smiling in that "Hi! What's for dinner?" way that dogs have. Mac came in behind them, smiling but not wagging. "How did the summit conference go?" he asked.

"Well, I guess it was a good news, bad news thing. From my standpoint, anyway." Colleen didn't look especially happy.

"Really?"

"Yeah. The good side of it is that Jeri Klein's a really smart person. Really. And I bet she'll deal with gender stuff as well as any of the rest of us. Probably better. The problem ... um, we'd better dish out some dog food, here, first. Or we'll have a revolt on our hands."

"I'll get it. Go ahead."

"Okay." Colleen followed him and the Shepherds out into the kitchen. "So, I don't know how Jenn and Alice came away from it, but I have sort of a bad taste in my mouth. We all three of us sat there and stereotyped that young lady. Badly. And I don't know if she saw it or not."

"Stereotyped how?"

"I think ... class, I guess. With a bit of race thrown in, maybe. Did you know she's part way to a master's in Poli Sci?"

"I keep telling people I don't know a damn thing about her. But, really? She's been down the academic path?"

"She has. And her father was in the State Department. The big league, US of A, full-blown State Department."

"So why ...?"

"I know. Why is she working small town cop jobs? We didn't get into that. But I just have this uncomfortable feeling that we were ... talking down to her for a while. And maybe she corrected us. Very subtly. Diplomatically."

"But it was all friendly? Amicable?"

"Yeah. We kind of got recruited, I think. We signed up, figuratively, to keep on having these little chats. And that was her idea."

"Huh. So what's the next step?"

"Would you consider calling her, in a kind of follow-up way? Ask her how she liked it, if she got any useful ideas?"

"Yeah, I will. I'm curious, now. And maybe I'll hint at getting invited to join the club."

"Good, good. I did enjoy talking to her. All of them, of course. I just wish I hadn't ... made quite so many assumptions."

Ricky sat in his car, debating with himself. Among the many things he disliked was exposing himself to other people who knew more about something than he did. He dragged out his wallet and extracted a blue laminated card. It had a cheap looking headshot of himself; boxes for his height, sex, and eye color; and the signature of the Washtenaw County clerk. Across the top, it said "Michigan Concealed Pistol License". Getting it had cost a day of his time, spent in a very elementary training class, and then some fussing with local government. It meant that he could walk into this store, safely outside Ann Arbor where he might see somebody he knew, and purchase a weapon. It didn't mean that he knew one end of a gun from another, and he was going to have to walk in, reveal himself as largely clueless, and take a stranger's advice.

He put the card back in his wallet, sighed, and got out of the car. The shop was a single-story cement block rectangle, among a mile or more of the same thing, up in the north suburbs. He carefully locked up the Hyundai and took a deep breath.

The store was jammed from one end to the other with non-lethal goods on racks and shelves and in cases. There was clothing of all kinds, there were bags and slings, ammunition storage boxes, sunglasses, hats. Right in his face were two different kinds of huge steel safes, designed for securing your personal arsenal. It was overwhelming, and he almost walked out, but there weren't many other customers, and a salesman was already greeting him from behind a long set of display cases. Trying to seem as though he knew what he was doing, Ricky nodded and walked over to the man.

"Good morning ... oops, afternoon, I mean," said the guy—and he was a 'guy' for sure, in all the traditional senses. He was tall, partly bald, overweight. His stomach was running a bit over each side of a wide leather belt. He was trying to be clean-shaven but it was already wearing off. He had a western-style shirt, tucked in, and a big, military-looking automatic in a web holster on his hip. "What can I help you with today?"

"Well, I was looking for ... for a handgun. A carry gun, sort of a sidearm."

"And I assume you mean concealed carry, sir? As opposed to a hunting weapon?"

"Yes, yes. Concealed carry. Sure." It hadn't occurred to Ricky that there was such a thing as hunting with a pistol. The wall behind the cases was crowded with long guns, and in what he remembered from his Alabama upbringing, those were the sort of weapons you needed to shoot ducks and, um, whatever else.

"All right, sir. Just over here to your left, we have quite a selection. And if you don't mind, I'm training Steve, here ..." He gestured at a younger man. "Steve, you want to come over here and observe? This gentleman is looking for a carry gun."

"Oh, ah, fine," Ricky said. He didn't really want anyone else in the deal, but at least a trainee wouldn't contribute much to his personal inadequacy.

"My name, by the way, is Bob," said Bob. He stuck out his hand. Ricky shook it, mumbling, "Richard".

"Now, sir, can I ask you a bit about how you want to carry? On your belt? Inside the waistband? Or in a shoulder holster?"

None of that, of course, was anything Ricky had considered. "Ah, probably in a pocket, I guess."

"In a pocket? Sure. Now that does impose some size and weight, um, restrictions. Can I suggest ..." He opened the case with a key from his pocket. "... this model, for example?" He bent down and then came back up with a pistol. He worked the action, peered into the breech, and then set it down, ostentatiously pointing it away from anyone. "That's a very popular handgun, if I do say so. Well made, too."

Ricky bent forward and looked it over. The grip and the trigger guard seemed to be all there was to it, barring a small slide and some rudimentary sights. Ricky picked it up gingerly. "It's, ah, not loaded, of course? I assume?"

Bob was right on top of that question. "No, sir. Of course as you know, the magazine isn't in place, and with the breech open, any round in the chamber would be clearly visible."

"Of course. May I ... ?

"Sure. Just point it over there." Ricky held the little weapon in his right hand and pointed it off in the direction of the back wall. His last finger and part of the one above it fell below the grip.

"The, uh, that is, the handle seems a bit small for me."

"It is small, sir, yes. But you see the magazine sticks down below, there, when it's in place, and it has a finger grip built in."

"Oh, yeah. Yeah. Right."

"And if you pull the slide back just a bit, it'll go forward. That'll be the position you'll fire it."

"Right," said Ricky. He shifted hands, holding the gun with his left and pulling back cautiously on the upper part. It was the only thing he could see that might be a 'slide'. It did move back, slightly, and when he let go of it, it sprang forward and stopped. He looked at Bob.

"Just like that," Bob said. "And when you're starting out, that's what you'll do. Just put the magazine in 'til it clicks, then pull the slide back and let her go. You're ready to shoot."

"Right. Right. Just what I'd expect."

"Have you fired one of these before?"

"No. Not one of these, specifically. Not as ... small as this, no."

"Well, you'll find it's an easy little gun. Not much recoil, not a lot of muzzle flip."

"How much, um, is it?" Ricky asked. He had a vague idea about recoil; 'muzzle flip' was beyond him.

"The MSRP on that firearm is ..." Bob picked up a ring binder from under the counter and squinted at it. "... let's see ... five hundred

125

and thirty-five dollars. But we could go ..." he flipped a page."... right now, four-ninety."

"Four-ninety? Well, ah, yes. I could do that."

When Ricky had dealt with the rather pro forma paperwork, agreed to add on a nylon pocket sleeve for carrying his new gear, and just remembered that he was "out of" ammunition, he got out the door for five hundred and thirty dollars.

"Goodbye now, sir. You have a good day!" Bob shouted after him. "Now," he said to Steve, the trainee, "you get a feel for that?"

"I don't know where to start."

"Okay, I'll run it down for you. That boy came in here not knowing dick about guns, and I had that spotted within about two sentences. He didn't know what he wanted, and he didn't want to seem dumb. So I showed him that damn little Beretta we've had in stock for eight months, casually made him seem even dumber than he knew he was, flat out lied about MSRP, and stuck him with it for list. And you know why it's been in the case for that long?"

"Nobody likes .32 ACP?"

"That's right. And nobody who knows dick would pay that much for a gun like that. Not when you can carry one of those ..." he pointed at a two-inch Smith and Wesson revolver "... for twenty dollars less, list price, and only two ounces heavier. And it shoots a real cartridge."

Steve nodded. When he grew up, he wanted to be just like Bob.

When I set out to write this memoir or autobiography, I intended to restrict myself to those facts and scenes about which I could speak from personal experience and knowledge. Where I have had to mention things that were beyond that scope, I have tried to make clear

126

that I was repeating what I learned at second-hand. Now, I have to do so again and with great emphasis.

Neither I nor my division took part in the battle called Shiloh. We were on our way there, ordered to move from Eastern Kentucky with General Buell's force, but because we had the farthest to go, we were at the end of the army, moving as well as we could over the very poor roads of that region, already traversed by other divisions and trampled into a morass. When we arrived on the north bank of the Tennessee River, the fight was over, and I have no personal glimpses of combat to record. For that reason, I will only touch on the points where I believe they illustrate my thesis, namely that careful preparation is the chief virtue of a commander, and when it is neglected, a terrible bloodletting, if not a complete defeat, can easily occur.

After Forts Henry and Donelson fell, Ulysses Grant and General Halleck had a misunderstanding of some form such that Grant was set aside for a short time. Shortly, though, Halleck appears to have had a change of heart or perhaps received a pointed question from the President; some writers have suggested this latter influence. At any rate both Grant and General Buell found themselves consolidated into Halleck's grand Army of the Mississippi. My division being under Buell, it was part of this new organization.

General Halleck's intention was to move south to the Tennessee River, cross it, and take Corinth, a town in Mississippi with significant road, rail, and telegraph connections. The general's view, and apparently one shared by General Grant, was that the defeats inflicted on the rebels so far had weakened them, and that the most they would do was to fortify and defend Corinth. There were two points neglected, however, and they led to a terrible outcome.

First, the Confederate government finally grasped the danger it faced in the west, and Generals Albert Johnston and P. G. T. Beauregard moved to combine their forces from the east and west, concentrating at Corinth. The second factor was the public and official criticism that had fallen on General Johnston after our fight at Mill Springs and the fall of Nashville. It gave him, some writers have claimed, a deeply felt need to give the rebellion a famous victory, and thus he insisted in the face of all argument that he would attack us at a crossing point on the Tennessee. His conception was clear enough, and it was one that I had recently used against his subordinate generals at Mill Springs, namely to attack an enemy who has just crossed a major river, defeat him, and attempt to crush his force against the water.

That is what General Johnston set out to do, declining the advice of his second in command, General Beauregard. His movement north from Corinth was slowed by poor weather, and it is reported that it was not quiet or stealthy. Again, just as they got within striking distance of our forces, General Beauregard argued for abandoning the attack and withdrawing back to Corinth. Johnston was adamant, though, and the attack went on.

Unfortunately, neither Grant nor General Sherman, who was present as a subordinate of Grant, believed that any rebel force was near or was strong enough to pose a threat. The position on the west bank of the river was not entrenched, Grant believing that his many new troops needed training in tactics and discipline, and that the time he spent waiting for our army, that is to say General Buell's army, to arrive would be better given over to instruction than to fortification.

Regardless of the reason, Johnston's attack was a complete surprise, and our forces were driven, over the course of the morning, back nearly to the river. We were fortunate, in the event, that the rebel troops were untried, many of them, and as before, poorly armed. Their fortunes were also affected by Johnston's death, early in the battle, from an untreated wound. He was shot in the leg and had nearly bled to death before acknowledging that he was badly hurt.

Beauregard took over, and the assault was pressed enthusiastically but without coordination. It stalled, eventually, with our line bent back on the left but anchored on the newly arrived division of General Wallace on the right. By then, the leading elements of General Buell's forces had arrived, including General McCook's division, and they were ferried across as quickly as possible.

In the morning, Grant and General Buell made a strong counter-attack, and although it was a bloody and sometimes desperate fight, the rebels were doomed by numbers from the start. It is to their credit, to speak from opinion, that they got away in reasonably good order.

To me, this battle seems to have been our first genuine experience of what fighting in the west would be like for the remainder of the war. Instead of the open ground, relatively speaking, of the eastern theatre with its well-developed network of roads and the potential for quick movements by rail, fighting in the dark forests and mountain ranges of Tennessee, Mississippi, and Georgia would demand almost superhuman capabilities in a successful general. He would have to do everything in his power to spy out the enemy's movements, secure his own camps and towns and flanks against surprise, and be rigorously conservative in his estimates of times and distances. Over and over again, the man who failed to do these things would come out the loser.

In an era of cubes and workstations and stand-up desks, Jenn counted herself fortunate. She had an office, two offices in fact. With doors and locks. One of them, out in the company's open area, was moderately decorated, and it was primarily for show. She used it for interviews and for dealing with vendors; when customers visited, it was part of the quick walk down executive row, demonstrating that Holcombe was a real company.

Her other home was in the closed area, and it was a more accurate reflection of herself and her work. There were two full-height steel bookshelves, packed with white and black ring binders. She had a combination-lock document safe beside her desk. On the desk, there were two desk phones, one secure and one not, and a pair of desktop computers, located a required distance apart from each other. As with the phones, one of them was on the company's secure internal net, and the other one was on the ordinary office wire. Neither of them had any kind of removable media or wireless technology.

She leaned back in her chair and looked at a photo of Andy. She kept it on the desktop, facing her, so that she could see it without doing more than shifting her eyes from a screen or from whoever was in one of her visitor chairs. Occasionally, it would occur to her that every married or partnered woman she'd ever known—those with desks, anyway—had a shot of her sweetie or a child or a dog in exactly the same place. Few of them, though, had anything like Jenn's other piece of decor. On the wall behind her she had a framed poster from the second *Alien* movie. Sigourney Weaver glared out at the viewer, holding an assault rifle.

At the moment, her visitor wasn't sitting. Viv Keyes was standing, with a portfolio under one arm and a cup of coffee. She was in transit from one place to another, coordinating things, asking questions, making sure that one hand knew what the other was doing; in essence, she was being a program manager. Jenn's office was a stop on the route.

"You remember LifeRigor changing their software lead on us?"

"I do," said Jenn. "The guy they swapped in just sat there in the design review. Every time he opened his mouth, Doctor M. cut him off. Not impressive."

"I agree. But you remember the woman he replaced?"

"Kathy or Cora or something like that? We only met her once."

"Look at this," said Viv. She set her coffee down, unzipped her bag, and fished out a stapled document. The first four words carried the whole message: *Resume: Corinne Dupuis-Baker.*

"Beautiful," said Jenn. "They pull her off the lead. Amazingly, she's not happy about it. But ... even if you had a slot, can we hire their people?"

"No. Unfortunately, we can't. Contract says so. And Izzy doesn't have any open reqs. But would you object if I brought her in, anyway?"

"Brought her in?"

"Interview her, just to get some insight. I told you, right? I have some real worries about what's going on over there. I'd like to hear what a disgruntled insider has to say."

"Is that kosher?"

"Well, the contract doesn't say we can't talk to people, informally. I wouldn't call it an interview, of course. And I'd be, ah, careful what *I* said. Let *her* do all the talking."

"What does Karolyn say?"

"I'll clear it with her, first. But are you okay with it, if she is?"

Not all that long ago, Jenn thought, *I'd have punted this.* Instead, she pushed her chair back, swiveled in Viv's direction, and crossed her legs. "Yeah, but if we do, I want to be in the conversation. I think their security is crap."

Apparently, Viv found Doctor Holcombe in short order. Jenn had only been through two messages on the classified computer when the President knocked on the door. She was a manager-by-walking-around, not a see-me-in-my-office type, and given the choice, she'd rather drop in on one of her people than pick up the phone.

"Jenn, Viv says you're all right with bringing this woman from LifeRigor in here for a chat?"

"Yeah, if we keep a lid on it. Viv's idea was to get her to talk to us, not so much the other way around, right?"

"That's what she said."

"Okay, then yes, I am. And Viv told you I want to be in on it? So I can get security dirt from her, if there is any?"

"Yes, she did. And I think that's a good idea. Let's just be circumspect, though." Holcombe smiled, making the word 'circumspect' sound as though it were in italics.

"That's our motto," said Jenn, making a gesture that you could interpret as taking in the Security department. "*Semper Circumspectus.*"

"But I wanted to ask you something," Karolyn said. "Sort of business, sort of personal."

"Oh, sure." Intense curiosity. Jenn didn't know her company President all that well, and so far, the only personal interest Karolyn had shown had been of the pro forma, "*How's your husband?*", kind.

"I get a lot of advertising mail," Karolyn started. "Paper mail, email, all of that." Jenn nodded.

"And the last month or so, there's been a lot of material about security. Personal security. 'Executive' security, some of them call it."

"Oh, yes. I get that, too. Some of it."

"Has something changed? Is there more of a threat, individually? To business people?"

Hell, Jenn thought. *Is this going to be the 'what-kind-of-gun-should-I-get?' conversation?* She took a breath. "If you wanted a proper

132

answer to that with some kind of analysis behind it, you'd have to do a lot of work on a lot of really poor-quality data. But a reasonable short answer is *no*. Not any specific threat."

"It just seems as though you see ... all these things in the news."

Ah. Right. She's thinking Mexico City. It was easy to forget that, working with Doctor Holcombe. She had no noticeable accent, and she seldom made any reference to her personal life. *She's thinking about executive kidnapping, families held for ransom, having to vary your routine, getting armor in your car panels ... Oh. Armor panels. Andy.* Jenn's business bag, carefully sanitized for bringing into the closed space, was sitting by the door. "Well," she said, "I, uh, can show you one thing I did."

She picked up the oversized shoulder bag and opened the main pocket. "I got this. It just fits in there, and it's, uh, bulletproof, to some extent."

"Really? But, *why* did you get it? What do you think ... what could happen, that you got that?"

How can I say 'I don't know'? How can I explain that my husband the Fed subtly suggested it, and he didn't say why, and I didn't ask? I'll sound like an idiot. She set the bag back down. A thought appeared.

"It's ... when I was in the police, we carried weapons, of course. But you never assumed you'd need it. It was ... just sensible. You knew, intellectually, that almost no one you'd run into was dangerous. But there was always that one chance ... so you carried your ... sidearm. And that's what I thought when I got that panel. It's not, um, heavy. And it doesn't get in the way. So I just have it."

"I see. So, you don't think you or I or anyone is any more ... threatened now?"

"I don't think so," Jenn said, and wondered if that was a lie or not.

"Well, that's good to hear. And ... I wanted to let you know something, just so you wouldn't be surprised if it came up, somehow. I have a license, and I carry, even in the office. So does Viv."

And I've been leaving mine out in the car, thought Jenn. *You learn something every day.*

Doctor Metharom's desk phone didn't have any fancy features. When it rang, it rang, and you had to take a chance on who was on the other end. It told him it was after five PM, but that didn't offer much information. He picked it up.

"This is Gardner, Doctor Metharom." The caller wasn't actually named Gardner, but Metharom didn't know that. He knew that it was a man with some kind of accent, a man representing people in Japan who might have money to invest. These people were willing to move quickly, but according to Mr. Gardner, they were quite professional, quite conservative, careful about the value of their capital, even in small amounts. He'd heard all of this twice before from Gardner, and he knew he was about to hear it again. What he didn't know was what he, Metharom, intended to do about it. Another thing he didn't know was that Gardner was Oleksiy Shulyayev, and all of the other things were arrant lies.

There were things Metharom wished he knew, but his caution was being sapped every day, the more clear it became that the rates in his Holcombe subcontract were three quarters or less of what they should have been. Put simply, LifeRigor was running out of cash, and he'd signed a contract that kept him from doing much about it. So the complete absence of anything on paper from 'Gardner' or his hypothetical backers was a warning sign he chose to set aside.

On the other end of the phone, Oleksiy was short of a few key facts, himself. He knew almost nothing about LifeRigor or its key technology. He'd found it in some science news content, looked up the papers Metharom had published, and decided it was something that could become an offering in his new line of business. His one local contact, "Ricardo" the waiter, hadn't been any use at all. To Oleksiy, the idea of stealing intellectual property was nothing new; it was his current profession, after all, and the profession of his acquaintances in Hong Kong. But the notion of stealing code from animals and making use of it intrigued him. It sounded safe. And cheap. Safe and cheap would play well with his market.

The important thing he didn't know about LifeRigor was how little the recording technology was useful, yet. Further, he didn't know that anything Metharom had to offer, other than the published, publically available research, would be ordinary, hand-cranked, human-written stuff, and the property of the US government. Even if it was working beautifully (which it wasn't), it wouldn't be anything his contacts couldn't recreate on their own. But the good news for him was that even if he'd known, it wouldn't have mattered, really, as long as certain other people didn't know it.

The reason was that he didn't intend to deliver anything at all, more than some teasers and samples. He hoped to get an increasing number of partial payments sent to himself, over a period of a few weeks. Then, when the pressure to deliver something really interesting got beyond a certain point, he would do something he'd become good at: vanish, taking the money and not much else. Both the supplier and the consumer of his product would be left holding the bag and in a poor position to complain. All the parties involved would have broken laws, after all, and would be quite publicity-shy. Oleksiy would ensure that.

Now it was time to push on this Thai PhD. Oleksiy already had a thousand dollars from his buyer, money he'd described as working cash, a term that both parties understood to mean "sweeteners" or frankly, bribes. Obviously, he hadn't bribed anyone yet, and the money, converted to Euros, was sitting in an envelope in a small safe under his bed. To get to the next cash point, he'd have to send Hong Kong something tangible, a document, a small snippet of code, something that would let him demand another, higher amount. He needed to run this game up to somewhere near fifty thousand, and then he would be in a position to disappear.

"Doctor Metharom," he said, "I have had a response verbal from Kyoto, and they are guardedly happy about your ideas. They told me, essentially, that they would be able to look at a proposal of you. But they will not to go on to that step ... you understand, it expenses them to have their experts evaluate things ... until they can some sample see of what they would gain interest in." He was having trouble speaking in syntactically correct English to someone on the phone; he didn't do it that often.

"Yes, I understand that. You have shown them my papers, I assume?"

"I have. But they ..." Oleksiy paused to look at some notes he'd made for himself. He had to come up with a plausible reason why the research articles weren't enough. He'd taken the trouble to call one of the journals, pretending to be an academic himself, and gotten an editor to say a few neutral things about the work they'd published. "... they say that your technical-mechanical techniques are well-presented, but the ways of transferring the data toward execution-able steps are difficultly understood."

"Do you mean the translation and transformation algorithms were hard to understand?"

"Yes, that is what they said to me."

"I see." Metharom wasn't pleased. For one thing, he thought he'd explained his ideas very clearly. For another, they were certainly something he'd been jealously trying to protect. Getting nerve impulse data from living *Platyhelminthes* wasn't all that hard, and his methods were only slightly improved from other peoples'. Doing something useful with the data was his own effort, though, and aside from a small retirement account and a moderately nice house in Ann Arbor, it was the only important thing he owned.

"Well, if your people will sign a non-disclosure agreement, I can put together something, I suppose. Something that will show them what can be done. They understand, I assume, that this is not yet a commercial process? That they would be ... supporting ... our work to make a viable ..."

"Yes, yes, yes. They understand that. They are always want ... wanting to be early on in. So they understand. And they will sign to protect your property." Oleksiy would of course be happy to sign anything Metharom sent him.

"All right. Will you send me the non-disclosure to review?"

"I will attach it to a mail, yes."

"But not to here, please. Mail it to another address." He gave Oleksiy his personal email account. He had no real grasp of information security, but he had a vague notion that keeping this correspondence away from LifeRigor.com might somehow be a smart thing to do. He had, after all, nothing more than a passing familiarity with the term "subpoena".

Oleksiy agreed, and they ended the call. Each man took away from it some actions and some concerns. The Doctor felt cornered; he could find the time to make up a small document with some code in it, but if the agreement went forward, he might find himself in the same old situation: committed to deliver something working and marketable. Oleksiy needed to mock up a non-disclosure agreement between a real, functioning company—one that might have a corporate council to review things—and a completely fictional entity. And the delay would be hard to explain to Hong Kong.

What I'll do, he thought, speaking fluently to himself in his native language, *is make a second contact. I'll see if I can get this engineer, this Peakes person, to be more cooperative.*

Alice Graves was a social person by upbringing and inclination. Her parents entertained people once or twice a week, wooing potential faculty or graduate students, making and maintaining relationships with colleagues, celebrating marriages, births, and birthdays. She enjoyed it, and when she'd had the final disagreement with her father over politics and genders, she tried to recreate the experience on her own. What she discovered was the difference between scheduling an event and making it happen, especially when you had no resident family or paid help. When you had to do it all yourself, it was a different experience. Paying for it on a graduate student or post doc income was just as much a challenge, even when the event was on a very minor scale. She got used to pot luck evenings and inexpensive wine.

Nothing about that had changed. But now she had a fingernail's grip on stability, with a prayer at least of an Associate Professorship. She had a partner, someone who could contribute financially to the household. And even more wonderfully, that person was earning her way through a belated bachelor's degree by working as a line cook! Jackie Langton knew one end of a kitchen from another, knew how to shop for ingredients, and was happy, apparently, to put food on the home table, nights when she wasn't cooking for the public. Of course, Alice tried hard to do her part, and whether or not she pitched in with the dinner, she could still be the greeter and mistress of ceremonies. Jackie, with her increasing restaurant experience, had another term for it, but since it was crude and their relationship was still new, she kept it to herself. Perhaps with the passage of time—after, for example, they'd made up their minds about marrying—she'd tell Alice that in restaurants most of the staff referred to the hostess as the door-whore.

There was still a constraint on their ability to entertain, and it was a physical one. They'd managed to leave Alice's old student efficiency apartment and rent a small house, but the emphasis was still on small. This particular evening, they had one guest only, and that made it easier and more comfortable, both in the living room and in the kitchen. Alice had told Jackie at length about the round table with Jeri Klein, and Jackie's reaction had been immediate and simple: "Invite her for dinner". Now, they were finishing the pasta—Jackie's take on *Alfredo*, modified slightly from her current employer's recipe—and talking about dogs.

"So do you bring your work dog home at night?" Jackie asked. "Does your home doggie get along with him?"

"I do bring him home, yes," said Jeri. "They get along well. He's adult, male, frankly the alpha dog. Cara's only a year old, and she's still trying to play rough with him. He's actually mellow about it, at least so far."

Alice raised her eyebrows slightly. "And you don't worry about, um, population growth?"

"Well, Cara's neutered, so, no."

"Ah."

"But you know," Jackie said, "Mom and Andy are talking about getting a pup of some kind. They've always liked the MacArthurs' dogs. Mom says."

"They're good friends with Mr. MacArthur and Colleen," said Alice. "You knew that, Jeri?"

"Yes, I did." She wound a quantity of pasta around her fork and ate it. "Oh, that's good, Jackie."

"Thanks. Yeah, that's Assif's formula—he's our chef. This week. We've had a few, lately."

"Do you think they're ready to do that?" Alice asked. "Jackie?"

"Sorry. Mouth full. Not to go out and get one. But it might be okay to go look at some."

"I got Cara from a rescue home. We could go out there. It'd have to be on a Wednesday, though. That's my day off."

"It would be hard for me to get away during the day. For the next few weeks," said Alice. "And I'm afraid of what I might come home with." Jackie rolled her eyes.

"But you know, Jeri, you might ask Mr. MacArthur to go along. He'd like it, I imagine. And he knows a lot about them. Too, I mean."

"I owe him a call," said Jeri. "I'll ask him. It might be nice break. If Jenn can get away."

"I'll call her," said Jackie. "I can talk her into it."

P51 and her yearlings kept on with their directed wandering. They were heading east, in general, but varying their route as they had to. They dodged back and forth during the day, finding wooded places to dart across roads, staying alert for edibles. Once, they spent an hour digging through garbage dumped at the end of a dirt two-track. Another day, they waited patiently in hiding, watching a

140

beaver dam. Eventually, a beaver climbed out of its den and waddled along the dam toward shore. They let it get ten feet inland before they rushed it.

Later on, they denned up for two days among the braided streams of a small river's flood plain. They went out to forage in the late evenings, and on the second night, they panicked a doe and her adolescent fawn. The chase went two miles through the woods, twisting through trees and brush. Finally, the doe remembered her size and her hoofs. She turned back on the wolves, confronting P51, rearing up and striking. As she did, though, the fawn kept running, and the two yearling cubs closed in. Their mother dodged the doe easily, circled around and stood her off while her own offspring brought the young whitetail down. Eventually, the doe gave up and bolted away. That meal alone was fuel for two days of travel.

Stones River

After the National forces recovered their poise and confidence following Shiloh, and after we completed our advance to Corinth, the war entered a time of confusion and delay. General Halleck, commanding in the West, and the government in Washington began to discover that the war in Virginia was not the only theatre in which success and failure could affect the outcome of the whole struggle. Eastern Tennessee became important not just to those of us serving west of the mountains, but to the strategists at several levels. Chattanooga, in particular, emerged as an important point for the movement of supplies to the rebel government, both from western states and from the port of New Orleans. It became our next objective. Unfortunately and at about the same time, those in Richmond reached a similar conclusion, and as we were taking steps to move east and seize it, so they made plans to defend it, to make it a base for attacks on Tennessee and Kentucky and a place from which to launch raids into states further north. These opposed desires set in motion two conflicting efforts.

Although we, in the sense of the northern army under General Buell, had several advantages, the orders given to us were formed on a grand strategic level by parties unfamiliar with the reality of conducting war in the west. Instead of taking a line of advance that would secure our supply line through Nashville and preempt any move that might be made against the central states, we were ordered to strike quickly due east toward Chattanooga, and at the same time, we were required to repair the damage to railroads and bridges as we went. Further, we were starved of cavalry, and so found it difficult to keep rebel horsemen from doing more damage, even as we repaired what had already been done. As we moved slowly east, General Bragg, who had assumed command of the rebellion's western forces, struck across the Tennessee River from Chattanooga, marching north to threaten either Nashville or Louisville. Our advance became a defensive movement, paralleling him as he went north.

In the campaign that followed, I freely admit that I was not in the forefront. Although General Buell frequently asked my advice, he seldom followed it. I presented my view that regardless of Bragg's target, to reach it he would have to expose his lines of supply to us or attack us in a prepared position. General Buell chose action instead of preparation, and marched north in step with Bragg, intending to intercept him and force him to a fight against our full force. This was not what I would have done. However, a commanding officer may only be persuaded, and if persuasion fails, he must be obeyed. I moved along with the army as it marched north, and eventually joined the rest of the force near Louisville, which had finally been revealed as Bragg's objective.

At this point, official discontent with General Buell reached a head, and we received an order, he and I, to the effect that I was to relieve him. This has been a well-reported event, especially given his later court-martial, and I will not go into it any detail. I will just say that, as is known, I declined to accept the position and advocated very strongly with General Halleck that General Buell be left in command. This is, as I say, well-known. What has been debated and guessed at for years are my reasons. I will set them out very simply here: General Buell had, at this point, combined his army, organized it for a fight, and set it in motion. To remove him before he had a chance to cross swords with Bragg would have been dangerous, regardless of who replaced him, and also unfair. He and I discussed it, I showed him the language I would use, and my request was accepted; Buell remained in charge. I was named second in command, and we set out to confront the rebel forces.

The fight that resulted was a victory for us in the sense that Bragg was forced to begin a long retreat back to Chattanooga, and he was kept from threatening Kentucky or Nashville and prevented from uniting effectively with his colleague, Kirby Smith. It was not, however, an ideal fight, and it cost more in casualties than could have been the case. Displeasure with General Buell became greater, and he was again relieved, this time being replaced with General Rosecrans. This change in command, the reorganization that followed, and our move south in late December, marked the beginning of the real Chattanooga campaign.

As we moved south, following Bragg, we marched with the intention of bringing him to battle and ending rebel control of Tennessee. Our object was nothing less than the destruction of Bragg's army, the seizure of Chattanooga, and the creation of a base from which we could eventually move on Atlanta. The first step, then, was to confront Bragg at the point he had chosen for his winter quarters. He paused in his withdrawal at Murfreesboro, thirty-some miles south east of Nashville, a small place on the east side of Stones River.

Ricky Peakes sat back on his couch, sticking his legs out all the way, stretching. Twelve and a half hours at the keyboard had not produced working code. Not integratable, not promotable, not, God damn it, *working*. What was worse, it wasn't just his code that was fouled up, now. There were three engineers flailing away, besides himself, and they were all checking in rubbish. Not even Corinne, that little weasel, was getting it right. And now he was in charge of it all. They weren't going to make a release to the prime contractor on time, the prime was already raising hell, and his own management didn't have a clue.

I told 'em, he thought. *I walked into Dormanski's office and told him we weren't gonna make it.* All Paul Dormanski had to say was, "You're the team lead. Kick some butt." *Useless bastard*, Ricky thought. And it was going to get even darker. He'd walked by the shared printer, and there was Corinne's resume laying on it. *Right*, he thought. *Beautiful. She can't cut it as lead, they put me in instead, and so she's gonna bail out. And if we can't replace her ...* At one point, he'd have been pleased to see her go, but now ... *Shit!* He looked at his watch; another ten minutes until the call.

In Windsor, Oleksiy Shulyayev was out on one of his security walks, wandering over to the riverside again. That he left his house and went out into public spaces for his conversations was more habit than anything learned. He'd acquired his business phone from a gentleman in Belarus, and he'd been assured that it was "secure". He thought that using it away from his home address was just an added layer of protection. He was in fact an amateur, and these little misconceptions were just confirmation of his amateurishness. When the digits on his watch told him it was time, he typed in Ricky's number and made the call.

Afterward, he thought that it seemed just a little too easy. Mister Peakes sounded tired and a bit anxious, and he offered only a few, weak objections to Oleksiy's requests. "*But you know, I could get in trouble*," was really the only sticking point. Oleksiy had that one covered. He retreated into his spy persona, suggested obliquely that there were ways of ensuring Ricky's personal security, hinted that money was also changing hands at higher levels. And then, he applied the closing argument.

"And of course, we will not be leaving you dry and high, you realize. That would be bad for us as well as you. For you, that is. If any things misfire, you can be certain we will get you out."

"Out?" said Ricky. "Out, how?"

"It is called extraction, you know. You have heard of it. If you have to go … and this never happens, never will happen, but if … we will take you out of the country. Give you new identifications. We can do this. We have done it. It is very sure. You could work with us, then."

"Are you serious?"

"Oh, yes. Very serious. We can do this."

Whether or not Ricky bought it, it was the last answer to objections Oleksiy had to provide. Peakes agreed to come up with a sample of the product.

Why are they all so foolish? Oleksiy asked himself. *All these little boys who know so much of some things and so little of the world?* A dispassionate observer might have asked the same question about him. But since his stock in trade was words, kind, reassuring words for the people he dealt with, his mind turned in that direction. Walking back to his house, he mulled over what he might say to someone who asked, "*How* would you get me out of the US?" What kind of semi-plausible tale could he tell, buying a few days for his own exit?

A story came to mind, something he'd read last year in the Windsor Star. Hard as it might be to believe, America had a surplus of little airports, small private landing strips with no full-time staff, no radar, no lights. And many of those places were in Michigan, up in the northern parts of the state. The story had been about drugs and people coming and going from similar sites in Ontario, flying low across the watery border in small planes. Landing, unloading quickly, and taking off again. That would do it. He'd find such a place on the map and give Peakes explicit instructions about being there at a given time. When, of course, no plane ever came, well … too bad. By then, Oleksiy's own exit strategy would be in operation.

Jenn and Vivienne walked Corinne Dupuis-Baker back out to the lobby. They said the required "Thank you for coming in. As we said, there aren't any open positions right now, but ..." things, and sent her on her way. Viv looked at Jenn and said, "Let's go in the back. Now."

Viv's office was nearer to the front of the closed area, so they went in there and shut the door. "That wasn't good," said Jenn.

"No. Not at all. We've got to do some damage control, like, right now."

First of all, Viv had heard a tale of technical and leadership issues that made her hair stand up. From a few initial interface problems, the code had devolved into a series of dissociated, overly complex little pieces, none of which was talking to any of the others correctly. Design discipline had gone out the window, with developers reacting frantically to problems as though they were isolated, whether or not the trouble with any one of them was internal or an artifact of undocumented interfaces. Their quality organization, bid at three engineers, was in fact one intern without even a BA. And that was just the technical aspect.

"Do you buy her story about the President?" Jenn asked.

"Doesn't matter. It reflects on the leadership." Corinne had stated as fact that she'd been taken off the lead position because she complained about sexual innuendo in the workplace and a general boys' town attitude. Her view was that she'd been discriminated against. That was not something Holcombe wanted to hear. If it was true, it was unacceptable. True or not, it was very bad press if it went public. Anything wrong at a subcontractor reflects on the prime. "And then, there's the security crap."

"Yes, indeed. If any of that is real, it isn't just unpleasant, it's illegal. The customer'd have a cow." Even in the closed area, it was "the customer," not the actual agency name. "This facilities guy, Norm? I never thought a lot of him, but she says, essentially, he hasn't got a clue."

"No. I don't think he does. What did she tell you?"

"She said, just for example, that there are personal cell phones all over their closed area. One was live and in use in the room during a call with Izzy on the secure line. We need to do something, right away."

"I agree. Absolutely. I think we need to get them all over here. Doctor Metharom, this Ricky Peakes, their operations guy, Dormanski. Maybe the so-called security guy, Norm."

"Yup," said Jenn. "And we need to do an all-in scolding. You and Izzy beat 'em up about the deliverables and their methods. I'll raise hell about the security. And you know what?"

"What?"

"We need Karolyn to run through the non-performance and cancellation-for-cause language, too. And another thing. I think we ought to start looking for a replacement."

"Yeah. I was going to say that. Just from a risk standpoint if nothing else." She paused. "I think we better go talk to her."

"Yup," Jenn said again. "Let's go ruin her day."

Ricky answered his phone with a new kind of caution, even if it showed him that the caller was just his father. He recognized Alabama area codes, and of course his dad was in his contacts list.

But any call from down home meant that somebody wanted something. At its most benign, it could be some girl from his high school class, trying to get people together for a reunion. At its worst, it might be some new family upheaval, death, divorce, birth, or something else that would make him pay attention and pretend to care. This time, it was a woman's voice calling, not his old man.

"Hi, Ricky. It's Paula." *Paula?* His half-sister? What the hell did she want?

"Yeah, hello," he said. "My phone says it's Dad's number."

"Yeah, my battery's down. Listen, I'm coming up there in a couple of days. I got a present for ya."

Ricky couldn't imagine what Paula might possibly have that he'd want. They hadn't been friends when they were growing up, and her mother's split with his father hadn't done anything to improve matters. He just waited, hoping it wouldn't be too bad.

"You there?"

"Yeah, I'm here. You got something for me?"

"Listen, I'm helpin' your dad clean up stuff and get rid of things, ya know? After Mom left? And he don't want her old car. She just left it in the back yard. And I'm comin' up that way, your way, you know, to see somebody, so he said I should drive it up and leave it with you and take the bus to Chicago." This kind of core-dump narrative style was one of the things Ricky hated about Paula.

"Hold up. Why are you bringing a car to me? I got a car. What the hell is it, anyway?"

"It's her four-door. You know, you seen it. Dad!" There was a pause. "Dad! Ricky says what kind of car is it? It's what?" Another pause. "Your dad says it's a Mercury Markwiss. A Grand Markwiss."

"A Marquis? That great big thing she had? You're going to drive that clear the hell up here?"

"He said it's in good shape. He always took care of it, he says. It's only ten years old, he says. What? Oh, he says it's only got sixty thousand miles on it."

"You better take out a loan. You'll be burning gas like crazy coming up here. And then you're going to Chicago?"

"Not in the car. It's Dad's in the divorce, and he don't want it down here. He says you can sell it or keep it or drive into a lake, for all he cares. He just wants it out of here. And I gotta go to Chicago to see somebody."

"Jesus, you know, I don't have a lot of ..." Ricky stopped short. He'd been about to argue against any such transfer of a bloated, gas-sucking monstrosity, but suddenly he had a thought. "Well, wait. How would we do a title switch, then? Who's going to sign it over to me?"

"Oh, he thought of that. He put it in my name now, and I'll just sign it off and leave the title with you."

"I see." *Interesting,* he thought. A car with an Alabama title and plates. In Paula's name. Whatever name she was using now, it wouldn't be Peakes. That might come in very handy.

"All right," he said. "I guess I can find a place for it. When you coming up?"

"I'm leavin' tomorrow morning. Probbly stay somewhere overnight, be up to your place the day after. You gotta give me your address."

"Yeah, well if I can get a storage place by then, I'll just have you meet me there. And then I'll take you to the bus station."

"I can meet ya, but ya don't get off that easy. I gotta sleep on your couch or something overnight. The bus don't go until the next morning." Pause. "You got a couch, right?"

"Right," said Ricky. "Yeah, I got a couch." It was a small price to pay, after all.

"I feel like hell, thanks," Harry Borowski answered, replying to Andy's polite "How are you?" It was eight-twenty in the morning, and Borowski had gotten home from the airport a bare four and half hours before. "I love and respect our superiors and our colleagues in other agencies, but I hate Dulles and I hate Metro and hate flying. When I'm not doing it myself, that is."

"Oh," said Andy. "Well ... the, um, the rest of the team is on their way down here now." The five employees of the Detroit FBI office who were directly concerned with Witthaya Metharom and his little software company were about to hear Borowski's debrief on a meeting in Washington. Since they were gathering in one of the two secure conference rooms, it was a given that at least one or two points would be sensitive in nature.

Besides Senior Agent Borowski and Andy, three others showed up: Andy's usual partner, Peter Corcoran, plus two more, Mike Sherman and Roger Bean. "We gotta wait a minute," said Borowski. "I pulled Sheila into this, too."

"Good," said Corcoran.

"Yeah, she was good with that financial company bullshit," Sherman added.

"Hi, Sheila," said Andy. He was the only one seated facing the door.

"Good morning, boys and boys," said Sheila Drew.

"Hey, Sheila," said Borowski. "Shut the door and let's get this over with. I got a headache." He arranged himself and his coffee. He did meetings like this without notes, let alone slides or agendas. "So, here's what I got from a bunch of folks in DC." He stretched both arms up over his head, grabbed one wrist with the other hand, and pulled. It didn't actually do anything, but it felt good. He really did hate flying.

"This is complex, just a little. There's a guy who isn't here at all, he's over in Canada. He's on a few lists at another agency we all know. He's got contacts somewhere in the P. R. of China. So far as that, it's just interesting gossip—for us, anyway. This guy I'm gonna call 'S' because I can't pronounce the name he's using and it isn't his real one, anyhow, sells tech secrets or stuff that's supposed to be secret. That pisses off a lot of people on our side. Defense Intelligence Agency, for one. And a couple of others. But again, our little family don't really care, yet."

"However, as you guys know," Sheila paid no attention to 'guys' there. She heard it nine times a day and was so used to it, it didn't even register. "... we know some of this already, because Mister S has been talking to people in our favorite little city, up Ann Arbor way. So, suddenly, we do care, sort of. None of that's new. But here's what is new."

"First new thing: some of the concern about S has slacked off a bit, because it turns out, he's never really sold anything. That we know of. His game is, he pretends he's got cool intel for sale, gets a big down payment, and then does a runner." Borowski had worked, recently, with a British agency, and he'd picked up some of their language. "That's part of why he changes names a lot."

"Next thing: he may be good at screwing companies and bootleg products people and like that, but he stays away from governments. I don't know exactly how the DC folks know that, but

151

they say they do. They say this guy is a freelancer and he deals with small fish."

"Third: he may be good at running these long cons on his customers, but he seems ... this was how they put it ... not to know much about communication security." He looked around the table, checking to see if people understood.

"They're listening to his calls?" asked Sheila.

"They didn't say that. But ... somebody is, 'cause they played me a translation of one."

"Wow."

"Yeah, wow. This time around, he and his friends off in the east talk to each other in Hungarian, for Christ's sake. No encryption or anything. The guy with the transcript said that in the meeting, and one of the other guys didn't look happy. Like that wasn't something they wanted to say. But that's what was said."

Andy looked over at Pete Corcoran. "They're reading his mail," he said, "and if he's talking to anybody at LifeRigor, that tells us who."

"Right. But," Pete said, looking at Borowski, "are we going to get the intel or just summaries of it? And if we charge somebody, can we use any of it in court?"

"So, here's the fourth new thing. DC has a new idea about all this. We, meaning us, get to go and frown very hard at the people at this company, and we try to lean on 'em to con Mr. S over here into our jurisdiction, so we can pick him up. Or if he won't come here, we pretend to do a meet with him over in Windsor and let the RCMP have him. Either way, somebody leans on him, then, to give up the people he knows, and ... you get the picture."

"Somebody, somewhere along the line, busts some IP crooks." Sheila paused. "And the Defense Intel people were okay with that? I thought they'd be interested in the software company over here?"

"Well," Borowski said, leaning back and stretching again, "we didn't go into that, but after the conference, one of the DIA guys pulled me aside, and he hinted, sort of, that when we got the first part of this done, the Defense Contracts people might want to take the rest of it."

"Ah," said Sheila.

Andy said nothing. His expression was carefully kept neutral. A DCMA investigation would look at financial things, not necessarily security flaws. Not necessarily. Probably not. He hoped.

 The fight at Stones River was a long day and a half, and for those who were not present, it can seem almost tedious. The rebel army attacked us repeatedly, were repeatedly repulsed, and eventually withdrew. It has been suggested that our forces won merely by failing to lose. In fact, it was a brutal episode, fought with tremendous loss of life, and there is an argument that it was the beginning of the end for the rebellion. What is often ignored is that we did not stand on the defensive by choice. General Rosecrans' plan was to attack with the left of our army, and we were preparing to do that when General Bragg attacked us with the left of *his* army. Fortunately for us, he attacked first, not at the same time we would have attacked him, and that allowed us to stand, adjust and reinforce our right, and defeat him. If we had attacked on his right as he was attacking ours, the fight might have become a pinwheel or a waltz. As it was, we were able to stand and repel him, both on the first day and on the second.

None of that is to say that it was not a terrible fight. The losses on both sides were extreme, and there were moments when the whole effort in the west hung in the balance. We were finally learning, however, how this business of war in the wild, uncivilized parts of the country had to

153

be conducted. With troops that were sufficiently experienced or at least sufficiently well-trained, the defensive became more and more the dominant posture. Although our intention at Stones River was, as I have said, to attack, we finished by winning the battle through defense. I began to see a method or to use a simpler term, a set of desirable conditions for fighting, one in which maneuver before the battle places you in a position where you have to be attacked, where you force your opponent to send his masses of men across open ground toward you, waiting in your woods or behind a stream or sheltered by entrenchments. You mass your own artillery to counter his, and you shoot down his gallant, helpless infantry as it rushes toward you.

This kind of fighting does not make good reading in the newspapers, nor does it satisfy political leaders who may have a need for quick action and glorious headlines. I do not mean to say, either, that offense and attack are useless. Far from it. The time for attack, however, is after your enemy has been allowed to frustrate himself, suffer large losses, deplete his supplies, and cast his army into a mental state of frustration and discouragement. Then is the time to advance, strike hard, and pursue. I cannot claim that Stones River was planned in that way, but as it turned out, it allowed us to adopt an attitude of that kind, and it carried us to Chattanooga, or perhaps I should say to Chickamauga.

All of that, though, is getting ahead of myself. To return to Stones River, at the end of the first day, General Rosecrans called together all of us, including most of his staff and his commanding officers. He wished to consider with us the outcome of the day's fight and to gather our opinions about the future. This meeting has been the subject of memoirs and histories, and a kind of folk tale has arisen regarding my part in it. Most of what has been said casts me in a dramatic form, whether it quotes me as saying simply that the army must not or cannot retreat, or whether it puts some kind of stirring rhetoric in my mouth regarding this battlefield being a good place to die.

I remember the event well, although my exact words are uncertain to me, and I can report with confidence that what I said was none of that. Rather, I told General Rosecrans and the others present what I believed to be the case, namely that Bragg was beaten. He had destroyed two-thirds of his army attacking us in a strong position, he had been thwarted, and now we were better supplied and better prepared to continue the fight than he could possibly be. If he attacked again in the morning, he would be beaten again, and then there would be nothing left for him to do but withdraw. I was very tired at the time, and I likely did not phrase it that clearly, but I can say with certainty that the sense of what I told them was "Bragg is finished".

As she moved eastward, P51 allowed her path to be guided by senses. Her hearing told her when humans were closer and in greater numbers than she cared for. They were noisy beasts, humans, worse than coyotes. If her pups were a little older and perhaps if the pack had one more member, coyotes might be a reasonable menu item. Now, being shorthanded—or perhaps short-pawed would be more precise—she stuck to prey species that were less intelligent.

Her nose told her another long list of location-specific characteristics. Food sources, hazards, water, the history of a locale; it was all written in odors. Humans of course left a range of smells, and those half-wolves they kept with them, dogs, were instantly recognizable. In general, both were something to avoid unless the scents were fading and edible garbage was present. It never occurred to her that humans were the source of trash, but she connected the two. Where humans had been, there might be tasty, unidentifiable things to eat. Conversely, where there was trash, watch out for humans. And dogs.

Her eyesight was not much like a human's nor as sharp as a cat's, but her temporal resolution was better. She could see movement and recognize it more quickly. In the blue-green world of her vision or even in the monochrome night, a mouse bolting from hiding would trigger a response even before she heard it. All of it together, sight, sound, and smell, worked together to give her a constantly changing picture of the neighborhood. As they moved east, trending a little north as well, they kept a bubble of wildness around them, dodging houses, crossing roads where the woods came down close to each side. They ate when food presented itself, and when it didn't they took steps to find it.

Due south of Marquette, the Escanaba River stood in their way. It was almost fifty yards wide, but they found a shallow stretch and waded across. Day after day, they kept going. In the evenings, P51 would try a howl, sometimes with the pups joining in. There was never a response.

The Chattanooga Campaign

Agent Sheila Drew was relatively short, and she wore her very dark hair in a short dome, coming low on the forehead and covering her ears and neck. *Like a Boeotian helmet*, she thought, glancing in the restroom mirror. She was just old enough to have had some humanities included in her mostly technical education. By the time she'd dried her hands, the thought was gone, replaced by the need to concoct a brief tactical plan. The conference room was ten minutes away, on a different floor, and she used the time to work out a mental draft.

Andy Patel was already in the room, along with Pete Corcoran. Mike and Roger were coming down the hall as she went in. Five people to plan for, all of whom could be counted on to follow the plan. Barring contingencies, that is. All fine except in the case of illness, injury, mechanical failures, acts of nature, and traffic problems. And that was the easy part. The plan was to drive to another city, visit a building none of them had ever entered, and have an unannounced set of conversations with four or five people who would, at least, be surprised. Some of them might be terrified or enraged. A few of them might have plans of their own, worked out as backups. And of course, there was always the chance that the visit *wouldn't* be a surprise. To put it a lot more simply, the plan was to drop in on a company, some of whose people were suspected of doing things illegal. *We're from the government, and we're here to help*, she thought. Not what people like to hear at eight-thirty in the morning.

The usual before-meeting pleasantries ended quickly. Sheila took the chalk, metaphorically speaking. "So, I'm thinking we take two cars from here, and we meet Andy someplace in Ann Arbor. Then, it's Andy and me in one, you guys," she indicated Pete, Mike, and Roger, "in the other. Andy and Pete know Ann Arbor, and so nobody gets too lost."

"Well, maybe Andy knows," said Pete. "But I'm not much of an expert. That downtown of theirs is wacky."

"Yeah, Pete," Andy said, "but we're not going downtown. The place is out on the northeast side, right off 23. Easy to find. And somebody can put the address in their phone, anyway."

"Andy, you want to pick a place close to that and meet us?"

"Right. You come off 23 at Plymouth Road, and go west. Right away, there's a shopping center on the left, and there's a Coney Island in there. Mark's. Pete knows it."

"Okay, and so we meet and head over to the company. We rendezvous at the visitor parking or whatever they have by the front, and we go in together. Andy, you want to announce us to the front desk or whatever?'

"Sure."

"And we ID ourselves, say we need to talk to, let's see here," she consulted a list, "The Pres, his Ops guy Dormanski, the security lead ... that's, ah, Todarcz, and especially your good friend and mine, Mr. Peakes."

"All in separate offices or meeting rooms," said Roger.

"Yup, and then of course, we run into the usual stuff."

"Nobody home," said Andy.

"Right, nobody home. Out of the office, in a meeting, in the hospital, missing, dead ..." Sheila paused for breath, "In which case, as per usual, we try to get 'em to come back in, we talk to 'someone else with knowledge', set up future interviews ... the usual." Everybody nodded. Nothing new there.

"What about the ex-VP? This Doctor Kasimir? The one who left?"

"Not today. She won't be at the office, anyway, of course. I think we set up a separate date with her."

"Is she really suing the company?" Pete asked.

"Nothing's filed so far," Andy said, "But regardless, you got somebody at her level, faculty at the U, kicked out of an exec job ... not possible she doesn't have a lawyer, suing or not suing."

"Okay," Sheila agreed, "so we talk to her later, separately. What about legal beagles for the rest of 'em?"

"You know," said Roger, "that's a little odd, but I can't find anything of record, there. I mean, they're a government contractor and all, but nothing about corporate counsel, no contact address for legal matters. Unusual, seems like."

"I guess we'll get that from the Pres or Dormanski," Andy said, "Now, I got another item. Pete and I did the criminal and firearms thing on everybody, and *nothing*. Nobody's got any sketchy Internet stuff, no NRA memberships, no arrests. Only this Todarcz guy even shows up in hunting license checks."

"But personally, I don't ever relax anymore," Mike Sherman said. "Hell, Andy, remember that other Ann Arbor thing? Back in the winter? You and Pete went in there thinking 'sketchy loan company' and the next thing, the execs are shooting at each other?"

"Agree, agree," said Andy. "We got no particular alerts here. But we know two of these folks are talking to an east Europe guy. Crimea, for God's sake. That's enough for me, right there. So we keep our eyes open. Me, I'm gonna wear a vest." There were nods around the table. "Oh, and by the way, there's another guy, another car. We let the local cops know this was happening, and they wanted to have one of their detectives there. Guy's named Burke. Louis Burke. I know him a little."

"Oh, joy. Local cops," Sheila said, grabbing the virtual chalk again. "So that's the basics. Now, let's work out what we ask whom and what kind of answers we think we'll get." That process took another two hours.

"Done, then, I guess," she said, when they had a detailed list of the intelligence they wanted, plus an assessment of how reliable each item might be, crossed with each potential subject. "Far as I'm concerned, it's 'see you tomorrow'."

"Bright and early." The people coming up from Detroit or the suburbs groaned, inwardly. Andy, on the other hand, just felt another twinge of worry.

 After Stones River, our army paused, repaired its damage, and quarreled with General Halleck and with Washington in general. I cannot claim that the analysis occurred to me at the time, but in the years since the war, I have extended my reading in the history of warfare back beyond the time of Napoleon, and I have come to the conclusion that our manner of fighting and the manner of fighting that is most admired and approved of, is an imitation of the practices of that great

Frenchman and his worthy opponents. We have, however, neglected to study the reasons that Napoleonic wars were fought as they were. We have failed to look back to the period before the beginning of our century. In the eighteenth century, in the time preceding the French Revolution, the great captains did not place all their hopes on the attack, did not see large and bloody battles as the true outcome of war and the thing to be most sought after. Rather, from the time of the first truly national armies and even before, back to the period when armies were purchased and were an asset to be preserved, not thrown away, excellence in a commander was often measured by his ability to defeat his enemy without fighting.

The countries of Europe were able to take that approach because they were led by monarchs, and the opinions and beliefs of their citizens were not, until late in the eighteenth century, of any real concern. There was no upcoming election to threaten the leadership, no political party feeling to place pressure on kings and emperors. Economic limitations, dynastic disputes, access to resources and markets—those things were present and important. Except, however, in the most extreme situations, what the monarch and the few powerful men around him ordered was the thing that was done. What monarchs wanted, most often, was the accomplishment of their aims without the risk and expense of mass warfare. What the people and the press, such as there was of it, may have thought became only gradually important as the century drew to its close.

This is not an acceptable way for a free nation to be governed, and I do not and I will never advocate it. It does, however, make the practice of arms and the command of armies in the field a more complicated and dangerous profession than it was before the advent of social freedoms and elected governments. This is the situation in which General Rosecrans and his corps commanders, myself among them, found ourselves in 1863.

Despite having won our fight at Stones River and thrown Bragg out of central Tennessee, we faced afterward, as did he, a bitter winter and a shortage of everything an army requires to carry on a campaign. Washington, where General Rosecrans was not the most popular of our commanders, applied pressure at all times to move on, to defeat Bragg finally and dramatically, and to seize Chattanooga. The gentlemen who issued these orders were either ignorant of the facts or had reasons to ignore them. For General Rosecrans to have obeyed literally any of the peremptorily demanding orders he received would have been simple murder. To do so, he (and we) would have acquiesced in the death of thousands of men and achieved nothing for it. Instead, to his eternal credit, General Rosecrans resisted until the middle of the year the foolish calls for action and a traditional offensive. Then, beginning in the first part of August, he deceived Bragg repeatedly, sidestepped him, flanked him, fought small fights for key passes in the hills and mountains, and eventually humbugged him back to Chattanooga and then out of there as well. Our losses were minimal.

It was at this point, unfortunately, that we allowed ourselves to be humbugged in return. General Rosecrans was certain, as I am in a position to know, that we had crushed the spirit if not the physical existence of Bragg's army. Intelligence we received from deserters and prisoners and country people appeared to confirm this impression. I had some doubts about the details of the intelligence, but I did not doubt the initial evidence that our limited scouting supplied. At any rate, the General determined to act on the assumption that Bragg was withdrawing in disorder and was very much weaker in ready troops than we. We occupied Chattanooga with a small force and then took the remainder of the Army on another attempt to move more quickly through the mountains than the enemy, hoping to catch him, surround him, and defeat him in detail. As the days of September ticked away, however, evidence began to mount, showing that the rebellion had not been as thoroughly crushed as we thought.

"Are you feeling all right?" Jenn asked.

"Oh ... well ..." Andy was not exactly surprised by the question. "We, ah, have a few issues going on at work."

"I have the feeling that somehow that's not an entirely candid answer."

He caught her eye, and a bit changed state in his brain, going from zero to one. "It isn't," he said. "I'm sorry."

"I get that. And I did sort of implicitly agree not to pry, but if it's something ..."

"No, it's not anything about ..." He was going to say "about you", but that would have been an egregious lie. A loud and scornful voice spoke in his ear, using that fast and efficient symbolic language we've evolved for scolding ourselves. "*Hey, boy. That's your wife over there. You married her, remember?*"

"Mmm," Jenn said, making it neither a statement nor a question, just a placeholder.

"Okay," he started. "You ... you deal with security for more than just Holcombe, internally, right?"

"I do."

"Like, for subs ... subcontractors."

"Yes."

"How many, roughly?"

"Current ones, three."

"If you knew ... if you found out that maybe an agency was looking at one of 'em. What would you do?"

"Immediately? I'd let the executive team know. With their approval, I'd let the customer know. And then I'd start ... looking harder at them ... myself." She paused. "It'd depend on how much I knew. And where I got the information." She was looking straight into his eyes, now.

"Tomorrow, there's a good chance you might hear something along those lines. About one of those subs. And I have to ask you ... you know why ... not to do anything with that, between now and then."

Jenn looked away for a moment. She looked back at Andy and said, "Okay. I see. I ... can probably guess at which one it is, too."

"You can? Good. That's really good. Um, are you on paper with that? At all? Anything that would, ah, show that you were ... concerned about them?"

"Doctor Holcombe knows. We talked about it just today. And our program manager."

"But it's not on paper? Or an email?"

"No."

"You know what might be a good idea? We could go back to your office, I'll wait for you outside. And you go in and send a message to, oh, at least your President. Recapping what you told her or something like that. And then we could go downtown and have dinner."

"Tonight?"

"Yeah."

"Because something might happen tomorrow?"

"Something might. Yes."

"I'll get my bag. Let's go."

Andy had an overwhelming sense of having done the right thing. It was very much like his reaction to asking Jenn to marry him, back in the middle of a terrible winter. He felt relieved, too, much as he'd felt the day after that, listening to her voice mail message and hearing her say "yes".

It was not, of course, the first time Holcombe had called one of its subcontractors in for a spanking. It wasn't a thing they did with any pleasure, though. Bad performance by a sub always reflected poorly on the prime contractor, and in the case of a company run by Karolyn Holcombe, it was doubly embarrassing. Her underlying development method cautioned against outsourcing anything important, and if you had to, it stressed the need for clear deliverables, rigorous management, and frequent check-ups. In many companies, a screwed up subcontract would be something you'd keep close to the chest. Karolyn, though, believed in being absolutely straight with her customers, and when problems happened, they were invited to assist in correcting the problem.

In keeping with that policy, an employee, a civilian, who had certain levels of contractor oversight responsibility at a branch of the Department of Defense, would be dialed in to this morning's meeting. He'd already had a talk with Karolyn, and in the last month, he'd been in two other conferences just like this one. They were with different companies, but they all followed the same general format. He knew from education and experience that no program plan ever written survives contact with the enemy, so to speak, "enemy" being time, money, and functionality. He was concerned but not panicked.

"The front desk says LifeRigor just arrived," Vivienne Keyes said. "I'll go collect them."

Eleven miles away by the fastest route, Andy sat down at a booth in a Coney Island and ordered a coffee. Before it arrived, a young man in a suit came in the door, looked around, and approached.

"Are you, uh, Andy Patel?" he asked. Andy remembered him slightly: Louie Burke, the new detective who'd picked up most of Jenn's workload when she left the Ann Arbor department.

"Hi, Detective Burke," he said. "Slide in. The rest of my folks will be here in a bit."

"Okay, thanks. I didn't really get any information on this, so, uh, what are we doin'?"

"I'll give you a little brief when we're outside, you know? Better that way."

"Oh. All right." Burke was not an impressive figure, physically. When he first started out in a detective slot, he hadn't been all that professionally impressive, either. But having been thrown right into a full-blown list of cases, he'd improved. He'd learned to pay attention to office chatter and to the tales of older cops. He understood, for example, a few things about outside law enforcement agencies, especially at the federal level. He knew they were usually reticent about details. He knew they didn't particularly like working with local departments unless they were teamed up with people they already knew and trusted. He knew that the last AAPD people the Detroit FBI office really knew and trusted were Mac MacArthur and Jenn Langton, both of whom were now gone. And he, Burke, was sorry that Mac hadn't been able to talk last night, at eleven PM. Mrs. MacArthur had been very clear about that. He ordered his own coffee, and when he turned back from the waitress, saw that Patel was on his phone.

"You're kidding? Well, not surprising, I guess. We'll, uh, just hang on here, then. What? Oh, the local guy's here with me. Okay, see you when you get here." Andy closed the call.

"The rest of the group's hung up in traffic. Something wrong at 275 and 94. So we wait."

"Oh, too bad. Yeah, things are getting, uh, bad. On the freeways." Burke ran out of things to say about traffic. "How's your ... how's Jenn?"

Andy didn't look as pleased as he might have. "She's ... all right. Working really hard. But good. She likes it over there."

"Oh, good. Good. Yeah, we've lost some other people, too. One of the older guy's retiring, Chief's retiring. Lost a patrol officer to the County." He ran dry again.

At Holcombe, diagonally across town, the people from LifeRigor came into the conference room and sat down. Ominously, the available seats were all on one side of the table. Karolyn, Jenn, Vivienne, and Izzy McLeroy were all on the other side. The speaker phone was in the middle of the table.

"All right," said Karolyn. "Let's get started. On the phone, we have Mr. West who is representing the customer. Some of you have spoken with him before. From our side, we have Jenn Langton, Viv Keyes, Israel McLeroy, and myself. And from LifeRigor, we're joined by ..."

As she introduced his people, Doctor Metharom sat very still, holding himself in a state of rigid control. He was a nervous man in general. His family had not been an important or wealthy one in Thailand, although extremely respectable. He'd had to work very hard to get into a college, move along the degree path, find a way to come to the US, and then get a permanent position. All his ideas were those of a man building an academic career. He'd never planned on becoming a businessman. It was just one step after another.

166

All of those steps had been the right ones, right up until now. He'd started a company to fund work on his ideas. He'd found a customer. He'd signed contracts. And now, after all those years of just doing what was necessary, doing what he thought was the expected thing, now it was clear to him, horribly clear. There were customs and practices he knew nothing about, circumstances in which he had no idea how to behave. He'd overstepped himself.

Down the table, Ricky Peakes was in almost the same state and for almost the same reasons. His background wasn't even middle class, let alone upper middle, and he came from Alabama and not Bangkok, but he had the same sinking feeling, the same desperate sense of waters rising around him. Like Metharom, he saw traps and disasters ahead. But the difference between them was fundamental. The Thai doctor saw now that the fault was mostly his own, that he'd made his own bed and would somehow have to sleep in it. Ricky, though, saw nothing but malice closing in. He couldn't even begin to blame himself. He had a living to make, he had rent to pay; sooner or later, somebody would want him to pay for his father's old age. He'd had to do what had to be done, and when it hadn't been enough, it had to be somebody else's fault. There were people in psychology and even in medicine who saw this set of reactions as symptoms, symptoms of a borderline mental illness. Peakes didn't know that, and if he did, he would have, of course, rejected the idea. If anybody was crazy, it was someone else.

Karolyn finished naming names. "We're going to review a series of issues with the status of LifeRigor's deliverables. Mr. McLeroy will deal with the specific software topics, and Vivienne Keyes will list dates and commitments. And then, I want Jenn Langton to go over what we feel are some very serious flaws in the security plan and its compliance with the contract and with both policy and legal requirements."

Ricky felt chilled. *Security? Legal? Oh, my, God!* Holcombe was finishing.

"We will conclude with a set of actions, both for LifeRigor and for Holcombe, intended to bring this program back into compliance with the contract. That will include complete revised schedules for development and review activities. It will include an analysis of current costs against bid. And we will review the rates that were in the proposals."

Metharom's lips contracted involuntarily. *Rates! Not rates!* He glanced at Roger Dormanski. Could he rely on Dormanski to get all this rates business brought into line? Dormanski looked serious but not panicked.

"And we will set a deadline for having this plan in place and committed to. I believe seven working days should be sufficient."

Everyone on the LifeRigor side of the table stiffened. There's nothing like a deadline to get your attention.

At 275 and 94, Sheila and the other Feds (*Good name for a band*, she thought), finally got free of the traffic. It had been slow at the interchange, as usual, but this time the dead stop had been caused by police investigating a body. Road workers found it in a swampy area, just off the highways as they came together. It was one of three bodies called in that morning, scattered around the Detroit metro area. No one in the car was particularly surprised or shocked. Pete Corcoran kept a running total, just of such incidents as were on local news sites.

"Three today, here," he said. "But Chicago says they had four." Roger brought his left arm in close to his chest, almost reflexively checking that he'd remembered his sidearm. He never forgot it, in fact, and yet he still kept checking. Behind the wheel, Sheila did her own little gear-check movement, a slight shrug, confirming that her vest was there. Pete sent Andy a text message: *Moving. 20 minutes ETA.*

At the Coney Island, Andy and Burke paid for their coffees. "Let's go outside," he said to Burke. "I can give you some more details."

After more than twenty minutes, Google maps being optimistic about the trip time north from 94 up M23 to Plymouth Road, the forces of law made their rendezvous. Andy did quick introductions with Louie Burke and said, "I've briefed him in on, uh, today. Today's plans."

"Where do we go?" Sheila asked. "Over there, somewhere, right?" She swung an arm off to the north.

"Right. We just go out of the lot here, over that way," pointing west toward Green Road. "Go right, go through the light, and it's the first left after that. I mean, there's a turn-in before that, into a parking lot, but it's the first real road on the left. Commonwealth. And the building's on the left."

"Okay. Like we said, I'll go with Andy. Pete and you guys in our car. And, um, Detective Burke, you got your own car, right?"

"Yes. I do."

"And you know where we're going?"

"Andy told me."

"All right then. Let's go."

In the conference room at Holcombe, the list of technical shortcomings had been covered. In almost every case, the pattern had repeated itself. Izzy McLeroy would describe a capability that was supposed to be functional, frozen, and delivered to his team. He would point out that it hadn't been. He'd ask Ricky why not. Ricky would make some general statement or, if he actually knew, he would start describing details of difficulty, unforeseen problems, or priority shifts. Before he could get far into them, Viv Keyes would cut him off. She would point out that his company had supposedly conducted a design process that should, hypothetically, identify such problems before they came up. Karolyn would then suspend debate by making the problem one more item to be addressed by LifeRigor's ever-growing mitigation plan. This went on for almost an hour. Then the action shifted to program management.

The process was similar. Now, Viv was pitching strikes at Metharom and Dormanski, asking for plans she knew didn't exist, records of design activities that she was sure wouldn't be forthcoming—in general, dragging them nude along a gravel path, scattered with broken glass. Dormanski's broad white face began to turn red, and his answers became more defensive. Metharom seemed to be withdrawing, giving shorter and more monosyllabic answers as time went on. Peakes, no longer directly on the hot seat, had time to ponder the upcoming agenda item: security. Meanwhile, the customer on the phone turned down the volume and began going through email messages. He'd seen at least two worse messes just in the last month.

The parking lot at LifeRigor's building was small enough that nobody except Louie Burke noticed that it was lightly populated. *Not many cars here*, he thought, *at nine-fifteen.* Still slightly awed at the army of dark-suited, serious Feds he was accompanying, he kept his mouth shut. That was almost exactly the instructions his sergeant had given him, anyway. That and "stay out of the way."

The team seemed to know what they were doing. There was no huddle at the parked cars, just a calm stroll up to the door, Sheila and Andy in the lead, the other three behind them, and Burke coming last. Even though every one of them was wearing a suit of some subdued kind, they were still an ominous crew, unusual almost anywhere in Ann Arbor, and not anything like the vendors and delivery people who made up almost all of the visitors to LifeRigor, Inc. The bright-eyed and attractive young person at the front desk was a bit startled.

"Hi! Ah, hello. Can I help you?"

Andy returned the greeting and asked for Metharom. He wasn't at all surprised to hear that the President was out. How about Mr. Dormanski, then? No? Well, then ...

Their contingency planning hit its second surprise of the day. That every last person they wanted to see would be "out" had seemed very unlikely. Inquiries were made about where they all were. All at one meeting? Wasn't that unusual? The reception person hadn't been briefed at all about security, and she was happy to explain where all the important people had gone. They were visiting the customer.

"I see," said Sheila. "Would you excuse us for a minute?" She nodded her head at the team, and they withdrew to the entrance way. "Do you buy this?"

The team had different views. Most were inclined to accept it at face value. Andy was skeptical, concerned that somehow LifeRigor had been alerted. There was a pause, and Louie Burke stepped into it.

"Is this customer out of town?"

"What?" said Sheila.

"No," said Andy. "They're here. Other side of town. Why?"

"Well, I thought ... maybe some of us could go over there and see."

The fight that we fought along the Chickamauga stream is not a soft or easy thing to remember. It was not a grand, sweeping spectacle of glittering armies advancing

171

and withdrawing under the impartial eye of God and nature. It was a blundering collision of armies seeking each other's destruction, fought in isolated pieces in dense woods along a dark and slowly-flowing stream. You will read in some of the more popularized descriptions that "Chickamauga" means "Bloody Stream" in the Cherokee language. That is an invention of the press. The most likely answer I have ever received as to its meaning is from an elderly local man who knew the last few Indian residents, and he told me that it means "Stagnant Flow". Regardless, it runs slowly through a valley called McLemore's Cove, and throughout the length of the valley, there are only scattered fields. The rest is dark, tangled forest. It was in this depression southwest of Chattanooga that our army hurried to reconcentrate, to join each of the corps one to another, and to present Bragg with our full strength. This became our only goal after it was accepted that the rebels had deceived us, had been reinforced, and were preparing to strike at each of our separate parties, individually. If General Bragg had not been so poorly served by his subordinate generals, he might have succeeded.

As it was, on three separate days he gave orders for specific attacks, only to find his commands ignored, performed poorly, or carried out in some different and mistaken way. In the tangled woods, men fought and died, but without coordinated effort. As we were all discovering, both the National forces and the men of the rebellion, in the uncivilized and primordial lands of this continent, the defense stands at a large advantage. The battle along the Chickamauga creek demonstrated this principle.

Finally, on the third day since our forces had come together, Bragg made his final effort. He had been reinforced overnight by General James Longstreet and three brigades sent by Lee from Virginia. In the morning, my corps and the troops that had been attached to it were attacked strongly, standing where we did on the left flank of our army. By the middle of the day, the rebel assaults on us had been held off, and although we expected more, we were still in position, and Bragg apparently believed that his strike at us had failed. Consequently, at about eleven-thirty, he sent General Longstreet straight ahead at the center of our forces, just as one of our brigades, directly in their path, was ordered to move north and reinforce my corps. Longstreet's men ran, by pure chance, straight into the gap left by this movement, cutting our army in two.

As it had been doing all along, the landscape again laid its hand on the events of the day. We could not see the extent of the disaster happening to the south of our position, nor could those who were scattered by Longstreet's advance see that we were still standing. General Rosecrans, General McCook, General Crittenden, and most of their forces, literally our whole right and center, withdrew toward Chattanooga, assuming that we also had been forced from the field. We, on our part, received no order to withdraw, nor for some time did we even know the extent of the defeat. What I did know was that our position had already repulsed heavy attacks and was prepared to continue doing so. When Longstreet turned north and came against our flank, the fact that we were in a semi-circular arrangement around a small hill saved us and allowed us to beat off every assault. General Steedman, coming down from General Granger's corps on the Chattanooga road, reinforced us with his brigade just at a most critical moment, and so we continued to stand as Bragg continued to do as he had done at Stones River, namely dash his army again and again at a determined and prepared defense. By nightfall, we were still standing, and I received orders from General Rosecrans to withdraw and join him at Chattanooga.

In the days that followed, we prepared the city for defense, but it became clear that Bragg was willing to do nothing more than besiege us. He used his cavalry to interfere with our supplies, and from his position on the mountains facing Chattanooga directly to its south and east, he could also keep us from using the river as we had been. He did not, however, move against us, and as time went on and he could not agree with his subordinates, he sent Longstreet away to menace General Burnside at Knoxville, weakening his own force in front of us by twenty thousand men. We still stood in front of him, our army was reforming and recovering itself, and we were being reinforced in a number of ways. I do not recall ever saying it, this time, to anyone, but the opinion I held after Stones River remained: Bragg was finished. It came at a terrible cost to both parties, Chickamauga being the bloodiest fight of the war, reckoned as a proportion of the men engaged, but still the thought stood with me. Bragg was finished.

"So here's what I want to do," Andy said to Burke. "I want to go over there and just watch. We've got some license numbers, we can see if any cars in the lot are hooked up with any of these folks. But we can't go busting in on 'em. Holc ... this other company, we aren't looking at. They might not appreciate us hassling their subcontractors, right in their front office."

"Got it. Where is it, again?" Andy gave him the address. "It's in that something-Farms complex, over there on State."

"Right. I'll follow you?"

"Sure. And then we sit and watch to see if they come out. And if they do, we just quietly follow. If they go anywhere but back here,"—he pointed down at the LifeRigor parking lot—"we call in the rest of the crew." He waved his arm at his colleagues. "Otherwise, well, we call anyway, but we just follow 'em back here."

Burke nodded. Sheila nodded at Andy. He nodded back and walked off toward his car. Burke followed.

Meanwhile, in Holcomb's closed area, the Spanish Inquisition had finished. Doctor Holcombe had supervised the construction of a lengthy action item list, and Doctor Metharom had been given no real chance to object. Jenn had raised a grim, polite, and unanswerable kind of hell about security violations. Before the meeting, she'd checked her list of issues against a simple test: *Am I asking this because of what I know or because I'm aware of Andy being up to something?* If the latter, she left it off her list.

It was still a long list. She asked Norm Todarcz to explain how his systems kept people from simply copying code onto some kind of media and taking it home. He explained that no one was allowed to do that. Jenn pointed out that no one was allowed to set the building on fire, either. Norm looked puzzled by the analogy. Ricky had no way of knowing that she'd pulled that question out of the air, based on Corinne's tales of phones in the secure space. He, of course, had copied a large amount of code onto a thumb drive, taken it home, and emailed the content to Oleksiy. He turned a whiter shade of pale.

Karolyn finished up with a sermon whose text was essentially "Go and sin no more," and the customer said a few solemn things about national priorities. People gathered up their pens and pencils, left any notes to be transcribed and sent out on the secure net, and the prosecution and the accused filed out and down the single flight of stairs. Karolyn, Vivienne, and Jenn stood in a semi-circle as the visitors went out the door.

Except for one small grass pad, the lozenge-shaped building was enclosed with a paved parking lot. Andy and Burke were parked along the south side, situated where they could see the building entrance. Burke had joined Andy in Andy's car. They'd confirmed that two vehicles in the visitor parking belonged to Metharom and to Roger Dormanski, and they assumed that the other two subjects had been passengers. This was only partly right. Ricky had come in his own car, and for no special reason, he'd parked it on the north side of the building, out of direct sight of anyone parked where the Fed and the cop were now sitting. As they watched, another car pulled into the lot, seemed to hesitate, and then took one of the remaining visitor spots.

The entrance doors of the building opened. "Here we go, maybe," said Burke. Both he and Andy focused in that direction. Andy had a fairly clear picture in his mind of the people he was seeking, but the proof of identity, obviously, would be the cars they went to. Someone held one of the building doors open for someone else, but the next person out ignored it and opened the opposite door for himself. Andy raised a small pair of binoculars.

Burke said, "Hey! Isn't that Jeri Klein?"

In fact, it was Jeri, not at the doors but walking toward them from her car which she'd parked between those of the LifeRigor execs. Andy had missed it because of the narrow field of his binoculars. Right behind Jeri was Jackie Langton and behind her, Mac MacArthur, limping slightly. They'd arrived a few minutes early, intending to take Jenn off to lunch and to a preliminary dog viewing at the rescue house.

"What?" said Andy, lowering the binoculars and looking off at where Burke was pointing.

Up on the top steps of the building entrance, Ricky let go of the door he'd been pointlessly holding open for Metharom. People moving toward the building caught his eye. He was in a state of severe paranoia, and virtually anything in sight could represent a threat. He looked at the trio of people, saw an older man, a young woman unfamiliar to him, and ... his breath caught in his throat! That terrifying woman cop! Jeri's face and posture were engraved in his memory and linked, actually or psychically, with two of the most terrifying and humiliating episodes of his life. He'd just undergone the third such trauma, and his entirely self-centered world view immediately jumped to a string of crisis delusions. They'd come for him!

Looking through the door and past him, Jenn saw her daughter and the others. She stepped forward, meaning to greet them and ask for five minutes to gather herself up for an hour away from work. Ricky let go of the door, and it swung back into Jenn's way. She blocked it with an arm and swore without meaning to. Ricky heard that, turned back, and saw only that impossible, demanding, threatening security bitch. He looked desperately back at Jeri, but stopped in half-turn as he saw two other men, dressed in dark suits and walking quickly toward him.

Andy was intensely worried by the intrusion of three more of his family and friends into a situation that already involved his wife. He left his car, and he was moving in to exert some as yet unplanned influence on the situation. Burke, still very much in the dark about everything, could only follow. His only coherent thought was, *I won't do any good sitting in the car.*

Ricky jerked his head back around toward Jeri. She had both a good memory and very good eyesight, and in quick sequence recognized him and identified his visible signs of distress. Knowing nothing else about him except his being present at that one crazy-lady episode, her thought was that he needed some kind of help. She was still ten yards away, she and her party just walking past the other three LifeRigor people. She held out one hand in Ricky's direction and said, "Hold on!" She meant "wait and I'll see if I can help" but to Ricky, anything she'd said would have been a threat. He made an incoherent noise and began to run, taking his first steps away from the doors and then turning left, running for his car.

Jenn, having just cleared the doors, looked after him and said, "What the hell?" loudly. Viv heard this, whirled around, and started out the doors herself. Andy and Burke only heard shouting and saw someone start to run. "Stop," Andy shouted. His voice blended with Jeri's as she, still thinking of Ricky as a victim of something, yelled, "Wait!" Doctor Metharom said something in Thai, and both of his companions whirled and stared.

Ricky took one more running step and stumbled. As he recovered, his right hand brushed his sport coat pocket. There was another half a second's purely biomechanical movements, not at all controlled by his brain, and then he saw his hand, somehow holding his little automatic. He turned back, saw Jeri coming in his direction, and jerked the trigger.

A .32 doesn't make an extremely loud noise, but any unexpected gunshot is loud enough, especially when it comes from a gun with a very short barrel. Burke and Andy both reached for their holstered weapons, Viv Keyes jumped back inside, forming a clear mental picture of her own pistol, safely in her purse, on her desk, back in the closed area. Doctor Holcombe, heading back to her office, misunderstood the sound and kept walking. Jenn dropped to one knee and yanked on the grip of a small revolver, holstered under her left arm. Andy and Burke were both still coming on, and Andy shouted at Ricky again. Ricky saw him, and in a complete state of panic, emptied the Beretta in that general direction. He spun, threw the pistol away, and ran on, turning the corner of the building and disappearing from the immediate chaos.

Burke saw all this, and he kept running, not after Ricky but toward a small group clustered on the ground. Jackie Langton and MacArthur were crouching around Jeri Klein, and Jeri was lying on her back, with her left leg doubled up. She was holding onto her thigh and watching blood run between her fingers. Burke was three paces away when Mac saw him and waved him back. "I got this!" he yelled. "Go see Andy!"

"What?"

"Andy! Go see Andy! He's down, too!"

"But the shooter ..."

"He threw down the gun! Go see Andy!" Mac was unintentionally talking to Burke as he would one of his dogs. Burke turned obediently and saw that Patel was in fact lying on the pavement. Jenn was off the steps and running toward him. Mac bent over Jeri and gestured Jackie Langton in closer.

"Here," he said to Jackie, handing her his phone. "Dial 911, and then give it to Jeri! Let her give them the details!"

"I can't let go of this," Jeri said. "It's arterial." Her voice was almost entirely calm. There was just the hint of strain.

"I know," said Mac. "I'll hold the bleeder. You talk to dispatch. They'll remember you better than me. Tell 'em we have two down." By that point, Jackie was holding out Mac's phone to her. She let go of the wound, and Mac grabbed for it, found the entrance point below the denim of her jeans, and put his thumb on it, leaning in for pressure.

"This is a Washtenaw County deputy," Jeri said to the phone. "Active shooter at ... "

"I know the address," said Jackie. Jeri held the phone up to her, and they got the address across to a startled multi-agency dispatcher. Jeri took it back. Her face tightened up briefly as Mac bore down harder on the wound. "Two down. I'm one, and there's another one. He's ... what, FBI?" She looked at Mac.

"Right! Agent Andy Patel. Unknown condition, but down."

"Okay, an FBI agent down, too. We need officer backup and medical times two. Shooter is still at large, ran toward the back of the building at ..." she recited the address again.

Burke and Jenn reached Andy almost together. As they got there, he was rolling over onto his back or trying to.

"Where is it?" Jenn yelled at him. "Where are you hit?" She was operating in some kind of automatic mode, a temporary way of being that let her set aside everything but her focus on the wounded man. Burke arrived in the next second, putting his forearm behind Andy's head.

"Lay back," he said. "Keep still. There's help on the way. Mac's ... um, in charge." Neither Andy nor Jenn paid any attention to that.

"I think ... I think it's not ... bad," Andy said. "Just my shoulder." There was no obvious blood on his jacket, but there was a small hole.

"Burke, give me a knife," Jenn said. "My damn bag's inside."

"Right," he said, fishing in his right pants pocket. He handed over a small folder. Jenn took a quick look at the sleeve, and then drew the blade along the shoulder seam. It separated, and she then did the same for the long closure running down the outside of the arm. She stopped near the elbow and then opened the whole thing up like a package. She drew her breath in sharply. The white shirt sleeve below it was stained red in a patch five inches across.

"My ribs hurt, too," Andy said. Before anyone could internalize that, there was a loud automotive and mechanical noise. A small car came around the south side of the building, moving fast. It went past Burke's car, then braked sharply, turned hard right, and went over the parking lot curb, heading out onto a space of mowed grass between the Holcombe building and another one, just south. Burke stood up, drew his handgun again, and started running after it, but within twenty feet he gave up. The car accelerated fast, swerved left again, and ran straight out onto the street. Its wheels bounced off the opposite curb, and the driver obviously struggled to get it straightened out. Burke took a couple of steps more, but the car found its course again and took off due south, curving east with the road and going out of sight.

Hyundai, Burke thought, memorizing everything he'd seen of it. *Elantra, dark blue. No license plate seen. One white male occupant.* He turned around and ran back toward the building.

It was fortunate for Ricky that Ann Arbor was between morning drive time and high lunchtime. The level of traffic was lower than it might have been, and he was in a literal blind panic. Crescents of black danced around the outside of his field of vision, giving the effect of peering through binoculars. What he did see and process was the bare minimum necessary to keep his car on the road. It's not accurate to say that he was thinking; his mind was essentially looping, trying to execute instructions, failing, and starting over.

As far as his route was concerned, he had few choices while he was leaving the office park. When he came, finally, to an exit, he was stumped. It was not the way the team had come in. Instead, it was the south exit, still onto State Street, but well out past the line of intense business development. The impression was misleading, but to the terror-blurred eyes of a young man awash in adrenaline, it looked like countryside. He turned south in an instinctive effort to distance himself from the horror behind. He passed up—didn't even see, actually—a gravel road going east, then turned left at the first paved road he came to.

This turned out to be just another route through scattered industrial buildings, but it bent south and took him out to Textile Road. As he neared the intersection, a Pittsfield Township officer went by, lights on and heading west, responding to the shooting report. Ricky grasped that piece of information sufficiently to turn east. He was recovering enough of his wits to have a few more concrete goals; for one, he grasped the idea that his car was something that could betray him. That immediately generated a leap to the stored Marquis, sitting in a rented space some four and half miles straight off to his left. He accelerated, bumped over a set of railroad tracks, and took the next road.

Ann Arbor isn't an easy city to enter. It's hemmed in by freeways. But Ricky had one small portion of luck remaining; he'd chosen a small gravel road that ran north to another small gravel road, and one block of that led to yet another, still going north. That road turned into pavement, crossed a major street, jumped over I-94, and dropped him exactly where he wanted to be, namely Packard heading toward downtown. Long before he got there, though, he turned left onto a small residential street going west, slipped over a series of speed bumps, and parked three houses away from a small storage rental business, the first of several that marked the point where the street turned commercial. He gathered a few things he either wanted or didn't want to leave lying around, locked the Hyundai, and left it sitting there. By now, he was too far from the south side to hear the ambulances taking Andy Patel and Jeri Klein to UMHS Emergency.

An hour and a half later, he pulled off I-75 at a rural exit; flat agricultural land surrounding a gas station and a McDonalds. It took twenty minutes at the station, in the restroom, and at the fast food counter to collect his wits. He walked back outside and called Oleksiy.

That conversation took almost another fifteen minutes to complete. When Ricky disconnected, he knew where he had to go and by when he had to be there. He reviewed his cash supply and checked a state-run website. He separated out a five dollar bill from his other money and put it in a shirt pocket, ensuring that he'd have it ready when he had to cross the Mackinac Bridge.

In Windsor, Oleksiy was not panicking. Not completely, anyway. Instead, he complimented himself on having a script prepared for this call, although he admitted that the extreme nature of it had been a surprise. *Americans,* he thought. *Fucking cowboys! The first time something happens, they all start shooting.* Now his moves were clear, and they'd been thought out months before.

He had a set of plain cardboard shipping boxes in his basement. There were just enough of them to fill the seat and cargo area of his Forester, a four-year-old car he'd bought when he came to Windsor and one he seldom drove. It was always fueled up and ready to go. He sorted his belongings into boxes—clothes, a few tools and kitchen supplies, no electronics whatsoever. He walked out into the back yard, set his phone down on a paving stone, and picked up a cement block that someone had left lying around. He dropped the block onto the phone, lifted it again, and dropped it

182

again. Then he gathered up the bits and pieces and put them in a trash bag. The bag went on the front passenger's seat. He'd dispose of it in a dumpster, somewhere during the first ten minutes of his drive. *Time to go,* he thought. Vancouver was forty-six hundred miles away.

Sheila Drew and her boss, Harold Borowski, were having a tense little conversation. "So," she said, "we know where the little bastard is going and when, but so far, we don't have a fix on him."

"Past the phone call, you don't."

"Right. We know where that was, and we got a deputy up there to go look, but it was three hours later on. He must have just jumped back on 75 and kept going."

"And nothing on the car?"

"Nobody remembers any blue Hyundais. One lady at McDonalds thinks she might have served him a burger, but she wasn't sure. Anyway, we know he was there, burger or not."

"All right. I want you in charge of the team. We know he isn't going straight up to the airport. His pal in Windsor told him it'd take until the day after tomorrow to get the so-called 'pick up' ready. So we've got until then."

"Right."

"And I want you to do a sim with the team. Just as formal as we can. You run it. This thing has gone as far sideways as I'm interested in it going."

"I get it. What does Washington think?"

"What do you think they think?"

"As bad as that?"

"Yup."

"Are we absolutely sure that the Windsor guy is jerking the geek around? There really isn't any plane coming for him?"

"I'm not absolutely sure of anything, anymore, but nobody involved ..." he jerked a thumb generally southward, toward the nation's capital "... thinks so. They think Mr. Windsor is a cheap punk. No juice with anybody."

"And he's gone?"

"That's what the Mounties said. House mostly cleaned out, no car. And nobody's hearing anything on the ..." he almost said 'phone', then remembered that they weren't in a closed area. "Nobody's hearing anything from him."

"Okay, I'll go get a simulation ready."

"Make it a good one."

Four and a half hours later, the arrest team sat down around a conference table. Sheila got up and closed the door.

"Okay, we got all four of us. Pete, Roger, Mike, and me. Now, Pete, I know you and Andy did one of these things already. Roger, Mike?" Both of them shook their heads.

"So as briefly as possible, here's how we've been doing simulations. We give 'em a concrete time budget, so it can't get out of hand and slow a case down. I'm the umpire, and I get a three hour block to work out the details, by myself. Then, the team gets no more than four hours to do the sim. Afterwards, I get an hour to write it up. We're not going to have that much time, this time. We have to finish it up yet today." She looked around, collecting nods. There was a general sense of repressed anger coming from everybody. Ricky Peakes was not a popular individual around the Detroit FBI shop—or anywhere else, for that matter.

"The rules are kind of minimal. During the sim itself, no discussion of the method. No questioning whether it's useful, no pointing out typos, no ... I guess you'd say, 'meta topics'. We just do the sim. If there's anything to be said about sims in general, that's for afterward. We have support from above ..." She nodded in the general direction of the senior agent's office. "...for doing these."

"So, Sheila," said Roger, "When you say you're the umpire? What does that mean?"

"It means I'm not actively playing a role. Pete'll be playing both of us, since we'll be together in the real thing. You and Mike play yourselves. And what I'll be doing is being the voice of God. I've got a list of things, events, I guess, that I think could happen, and a likeliness score for each one. It's not rigorous. I just make it up, since we haven't figured out any better way yet. And I use dice to determine if any of the events happen."

"What's an example of the events?"

"Oh, simple stuff like 'Car two breaks down'. Or nasty stuff like 'It's a trap. Sniper opens fire on agents'. And you can ask me to throw the dice, too. To answer questions. Like, 'Has it stopped raining yet?'"

"So we're playing 'What could go wrong?' Something like that?"

"Right. I take lots of notes. And then afterward, we sit down with Borowski, look it all over. Make decisions about which of the problems we address before the real thing."

"Sounds a lot like risk management," said Mike.

"It is. We stole it from a project management book. Borowski didn't like some of the little surprises we were turning up, the last couple of years. So he gave this to me to figure out. Honestly? We're still playing with it."

Pete spoke up. "We better get going. We're eating into the time box."

Sheila sat down. She handed around single page copies of an outline. "This is the basic plan. It's what we're going to game out this afternoon. And ..." She picked up an icosahedronal die, bright red with white numbers from 1 to 20. She tossed it against the spine of her notebook. "... at seven-thirty PM, it's clouded over and drizzling."

They worked through the main points of movement. They assumed that the FBI team would be in place, hanging out in their cars, somewhere twenty miles or so from an isolated farm airport. They assumed the subject would have made it across the Mackinac Bridge without being spotted. If he was stopped there, after all, that would be that and the exercise would already be over. One of Sheila's random factors was related to the subject's average driving speed from the Saint Ignace side of the bridge, out fifty miles more or less to the airport. The die roll said they'd guessed right.

Then, when the team moved off to the airfield themselves, the first issue came up.

"Oh, dear," said Sheila. "The local cops haven't turned up yet. They're delayed ..." She rolled again. "... half an hour."

"So we don't have anybody on the ground but us."

"Right. And we asked for at least two bodies."

Pete said, "I'm calling their boss ... I'm noting that we need to be sure we have that contact info ... and complaining."

"But the dice say 'no'," said Sheila. "He's not answering his cell."

"We have to go anyway," said Roger. "There's still four of us."

The game went on, taking the team in two cars along a path in the gathering dark, down roads lined with tall pines and not much else, out to the last turn.

"All, right," said Pete. "We're driving north. The landing field is on the right side. No trees along the road now. Not on that side. Oh, and we blacked out before making that last turn. We're running without lights."

"There's ... no traffic," said Sheila. "But ... oh, oh. You're blacked out and you've missed the turnoff out into the field. You're beyond it. But your passenger noticed."

"Okay. Damn. So I'm braking, stopping. Brake lights come on. Car two sees that, slows. They see the turnout?"

Sheila rolled. "Yes, they're turning in."

"I'm turning around, then. Did we tip anybody off?"

"No, he's not there yet. You're still theoretically ... half an hour ahead of him."

So the team imagined parking their cars in tactically chosen spots, out of sight from someone driving in, well-placed to block the driveway once he was in. They imagined sitting in the cars, dodging the mosquitoes and the damp. Per Sheila's die rolls, the rain had stopped, but there was still mist and no stars or moon to be seen.

"There are lights on the road," said Sheila. "One car. It's the deputies, finally showing up. The car is turning into the drive."

"I'm flashing my lights at them," said Roger.

"Okay, they see you. They're ... leaving their car in sight ... in the drive ... and walking up to you."

"I'm telling them to conceal their car. On the south side of the drive, tucked in behind the trees, so it won't show up from the road."

"All right, they're doing that. One of them is. The other one is still hanging around, talking to you."

Sheila rolled the die again. "Lights on the road! One car, coming from the south."

"Roger, get that cop out of there," said Mike.

"Okay," he said, "He's running back south to his car."

"No," said Sheila. "He's walking. Just walking back. Car turning into the drive!"

"Shit!"

The die was hopping around. "Subject sees the cop! He's stopping. He's leaving his car and running ... west!"

"West?"

"Back across the road. He's in the woods. Cops are ... chasing. Cops ... stop at the edge of the road." West of the airport there was nothing whatsoever but mile after mile of National Forest.

"Local cops," said Mike.

"And of course, they didn't have a dog with them." Roger looked at Sheila. "Did they?"

"The dice say ... no. We lost the suspect."

The young man was a walking stack of illegality, a collection of misdemeanors that defined his existence almost as though no further description was necessary. He was on probation, most recently, for operating a vehicle while intoxicated. He was not allowed to drive. A previous conviction for violating game laws made it illegal for him to be in possession of a firearm. He was a month overdue on reporting to his probation officer, although that individual was so overworked that he hadn't yet noticed. It was not a hunting season of any kind. And yet the youth had driven his cousin's pickup truck out into the woods, taken a rifle from behind the seat, a gun that technically belonged to his uncle, and walked out into the underbrush, absolutely intent on hunting. Deer, specifically.

It took almost until dark before a doe and her fawn wandered across his path. He moved too quickly bringing the rifle up, and the deer heard him and bolted away. All the boy really saw was the flash of her white tail, but he fired anyway. The deer kept running, and he assumed a miss. He stood for a few minutes, and then gave up and walked back the way he came, heading for the truck and the beer under its seat. He never drank before hunting; it spoiled his aim.

Behind him, the doe stopped running. There was a sharp pain in her right hind leg. Without intending to, the anonymous young man had provided the main course of a future wolf meal, a crippled deer.

In the first few weeks after the battle along the Chickamauga, the government did not agree with my notion that the rebellion in the west was past its apex. We were besieged in Chattanooga, and unsurprisingly our commander was removed. General Rosecrans had not been given another chance in the way so many of our other leaders were. He was, in fairness, not at his best in the days after the fight, and the fatalistic tone of his communications must have been frightening to the War Department and to the President. Their reaction was predictable, I suppose, in that they chose the most recently successful general to take command of the entire western theatre of war. What I found mildly surprising was that General Grant in turn supported me as Rosecrans' replacement. I will make no secret that Grant and I were not easy with each other at that time, but the immediate challenges we faced in Chattanooga more than occupied my attention. I also had a number of commanders remaining to me who were highly capable, and by the time Grant, who had recently been injured by a fall, arrived, we were able to present him with a plan for restoring our supply lines and turning a defeat into an unassailable defense and then into an attack on Bragg as he sat looking down on us from Missionary Ridge.

The story of the 'cracker line' has been told many times, and its hero is General W. F. Smith, the man who built a river-going navy out of nothing, created a plan that hoodwinked both Bragg and Longstreet, and brought us back to a condition of health and plenty. Within a remarkably short time, carrying out Smith's plan, we sent General Hooker across the river and onto Bragg's extreme left. From there, our supplies could begin flowing again, and when we, meaning General Grant, General Sherman, and I, had created a plan for driving Bragg from the high ground across from us, our army was again in condition to carry it out. Acting in our favor was General Bragg's increasingly evident inability to resist an assault.

The plan that General Grant made was, essentially, a double envelopment. Across the river from us, to the east, Bragg held a line from Lookout Mountain on the south, running north through the assorted hills that make up Missionary Ridge and ending short of the Tennessee River. If you make a fist with your left hand and then bring your right open palm against it at the knuckles, you will see how the geography was. Your fist is Chattanooga where we were. Your right hand, seen edge-on, is Missionary Ridge, with Lookout Mountain being represented by your thumb. Along that line was where Bragg's men stood.

Grant's intent was to draw Bragg's attention by attacking and securing Lookout Mountain, driving his forces off it and opening a way to attack him on his left. Meanwhile, General Sherman would stage a crossing of the river opposite his right, taking the northern end of the great ridge by surprise. The rest of our army, standing before Chattanooga and facing Bragg's center, would threaten him with a direct assault and, when the flank attacks achieved their goals, it was my belief, if not necessarily Grant's, that this was where we would strike the death blow.

In the beginning, things went according to that plan. General Hooker drove the rebels off Lookout Mountain, advanced across the valley and stream separating it from the ridge, and were well positioned to make their flanking attack on the next day. But due to some mistaken ideas about the geography of the northern end of the ridge, Sherman's attack stalled. The arrangement of the three small hills at that end and the defenses Bragg had managed to assemble, once he knew that he was threatened there, held up the plan. Grant, standing with me in the center, ordered me to make a limited attack on just Bragg's initial line of rifle pits, directly opposite us in the center, hoping to draw troops away from those defending against Sherman. I ordered exactly that, and with speed and precision, it was accomplished.

But when our divisions in the center had overrun that first line of the rebel defense, literally at the foot of the ridge, they did not stop. Inspired by anger at our losses at Chickamauga and by the weeks of near-starvation afterward, and finding themselves under fire from the positions further up the ridge, by brigades and individual regiments they went on, making a bayonet charge up the side of a near-mountain. The rebels were taken by surprise at first, then they were gripped with a growing panic as our men kept coming, and as their fire served only to urge our divisions to come on faster, they broke. Bragg himself was nearly captured, and he was obliged to join the two-thirds of his army that fled down the east slope of Missionary Ridge.

General Grant was initially dismayed as the men went up the hill, fearing the outcome of such a seemingly desperate charge. But as a good commander does when presented with an unexpected success, he accepted the gift graciously. The rest is detail as we pursued Bragg and sent forces after the recently-departed Longstreet, ensuring that General Burnside would remain secure in Knoxville. I confess to a bit of superstition regarding predictions, and so I kept to myself the pleasure of having been right. The nemesis that I sensed hovering around General Bragg's shoulders as far back as Stones River had exacted its toll. He was indeed finished.

The Battle of Nashville

Just shy of eighty thousand times a year, people show up at the University's Emergency Department. Typically, one of them needs medical care and one or more others are there in support. When law enforcement personnel are the patients, the visitors become a touch more diverse. Among the people who were there as a result of the Holcombe parking lot skirmish, there was a small group sitting around a set of couches in the waiting room. Mac and Colleen were there and Jackie Langton, too.

An older woman came in the sliding doors, looked around, and then approached the reception desk. She spoke briefly with the people there, then came over to the couches.

"Excuse me," she said. "I'm Gloria Klein. Jerilynn's mother? They said you were here with her?"

"Oh, yes, we are," Mac said. "I'm Mac MacArthur, this is Colleen. And Jackie Langton. We're friends of Jeri's."

"They say she's in surgery now," said Jeri's mother. She was tall, with Jeri's Nilotic face and an east coast accent. "Do you have any idea how she is?"

"She should be all right," Colleen said. "That's what the surgeon told us."

"Right," added Jackie. "She was okay, talking, calling in the shooting. They've just got to get the bleeding fixed."

"But what on earth happened? Was she on duty?"

"No," said Mac. "We were just going to pick up Jackie's mother and go to lunch. We walked into something. Please, sit down." He waved to a couch. "We don't really know anything." *Another lie*, he thought.

Mrs. Klein took the offered seat. "She just seems to attract this kind of thing. She was hurt back in the winter, too."

"This was different, though. Seriously. She just got out of her car and ... somebody started shooting. No sense at all." MacArthur was running around the circle of faces, trying to remember who know what. Colleen knew that Andy was hurt, too, and she knew, of course, what he did for a living. She knew who Andy was married to and where she worked. Jackie knew all that, but probably less of the Andy story. And himself? Well, what the hell *did* he know? He knew that Holcombe had something to do with another company that Andy was interested in. He knew that Andy wasn't there to go to lunch with them and check out rescue dogs. Mac had seen the same events Jackie had: something going completely casters-up in that damn parking lot. But beyond that? Not a thing.

"Oh, here's Mom," Jackie said. Jenn was coming toward them from the swinging doors of the patient area. "How is he?"

"The dumb bastard," Jenn said. "He'll be okay. He's worried about playing his guitar, for God's sake." She was holding herself very strongly in control, and her face was tightened with the effort of it.

"Jenn, this is Jeri's mother," said Colleen. "Mrs. Klein, this is Jenn Langton. Her husband was hurt, too."

"I'm so sorry. Will he be all right?"

"Yes. He was lucky." Jenn hadn't shifted from police mode yet. She'd been talking to Andy, Louie Burke, and a pair of Andy's fellow Feds. "He took one hit in the shoulder, and it really just bounced off the bone. Another one in the side; came in through the arm hole of his vest, scraped him and then kept on going. Just a graze." She stopped, realizing that three out of four people listening were not being comforted by this narrative style. "So, um, yes, he'll be okay."

"Do you have *any* idea ... do you know what happened?"

I know that I read the riot act to a crew of incompetents, and then one of them shot my husband, Jenn thought. *I know that I'm probably to blame for not finding out what a cesspit of morons LifeRigor was.* Her use of the past tense was instinctive but accurate. That company was dead in the water, now. *I don't know if I still have a job.* "No, Mrs. Klein, we ... just don't know why ... what was going on. I wish I did."

"People like that," said Gloria Klein, "people who just start shooting." She shook her head. "How can you ... guard yourself from that sort of thing?"

Jenn looked at Mac. He arched his eyebrows and shook his head slightly, making a "beats me" face. "I don't know," she said. "I don't really think you can." She drew in a breath and stifled a sound that might have become a sob, left to itself. She brushed her hand across one cheek. "Apparently, you can't."

Ricky was a tired boy. He'd managed to spend two nights in his car, finding obscure places to park in the countryside around Mackinac City. No bored local police officers had stumbled on him. He'd eaten junk food and stayed away from the caffeinated sodas he usually drank. What sleep he got was sporadic and uneasy. Now it was time to move on. He fumbled in a convenience store bag and dug out a disposable razor. Looking in the rearview mirror, he scraped off the dark beard hairs that were making him look even more suspicious than he actually was. *Like some kind of terrorist,* he thought, missing the irony.

The makeover was important today. For the first time since the shooting, he was going to interact with someone more official than store clerks. The sun was low in the west, shining in the back window of the Marquis as he got back on I-75 north and drove up onto the Mackinac Bridge. The toll gates were on the far side, five miles north across the straits, and you had all the time it took, driving at thirty-five or forty miles an hour, to think about handing your money to that person in the booth, that person who might have been given a picture of you or a description. Or even the license plate of your car, if things hadn't worked out in your favor, back in Ann Arbor. He tensed as his turn at the window came, but the woman just said, "Four dollars, please," and then, "Thank you" as she raised the gate. He rolled through, exited into St. Ignace, and then headed out on a series of two-lanes in the fading daylight. It took him fifty odd miles northwest, through Trout Lake and on further, heading for a very rural, very obscure little farm landing strip, right in the middle of the Sault Sainte Marie state forest.

As night came on, other cars began to converge on that same strip. The FBI didn't know where Ricky was, specifically, but they knew where he'd have to be at a given time on a given night, believing that a plane was coming to pick him up. They knew he was headed north, and they assumed he'd been dumb enough to take Oleksiy's promise at face value. They knew that he'd thrown away his little pocket pistol, but they had no idea what other hardware he might have with him. They knew he'd shot one of their colleagues and a random bystander for no reason anyone had been able to work out. And they had the negative outcome of their simulation exercise. They were determined to get their hands on Ricky Peakes.

Sheila Drew was as determined as anybody, but she was also concerned. She'd done everything she could think of to ensure success, but one of her plans had been altered from above. She'd wanted to brief the local police—Sheriff's Deputies, to be specific—very fully. In keeping with the agency's general attitude toward life, that had been denied. All the four local cops had been told was that the Feds were going to make an arrest at a very isolated farm landing strip in their jurisdiction, around nine o'clock at night. They were told to be there, take direction from the agents, and to bring their canine unit. The Sheriff himself was very anxious to please, since he was in the middle of a deal to get some surplus gear from the Army. Unlike the problem in the simulation, his people would be there.

But the trouble was, they didn't know why. Gathering at their headquarters beforehand, they ran over what little they did know—Feds, after dark, unmanned landing strip, dog—and concluded that it was a drug thing. Critically, they assumed that there really would be a plane coming in.

It was a very quiet patch of woods. P51 and the yearlings were comfortable being there, even though there was a road nearby. The human noises from the road and from one farm house half a mile south tapered off almost entirely when it became dark. They were well-fed, having encountered a crippled doe two nights before. She was in no shape to avoid them, and her death was relatively quick. They ate a large part of her, starting with internal organs, tasty lungs, delicious liver. They slept, and in the morning, P51 had trotted off a half mile to the east, two hundred yards or so from a road, and cached one hind leg from the kill. She covered it with scratched up leaves and humus, and she dragged a downed branch over the meat. It was a usual thing with her, especially since her pack was so small. Food needed to be preserved, away from the kill site so that scavengers, especially those damn persistent ravens, would be denied more than their fair share. Her nose told her that this was as good a place as any; there were no dog smells or coyote smells, and the tree cover would keep turkey vultures from spotting the stash. She and the young ones moved away a short distance and bedded down. She roused herself once, hearing the sound of cars on the road, but the noises stopped, and she relaxed again.

One at a time, four vehicles turned off the pavement, heading away from the wolves and their food. The cars went a short way down the gravel entrance to an airfield, then shuffled back and forth, getting into position for a pursuit. The Federals backed into a small north-south gap in the trees, and the two Sheriff's cars went a bit further east, picking a spot where they'd be hidden from the road and from anything coming down onto the grass landing strip. That was all the "airport" was; just six hundred yards of level ground in a straight north-south line. There was a shed of some kind, halfway down, and Roger Bean jogged down to it, saw that it was padlocked and windowless, and he came back to the cars.

"No getting into it without a key," he said to his fellow Feds. The deputies were out of earshot. "Unless this is more than just a fantasy, he can't get in there."

"Hard to imagine him knowing about it, let alone having keys," said Sheila. "I think we can forget it."

"Agreed."

Three miles due south, Ricky was driving slowly through a minuscule town. It seemed to have no commercial nature at all, just a few blocks of small, dark houses. Some room lights or flickering blue TV screens suggested life in progress. It might have been depressing to someone with an urban background, but to Ricky it seemed familiar. Back in Alabama, between his home town and anywhere else, there were hamlets like this one, places where everybody knew everybody, and the stranger knew nobody at all. To a terrified young man, passing through in the dark and in the

197

summer, it showed its best face. In a couple of minutes, he was through and the woods closed back in on each side of the road. The asphalt was gray with age, and the crack sealant made long, wavy serpent tracks in his headlights.

At the airstrip, the darkness was complete. Nothing showed except starlight and a jet, twenty-six thousand feet up and headed for Europe. Its contrail made a slightly paler streak. In one of the Sheriff's cars, Garvey the K9 officer curled up on the back seat, sighed, and closed his eyes. Two hundred yards away, Pete Corcoran shaded his watch with one hand, pressed the button for illumination, and looked at the display.

"Nine-seventeen. Now we wait."

A mile north, a large pickup truck came around a corner. The road past the airstrip bent behind it, but ahead was just a dark straight line. The truck's lights went off. Inside, two young men blinked, trying to get their night vision back. The truck was noisy, its exhaust pipes suffering the effects of northern Michigan winters, and the driver slowed down. It cut the sound and also let him watch for the driveway into the landing field. But the engine and the tires on the imperfect paving still made noise.

In the Sheriff's car, Garvey raised his head and whined. "What?" said his handler.

"You hear that?" said the other deputy. "Somebody's coming."

"Oh, yeah. And I hear something else, too. Call the Feds." Garvey was sitting up, alert, and not looking out the window. He was staring up at the roof of the car.

Just a half mile south, Ricky saw his last turn coming up and shut off his lights. He slowed and began watching the right side of the road for his turnoff. Sheila's push-to-talk radio said something. "Say again?" she asked.

"We got a vehicle coming. We can hear it," said the K9 handler. "And I can hear ..." He was about to say something but Garvey barked once, drowning him out.

"What?" said Sheila. "You hear what?" At that moment, the pickup truck turned into the drive. "Here we go," she said to Pete, and started the engine. Pete triggered his radio and said, "Execute." The truck drove across in front of them, turning south. It switched on its lights, pointing down the landing strip.

A hundred yards short of the driveway, Ricky saw a set of headlights come on, over on his right and far off the road. *Oh, shit!* was his most coherent thought, and without thinking about it, he turned on his own lights. Ahead was nothing but the road, trees on the left and the landing field on the right. And at the end of it, shining in his eyes, were those headlights.

In the truck, both parties saw Ricky light up, and they both said "Oh, shit!" or words to that effect. The driver blacked the pickup out again and slammed it into reverse.

The deputies, both cars of them, saw the truck go dark. One of them, at least, said "Oh, shit!" and since he was driving, hit the accelerator. Garvey began barking again.

"Go!" said Sheila, unnecessarily since she was at the wheel. She cut left over the uneven ground, moving in to block the truck's exit. A large bump dislodged the radio from Pete's hand. "Oh, shit!" he said. "Light 'em up!" Sheila turned on the headlights.

Coming down over the south end of the strip, a woman from Montreal cut back on the throttle of her small aircraft. She was used to flying in the dark, and a short flight like this one, over the water from a grass field in Ontario to a grass field in Michigan, was more routine than you'd think. To set down in the dark, though, wasn't really a good idea. She saw the pickup's headlights come on, then go off again. That was the agreed signal from the ground, and she switched on her landing lights.

"Plane! Here we go!" said the senior Deputy. Already the other Sheriff's car was moving, getting in position to block the plane once it stopped rolling. Along with Sheila, he turned on his lights. In the aircraft, the pilot said "Oh, *merde*!" and advanced her throttle. Looking left to make sure she cleared the one strand of power line that ran along the road, she saw Ricky's lights as well. "Merde, merde, merde!" The plane, carrying only a few kilos of product, was light and it executed a climbing turn, out to the west where she knew from experience there was nothing at all except trees.

The driver of the pickup saw nothing at first except headlights coming in his direction. But as the plane started its turn, the landing lights briefly showed him a car, no, two cars. Four, dammit! coming straight for him. There was a gap, though, and he came down hard on the gas, charging toward the hole between the Feds and the local cops. The landing lights moved on, leaving him blind, and he ran straight over a young spruce tree, ripping off most of the exhaust system. The truck kept going, though, and he pointed it in the general direction of the road.

Behind him, chaos lived. In one local car, a deputy was trying to call in the fleeing plane, following a standard procedure for this sort of event. Smuggling by clandestine aircraft was common enough that they'd worked out at least the rudiments of a who-calls-who plan. In the other patrol car, Garvey was barking "Stop!" in his own language, aimed at whoever it was out there who needed to be stopped. Being an Upper Peninsula police dog, he was used to bouncing around in off-road pursuits. The deputies with him were trying to see where the fugitives in the truck were going.

In Sheila's car, Pete was scrabbling around on the floor, trying to find his radio. Sheila was trying to get onto the driveway and cut off the truck. Roger and Mike were doing the same, and arguing about whether that had actually been a plane or what?

And out on the road, Ricky had again lost all rational control. Just as his body had taken over in the parking lot of Holcombe, causing him to start spraying small caliber bullets around in general, so here his animal instinct took over. Rationally, his situation couldn't be helped by anything other than slowly and innocently driving on by and vanishing. But rationality was shut down. It was fight or flee, again, and he fled. He jumped out, leaving the lights on and the engine running. He dashed across the road and into the woods.

An especially vicious bump made Sheila wince. Her partly-closed eyelids somehow improved her view of the absurd situation, giving her a sudden impression of movement on her left. She stared for half a second, then jerked the wheel right, making Pete drop the radio again. Before she could yell a warning, she ran the left fender squarely into the passenger's side door of the pickup truck. The driver didn't see it coming, and he reacted in a panic, yanking his own wheel left. It vectored him off the driveway and straight into a tree thick enough to stop him dead. Both he and his passenger knocked heads on the dashboard. Sheila's car ended up parallel to the truck, a couple of feet away, and she got the door open as quickly as she could. Pete recovered himself enough to follow, drawing his sidearm and shouting at the truck in general. Sheila yanked its right side door open and stopped. "What the hell?" There were *two* people inside. That the subject might bring a friend hadn't been part of the simulation.

By now, only fifty or so yards away, the deputies had given up on the plane. It was clearly gone, and it would be up to somebody else—maybe the immigration agents who hung out on Drummond Island—to worry about it. But right here, up close, there was a crashed truck and people shouting, and another car full of Feds pulling up. The locals stopped and jumped out, bringing Garvey along, still barking.

201

Fifteen yards or so into the woods, Ricky stopped to let his heart slow down. He looked around. He could see only a few feet in any direction, and that was all. He looked down at his feet, and there was just a surface of dead leaves, small branches, foliage. Overhead, what he could see of sky was only a slightly lighter darkness, crisscrossed with trees. Behind, he could hear shouting, barking, and a set of mechanical noises, a crash, and then just voices again. He tried to think, struggling to plan something, some course of action other than simply getting away from those noises. Nothing came to mind, and he started walking carefully, moving in a direction that just happened to be west. It was slow going.

Feds and deputies swarmed the pickup truck. The passengers were being extracted, and over the sound of Garvey's insults, Sheila heard one of the deputies say, "Hey, I know this guy."

"Yeah, said his partner. "We got him over in Fibre, doin' that B and E."

"You know these kids?" Sheila yelled. "Both of them?"

"Yeah, this one ... and oh, yeah, his buddy, too. Mostly they just do larcenies, though. Nothing big like this."

"Oh, Jesus H. Christ!" she said. "These are the wrong ones!"

"Sheila! Hey, Sheila!" It was Mike Sherman, trying to get her attention. "There's another car! Over on the road!"

"What? Well, get somebody over there. Mike, you and Roger ..."

"Yeah?"

"Take, um, take that guy and his dog! Go check that car!"

P51 was awake. In the distance, she could hear human noises. Motors and voices and a dog barking. Her yearlings were awake as well, listening, looking at her for cues. She stood up and focused all her intelligence-gathering abilities toward the east. She wasn't interested in eating, but the delicious venison concealed a few yards away was decidedly on her mind. There was a slight breeze at treetop level, but on the ground there was no movement of air at all. There were woods smells and the unique signatures of the pups, but beyond that, there was only the deer, announcing itself. A long way off, closer than the noises, but still a good way off, she could hear something moving clumsily through the woods. It was getting nearer.

Ricky was getting near his limit. He'd had little or no sleep. He'd been tense and afraid at the bridge crossing, and then the adrenaline had subsided, leaving him fighting to stay alert on the drive through these endless back roads. Now, he'd watched his escape blow up and disappear. It had not occurred to him that there wouldn't be a plane coming for him. Sure enough, it had been there, but so had the authorities. He had no real idea who'd be after him, but he never questioned that there'd be someone. And they'd known! They'd known exactly when and where to find him! He tripped on a tree root, stumbled, and paused. For the first time, he thought about what he'd abandoned in the car. Clothes, some leftover junk food. But his phone! It was still on his belt! He could call!

He scrabbled at the phone, managing to get it unholstered without dropping it. He crouched down and cupped it in his hands, aware that the screen would light up and be visible. He pressed the button. The usual greeting appeared, calling for a PIN. He mistyped it twice, then got it right. It displayed the home screen. In the upper right corner, the signal monitor appeared. He stared at it, waiting. Ten seconds went by, but it remained at zero. No bars. No connection. He made a noise that was a combination of a cough and a sob.

Behind him, Mike, Roger, the deputy, and Garvey left the abandoned Mercury. Garvey led them across the dark road and into the darker woods. "Better let me go first," said Garvey's human. "I'm used to keeping up with him."

Ricky gathered himself up and began to move on. He had no real sense of his direction, and there was no longer noise from the airstrip to get away from. For a boy from the countryside, he had almost no outdoor skills, and he struggled blindly ahead. Behind him, Garvey was in his element, easily following the scent trail of a panicked, sweating young man. Ahead, P51 became more concerned. Something was coming, and the still air wasn't telling her what it might be.

"I'm glad we did ... that simulation," Mike said to Roger, talking between breaths. "At least I dressed for this." Roger said something that indicated general agreement; he was focused on his feet and where he was putting them. The deputy was trying to keep up with the dog, but Garvey was getting ahead of them, following Ricky's wavering path. Besides the scent trail, he could hear him now. Ricky was breathing harder than anybody.

The things, whatever they were, were getting closer, but P51 relaxed slightly. The sounds were drawing off to the south. They weren't heading directly for the little pack or its cache. Then, it changed. The nearest thing made a louder noise, something that sounded like falling down. And from farther away, a dog barked!

Ricky put a foot wrong again, and this time he actually fell. A dead branch broke under his weight and made a loud crack. Garvey heard most of the event, and increased his pace, barking once, encouraging the humans to hurry up. Ricky heard that, got to his feet again, and tried to run, blundering into the undergrowth and making more noise. He changed his direction, too, shifting to the right and heading straight for the wolves. P51 raised her hackles, and her lips drew back. Whatever was out there sounded big. The pups drew in close behind her.

Ahead of Ricky, an eight-inch tree trunk lay on the ground, slowly decomposing. A wind storm had put it there, years ago. He came to it, saw it at the last minute, and tried to jump. One foot went over, but the other one caught its toe on the stub of a branch, and he fell violently on his face, square across P51's deer haunch. The pups jumped back, but their mother stood her ground, growling and making her best aggression face. A gap in the overhead branches offered a minimal amount of light. Ricky looked up and into the wolf's eyes, and his horror-stricken mind could only offer one image: that woman in Tuscaloosa, staring at him as she smashed his laptop. He shrieked and tried to roll over, tried to curl into a fetal ball. And then into the little scene came Garvey. He saw P51 just as she saw him. He skidded to a stop, and their eyes locked.

The action froze. Neither the wolf nor the dog had ever been this close to one of their cousins before. Garvey had never seen or smelled a wolf, and P51 had tried to steer clear of dogs. But this was a different situation. Each of them had something to lose.

P51 broke the silence, symbolically. What she said was not verbal. It didn't make any actual sound at all. But still keeping her eyes locked on Garvey's, she put out her right paw and laid it on the deer meat. "Mine," she said. One of the pups growled slightly.

Garvey stared back, then looked at the haunch of meat. Ricky moaned. Garvey shifted his look toward him and put his paw on Ricky's shaking back. "Mine," he said.

There was noise and light behind the dog. The deputy was catching up, shouting at whoever it was his dog was chasing, waving his flashlight around. He still knew nothing about anything, but the fact that Garvey had gone quiet was worrisome. Behind him, the Feds staggered along in the dark. P51 stepped one pace forward, grabbed the deer meat with her teeth, and turned. She and the yearlings vanished in the dark. Garvey glanced after her, then grabbed Ricky by his shoulder and began shaking him, snarling.

When the posse arrived and called Garvey off, Ricky was too traumatized even to be grateful.

 General John Bell Hood lost an arm at Gettysburg. Lee sent him west to assist Bragg, and he lost a leg in our fight at Chickamauga. He ought to have gone home at that point, but he was a stubborn officer and, for better or for worse, committed to the rebellion. General Bragg was called home after his loss in front of Chattanooga, and they brought Joseph Johnston back. Despite their names, this man was not related to the Johnston who died at Shiloh, and he was a more effective commander by far.

Johnston did all he could to hinder us, but we eventually overwhelmed him and took Atlanta. The government in Richmond relieved Johnston for not having done the impossible, and they put Hood in charge. When he had even partly healed from his wounds, he resumed the fight. That one decision, to put a man of Hood's disposition, a man with half his body shot away and who had supreme courage and little more than that, in command of the last rebel force not tied down by Grant in the east, that decision sounded the death knell of the rebellion. At first glance, though, it seemed sound enough.

To understand what Hood was ordered to do, consider the war in the west and in the east as having become one long battle line. With the rebellion facing north, its right wing was entirely occupied with General Grant's unceasing blows against Virginia, intended to drive Lee's forces back, one bloody fight at a time, upon Richmond. In the center, we—Sherman and his command of several armies, including mine—had taken Atlanta. We were poised to strike through their line, turn on them, and cut them off from behind. Only on their far left, west of our forces in Georgia, was there an opportunity, and Hood was sent to exploit it. His challenge was to strike past us, north into Tennessee, and discredit the National government by threatening an attack into Kentucky and even Ohio. No one believed, on our side or theirs, that this attack could be sustained, militarily, but the damage it could do to the President's loyalty among people of the north might be enough to win some time for Richmond. Time was what they needed, and if

206

General Hood could embarrass us by making a raid on the northwest, a raid on a grand scale, true, but still no more than a raid, it would be a heavy blow to the Federal cause.

It would be pointless to dwell on the details of Hood's initial movements and on Washington's indecision about how best to counter him. It is enough simply to record that I was given a small core of forces, especially short of cavalry, and sent to keep Hood from succeeding in his mission. It became clear as the movement of troops sorted itself out that his first major goal would be the taking of Nashville, and in the same way, it became clear to me that, if I could gather the remainder of a reasonable force, Nashville would be the grave of Hood's hopes. As it turned out, I would have less difficulty mastering Hood than I would have in working through outright interference from the government, stricken as it was with panic, and from at least one of my own officers.

There was a general officer, one whose name I will not give here although he is well enough known as a critic of the campaign and of its management, who was in clandestine communication with Washington. I was not aware of this at first, until it was reported to me by others in our army, and even then, his behavior was just short of a line which would have justified my taking action against him. By the barest margin, he failed in what was a clear and demonstrated effort to have me removed from command, on the same grounds that were always used when my name was being compared to that of others. I was widely considered "slow". When I wished to act in a professional way, preparing my force completely and then striking my opposition in a place and at a time that I judged would result in his destruction and a minimal loss to our armies, I was criticized in comparison to other commanders who flung masses of unprepared and ill-supplied men into wild adventures, apparently in the belief that action was better than preparation, regardless of the outcome. At Nashville, I prepared the utter destruction of Hood's army, but it was a near thing. I was almost removed from command before it could take place.

Hood attacked a part of my force south of the city at a town called Franklin. He had a numeric advantage, but attacked without finesse and suffered heavily. Although the general in command of our forces withdrew, moving back to Nashville, those were his orders from me. He arrived back in the city at almost the same time as reinforcements came to us by the river, and we continued training our new recruits, gathering supplies, and especially acquiring mounts for our cavalry. This latter was crucial to my intentions, since once we had crushed and scattered Hood's army, I meant to pursue him mercilessly, as far back out of Tennessee as he could be driven. That alone, in my view and it must be said in the view of Washington as well, was the only outcome that would put a permanent end to the war in the west and reassure the voters that the rebellion was on its death bed.

Hood arrived in front of the city, and he made no immediate attempt to attack. We had prepared it extremely well to repulse any assault he might make, and all he was able to do was blockade us on the south and feint at the river crossings, east and west. Then, as we were ready to make our attack on him, the weather became an obstacle, with sleet and ice storms making the whole countryside impassible. The rebels suffered in their camps, we less so since were in the city and in some shelter. Hood had to feed his men from a long supply line running back south, since the countryside, in mid-winter, offered nothing to him.

This situation lasted two weeks, and during that time, I fought a battle with Washington, trying as hard as I knew how to show that all we waited for was favorable weather. They were afraid Hood would break away and move west or east around me, striking terror wherever he went. I explained that he could do no such thing, since it would mean leaving his source of supply and finding nothing locally. He could not do, to put it simply, what Sherman was able to do in the south. This conversation went on the whole time we waited.

Finally, on the 15th of December, the conditions improved, and we began the fight I intended to fight. Hood was in a semi-circular position in front of the city, and we began by sending our cavalry to flank him on his left. We drew his attention away from this move by sending General Steedman's division, including black troops, against his right, and they fought with great gallantry against entrenched positions. On Hood's left, he was repeatedly flanked and driven out of his individual lines. By the end of the day, he was sorely depleted in numbers and forced back into a second position.

On the next day, we repeated our tactics, sending in an attack on Hood's new right and then swinging a powerful force against his left. Meanwhile, our cavalry was almost in his rear. In the afternoon, I ordered one of my corps commanders to make an attack on a small hill the enemy had occupied. This officer argued that he was outnumbered and even feared an attack on his position. He was reinforced and still declined to advance. This was the same gentleman who, as became known much later, had been urging my replacement. At the moment, though, a divisional commander who could see the condition in which the rebels found themselves issued an ultimatum, stating that unless specifically ordered not to, he was about to attack, whether the reluctant general supported him or not. I concurred, and the assault he made routed the rebel left entirely. The remainder of their army, with the exception of part of one corps, disintegrated. Hood was pursued out of Tennessee and into Alabama. The war in the west was effectively over.

What I did not know at the time was that General Grant himself had been preparing to come to Nashville with orders for my replacement. He was stopped by the telegrams reporting our complete victory. The insubordinate and political general to whom I have alluded went unpunished through the concealment of his actions and by the final and crushing nature of our battle. He was sent away to assist Sherman.

MacArthur wasn't used to visiting other people in the hospital. Usually, people visited him. And the visitor chair next to Jeri's bed was uncomfortable.

"So," she was saying, "Cara's staying with my mother. They get along well."

"Good," said Mac. "Are you going to stay with her, too? When you get out of here?"

"Yes. She's got a better car, for one thing. For getting in and out of."

"How long do they think you'll be off your feet?" He nodded at a wheelchair in the corner.

"They don't really say. A month, at least, according to one of them. He said I was lucky." A seriously bleeding artery in the thigh makes everyone think *femoral*, but Jeri had ducked that bullet, figuratively and literally. Ricky's shot severed the second perforating artery and lodged just behind it. According to the doctors, they'd been able to repair it with a kind of synthetic cuff.

"You know," Mac said, "keep in mind that we're all, ah, available. To help."

"Thank you. But, you realize, don't you, you've already helped? *Really* helped."

"Well, I suppose ..."

"No, I mean it. I don't think anyone else there would have known what to do. I could be in a lot worse shape, right now."

"That miserable little bastard." Mac usually tried to deliver summary judgments like that in a flat, neutral tone. It made better theatre, after all. But his voice trembled, just slightly, halfway through. "Just out of nowhere, start shooting like that." His disorganized memory suddenly reminded him of Albert Sidney Johnston, bleeding to death on the field at Shiloh. He'd been shot in the thigh, too.

"He was a guy I stopped, the week before. He was at a stop light and a meth user ran up to his window. A woman with a knife. It scared the hell out of him."

"You knew him?"

"I recognized him. I thought he was having an attack or something. Apparently he was."

Mac's phone went off. "I should take this, it's Jenn. Hi, Jenn." He listened. "Oh, good. I'm here with Jeri, I'll let her know. Thanks." Jeri looked at him with her eyebrows raised.

"They got Peakes," he said. "He was somewhere up in the Upper Peninsula, for some reason."

"Who got him?"

"The FBI. Andy's team. And Jenn said they had some local help, too. In fact, the local K9 was the one who actually got ahold of him."

"Good." She held out her hand. Mac gripped it. "Go, dogs," she said.

"Are you going to go back? Back to the county?"

"Well, that's a good question." She looked away, focusing on a piece of hospital art. "I talked to my mother about that. She ... wants me to go back to school. Law school, specifically."

"Law school?"

"Yes. She's an attorney, or she was. In Virginia. But she wants us both to qualify here. And then start doing ... "

"I can guess. Doing something about it."

"That's right. Sexual assault. Gender bias. She mentioned academic freedom, too. We'd have an advantage. We wouldn't absolutely have to turn a profit."

"Good. Very good. About goddamn time, in fact."

Surrender

So, as I have noted above, my part in the war came to an end. There were other battles fought, but the west was rendered secure by the destruction of the rebellion's last western army. Savage bloodletting around Richmond and Petersburg remained, but General Grant overwhelmed them in the end. General Sherman pushed aside Johnston's last efforts in the southeast, and Lee was finally forced to capitulate. Afterwards, the celebrations were cut short by the tragic and insane act of the President's assassin, and the task of reconstructing the rebel states became more harsh and repressive than it would otherwise have been.

I found that what remained of my family were not willing to accept (I will not use the word "forgive" since there is nothing in my choice of allegiances that requires forgiveness) the part I played, and my wife and I were finding our roots in her northern homeland anyway. So I did not return to Virginia. Sadly, the post-war reduction of the army brought about a discreditable series of quarrels over who, of the remaining general officers, should be given which posting. Although I would have preferred to remain in the east, I find myself now, with Mrs. Thomas, here in California, commanding our peacetime forces.

It cannot be seen as surprising, after a nation goes through an upheaval and ordeal such as our country did, that those who took part would feel compelled to record their experiences and opinions. Many of my former colleagues and opponents began to do so, and many more continue to. I have held my hand, because I am still a serving officer and it is not my place to comment on the successes and failures of other officers, men who were after all just men, some capable, some more fallible than a man in command ought to be. And yet, my own sense of injustice and what I feel is my duty to the soldiers who fought alongside me has now come to demand from me a response to what I can only call a set of outright, self-serving, and unprovoked lies. Whether this document I am preparing ever reaches the public is of less concern to me, now, than the simple act of refuting the discreditable opinions of General S ... *(here the manuscript ends).*

"So, I had a long talk with Doctor Holcombe," said Jenn. Andy was immediately alert, listening carefully. "It was a good talk." He relaxed slightly.

"We covered quite a bit of ground. Wide-ranging. She doesn't blame me. About LifeRigor. *She* accepted their bid, she says. Says it was *her* call, and she didn't look closely enough. Obviously, we're suing them for the damage they did to the contract and our reputation."

"Metharom bailed, though. Can you get at him, back in Thailand?"

"We'll get him home to testify. Karolyn has some juice in Washington. He'll be back."

"You know, you might want to talk to somebody else about that."

"Who?"

"Marian Kasimir. The exec LifeRigor fired. I hear she's suing them, too."

"Done," said Jenn. "Already happened." She paused. *How long have we been together?* she thought. *How sure am I that he knows the difference between how I feel about him and about certain other men? How will he react if I say what I'm about to say? Oh, hell, let's find out."* She looked straight into his eyes. "When Doctors Holcombe and Kasimir get done with them, there won't be a testicle left hanging."

Andy didn't blink. "Good. That's the general sentiment at my shop, too."

"Then we're all on the same page. But ..." Andy again went on mild alert. Jenn typically used the "but" conjunction to switch from one topic to a more serious one. "The next time you're about to raid one of my suppliers, can you warn me a *bit* more specifically? I mean, I bought one of those Kevlar panels, but I didn't even have my bag out there with me."

"Yes, dear," he said.

She patted his good hand, making him spill a piece of *tubetti* off his fork. "I won't tell if you don't."

In MacArthur's back yard, three domesticated wolves were engaged in a kind of familiarization dance. One of them, quite young and enthusiastic, was doing a German Shepherd version of "run and find out" in the sense Kipling meant it about a mongoose. She was dashing from one fence to another, sticking her nose between the bars, standing up to see if that was any better, turning around, running somewhere else. Her hosts, Mac's dogs, were stirred up by her, and they were running back and forth with her, pointing out important patches of ivy, appropriate places to urinate, and strategic positions, such as the place where a squirrel once fell out of a tree.

Jeri, sitting in a wheelchair on the deck, was watching closely. Cara was generally good with other dogs, but she wanted to keep an eye on things. Mac and Andy were there, too, ready to help Jeri back inside when the dogs were done with their rituals.

"I feel guilty," Andy said. "I know both of you want to know more about that little fiasco."

"Oh, no, not at all," said Mac. "Farthest thing from my mind."

"You're a little bit constrained, though, aren't you?" Jeri asked. "We're all going to be testifying about it, sooner or later, right?"

"Well ... I guess so. It wasn't supposed to go that way, but now ..." He trailed off.

"You mean it wasn't supposed to involve gunfire?"

"No, really, it was just another ... damn it, just a case. Just an investigation." Both Mac and Jeri looked at him. Mac made a circular gesture with one hand, somehow conveying "... and?"

"Okay, look. I'll try to ... try to give you the general, ah, picture. All right?"

"Fine," said Jeri. "I won't say a word."

"So we had ... there was a suspicion that those people weren't really ... playing by the rules. The security rules." He was looking hard at each of their faces, trying to see if they were following. "We knew ... it was known ... that both the head man and the little software lunatic were talking to ... another person. Somebody who was ... on some lists."

"Ah," said Mac. "A bus station kind of guy?" Jeri raised an eyebrow. "Andy once gave me an analogy about people who were anti-bus station. About not telling them where the bus station was." She dipped her head. It could mean she understood or simply "go on".

"It was along those lines, yes," Andy said. "And it was about a ... a new kind of bus station."

"I'm not sure I follow *that,*" said Jeri.

"He means, if I can paraphrase, that his employer knew about that company leaking things. Classified technology. I can say that because nobody told me. I figured it out by myself."

"That's your story, and you're sticking to it," she said, "in case anybody asks?"

"Especially anybody in a court room."

Andy was wearing an uncomfortable face. Mac guessed why, and he decided to smooth the way ahead. "And of course, if an old fool like me can figure something like that out, a smart security director probably could, too."

"Well," Andy started.

"No, no, I see it," said Jeri. "The other company. The one we, um, showed up to see. Where Jenn works. They only knew what they could figure out."

"That's how I see it. No reason for anybody there, even, say, a security director, to think of pistol-packin' little bit twisters going on a rampage. Just business."

"Well, I mean they ... No, you're right. They didn't have any idea ..."

"But, Agent Patel, let me ask this, and you can answer or not, as you're able. Did *you* know what a nut job that kid was?"

"No, Mac. No, I didn't. I wouldn't have let that ..."

"Say no more. I understand. I remember a little investigation you and I went on, once. Jenn, too. Nobody knew anything. And the body count was a whole lot larger."

"What was that?" said Jeri. "Oh, wait. I did hear about something along those lines. Out in the country, a few years ago?"

"That's a story for later," said Andy. "I wonder if they're ready to eat, inside there?" Like a dog, he was looking at the door wall, pointing with his gaze and his nose. He was feeling better.

In the kitchen, an assorted brunch menu was being set out. Mac had already made soup. Colleen and Jenn, Jackie and Alice, and Karolyn Holcombe were moving around in a kind of dance, not unlike the one the dogs were doing. Things were coming out of and going into the refrigerator. Jackie was doing knife work, rendering some late-season vegetables into small pieces. Karolyn was on her phone, talking her husband through the last couple of turns into the MacArthur's obscure little neighborhood. Alice was talking about comparative mythology.

"The trickster is so common," she was saying. "He shows up in so many cultures, and he's always interfering with people. Sometimes helping, sometimes tripping them up. But always there."

"I had a book of African folk tales when I was a kid," said Jackie. "There was a guy like that. A spider, I think."

"Anansi. Anansi the spider. That's one. And I read something the other day saying that Bugs Bunny belongs in the group, too. And the Chinese have The Monkey King."

Colleen looked up from slicing bread. "This sounds like something, what was it? An archetype? Or am I just making that up?"

"The one I always think of is Hermes," Alice said. "Messenger of the gods, supposedly. The Romans stole the idea and called him Mercury. But the thing about him is, he's the one who invented lying."

"Shame he didn't patent it," Karolyn said, hanging up, trusting her husband to find his own way. "He'd be a rich god by now."

The outside group came inside, bringing the dogs with them. There was some shuffling of dishes around, moving them safely back from the edges of the kitchen island.

"Mac," said Jenn, "You were telling me about a trickster in, oh, Ottawa mythology? Alice was talking about the invention of lying."

217

"I doubt lying had to be invented. I think it just came naturally. But are you thinking of Nanabozho? The Ojibwe great-uncle character? Why?"

"I was talking about how widespread the idea is, all over the world," said Alice. "Of a deity or a spirit or a fabulous animal. Who just messes with people and makes things happen."

Everybody here has that in mind right now, Jenn thought. *About how nothing goes the way you think it will.* She looked quickly around the room. *Everybody here's been through it. Best-laid-plans going random on you.* She thought of something else. "Andy, what was that Yiddish thing you were talking about? The two stereotypes?"

"Oh, schlemiel and schlimazel? The clumsy guy and the unlucky guy?"

"Right. What was the difference?"

"A schlemiel is the waiter who drops a tray of drinks. The schlimazel is the guy it falls on."

"Right. So, neither one those is a trickster. But the humans he fools are certainly schlimazels."

Peakes was the schlimazel, all right, Andy thought. *His pal in Windsor was the trickster. So what does that make me?*

The events at the air strip were disturbing to P51 and her youngsters. They withdrew a safe distance that night and ate the remainder of the deer. Then, during the next twenty-four hours, she led them back west almost fifteen miles, moving during the day. There was nothing at all to worry about in the daylight, since they had almost nothing but forest to move through. They stopped in the middle of a huge patch of wooded land, a place far from roads or anything else. Although nothing they'd seen suggested other members of their tribe, they howled, all three of them together. And this time, coming from a long way off to the north east, there was an answer.

It was just a single voice, but it was deep pitched, and it suggested maturity. It wasn't a howl they'd heard before. Five miles or more away, another adult wolf was calling, and it was a male.

The core of a wolf pack is a breeding pair, and P51 had lost her mate back in the winter. Soon, her yearlings would disperse, at least the young male. Her daughter might stay with her, or she, too, might go wandering. A single female would find it difficult to join another pack, even if there was one to join. She howled again and listened carefully to the reply. Again, there was just the one voice. She and the cubs stretched and began moving in single file, heading north east.

Ann Arbor hosts any number of public fairs, shows, and events. The pattern is usually a block or two of a street closed off, some booths set up for groups and food vendors, a separate tent for children's activities, and maybe an enclosed area for alcohol. Almost inevitably, there's a stage and a sound system. This particular evening, one of the smaller gatherings was laid on, and the music was all made by local bands. The head of a homeless and veterans' aid group was doing the announcing; a well-known jazz and jellyroll pianist had just finished his set.

"Now we just need to take a minute to move things around, here," the mistress of ceremonies said, "and then we'll welcome a brand new group. They're so new, they haven't even come up with a name, they tell me. But they said just to call them Four Local

Musicians, for the time being. So ... I see they're coming up now, so would you welcome ... Four Local Musicians!"

Two musicians climbed up onto the portable stage, one with a flute and one with a B flat trumpet. Behind them, people were helping a man who seemed to have some kind of disability in his left arm. Then with a bit more trouble, another woman was assisted up the steps. She stood on one foot while a wheelchair was arranged behind her. Someone rolled her forward to a microphone and handed her a violin. The man shifted his mic around awkwardly, using just one hand.

"Okay," he said. "Thanks for coming out. I do have an update. Jeri, it was your idea, do you want to ..."

"Sure," said the woman in the chair. Someone had already lowered her mic, and she pulled it a little closer. "It's no longer true that we don't have a name. We just thought of one, about five minutes ago. Andy and I," she nodded at the man, "and Li and Vicky took at a look at ourselves and decided we'd appear as *Didn't Duck*." Several people in the audience laughed, and a few others followed politely. Most of the small crowd didn't get it.

"Ready?" asked the man, gesturing with a harmonica at the others. "All right." They kicked off a reel set, Drowsy Maggie sliding into The Wise Maid. Not many people there had heard reels played with a woodwind, a horn, a fiddle, and a mouth harp, but for all its unorthodoxy, it stirred up a few children. Sitting in the front row of folding chairs, MacArthur nudged Colleen and pointed at a woman and twin five-year-olds, jumping and dancing around off to the side. Jackie Langton grabbed her mother's hand and more or less dragged her up to dance.

The reels came to their conclusion, and there was a round of applause. "Thank you," said the fiddler. "Now, here's one that was written as a poem by a good friend of ours. We had the privilege of

220

making a song out of it." She eye-checked the other three, and the horn started off by itself. After a bar, the flute and fiddle joined. The man had pocketed his harp, and he stepped closer to his microphone. He had a solid baritone, rich without being high. In operatic terms, he would have been close to the *Kavalierbariton*. *With instruction, he might have made Bizet happy.*

> *"Lately I find*
> *That I don't give*
> *One single flying damn*
> *For the things that keep you up at night*
> *And make you fly those banners on your car."*

It wound on, with bits of trumpet marking changes in feeling. The lyrics expressed growing discontent, as though accusing another party of breaking an unspoken agreement.

> *Katie, you must pick and choose*
> *Which one you lose*
> *Those lies or me*
> *What you believe*
> *Is not just false but wrong,*
> *And you are no longer free.*

The violin came in with a solemn set of phrases, by itself, and then the other instruments joined with two bars of resolution. The man finished the song.

> *So you go on ahead.*
> *Me, I'm headed for the bar.*
> *Such a dark and quiet holy place*
> *Where my old cronies are*
> *And any lessons to be learned*
> *Are not received but earned.*
> *Not received but earned.*

"Mac wrote that?" Jackie asked her mother. "What does the 'received' thing mean?"

"A received idea is something you take on faith. Something you just accept without questioning. Or so Mac says, anyway."

"Thank you," said the baritone. "Thank you. We have to get out of the way of some real musicians, here, but we're gonna leave you with one more. If I wasn't so banged up, I'd have a guitar for this, but I'll have to stick to the harp." He waved the harmonica at the woman in the wheelchair. "Jeri gives this quite a going over, though. So hold onto your seats." He took a breath and started out on an imitation of a fiddle. The woman in the chair put her violin in her lap, drew the mic in closer, and began.

Well, now tell me, Sean O'Farrell
Where the meetin' is to be.
In the old spot by the river,
Right well known to you and me.

"Rising of the moon," whispered Colleen. "This augurs ... something, anyway." The old Fenian ballad wound on, coming to its final verse.

There beside the singin' river,
That dark mass of souls was seen,
And above their shining weapons,
Hung their own beloved green.
Death to every foe and traitor,
Forward, strike the marchin' tune.
And arragh! me friends for freedom,
'Tis the risin' of the moon!

There weren't any cymbals to crash, but the voice and the horn stood in. There was a breath's worth of silence and then more than polite applause. On the stage, those who could took a bow. In the audience, only MacArthur noticed that the final verse changed the traditional "men" to "souls" and "boys" to "friends."

"Thank you! Thanks, everybody! On the flute, Li Kelsey! On the horn, Vicky Cordell! On the violin and with a voice that could bring the pikes together, Jeri Klein! I'm Andy Patel, good night!"

A note on the manuscript

I have been asked by a number of officers who served with and under my beloved late husband whether I would undertake to edit and prepare the document above, a document that appears to be something of an autobiography. To the everlasting loss of his family and his country, General Thomas died while writing it. I have agreed, to some extent against my better judgment, that I would review it and correct the occasional error in language, but I have sustained what I believe he would have wished, and I have made no changes in its sense and meaning. Neither will I try to expand it or to finish his complaint against a particular individual. I will just say in closing that I know full well who "General S" is, and I know that gentleman will recognize himself. I hope he will take my husband's words to heart.

(signed) Mrs. George Henry Thomas

🐆

Author's note on sources

This isn't an academic work. It's fiction, and fiction typically doesn't cite sources. But since I decided to make part of it a hypothetical "autobiography" of a real person, and to create characters—important characters, in fact—who are members of another species, and because it was so much more fun than doing the actual writing, I did quite a bit of research. If you're at all interested, here are a few books out of many that I found useful.

For General George Thomas and his military experience, a recent source is *George Henry Thomas: As True as Steel*, by Brian Steel Wills, 2012, University Press of Kansas. For a point of view closer in time to Thomas, consider *General George H. Thomas: A Critical Biography*, by Donn Piatt and Henry van Boynton, 1893, Robert Clarke and Company. (Digital reprint.)

For a readable and complete treatment of North American wolves, see *Wolves: Behavior, Ecology, and Conservation*, Edited by L. David Mech and Luigi Boitani, 2003, The University of Chicago Press.

Author photo: L. Bangert

Joseph McConnell describes himself as a retired technical bureaucrat. In and around his day jobs, he's been writing for decades, once sharing the cover of The Whole Earth Review with Allen Ginsberg. Born in (extremely) rural Michigan, he's lived in Ann Arbor since 1977 and—whether the city is prepared to admit it or not—considers himself a stakeholder. **A Lair for the Wolves** is his fourth novel.

Other books by Joseph McConnell:

Many Believable Lies	Kindle	Paperback
Clash By Night	Kindle	Paperback
The Least Weasel:	Kindle	Paperback

Made in the USA
Charleston, SC
15 October 2015